I0885903

MEMORIES by the SHORE

Tangerine Sky Book 4

M.J. HUXLEY

M.J. Huxley

First Edition: February 2025

Dedication

This book is dedicated to the women who've experienced a summer love you just can't shake. That raw, unconditional love that only makes sense to you. The kind you feel in the depths of your soul. The type of love that everything in life seems to tear you apart, but somehow, you always find your way back to one another.

Avery and Jasper's story is for you.

A Note from the Author

Your mental health and triggers matter.

Please be aware there is an on-page description of pregnancy loss. This book does include cheating, but **NOT** between the two main characters. There are also descriptions of depression and the effects it can have on a healthy person and their loved ones.

Playlist

"Past Lives"–BORNS

"Heart Skipped a Beat"–The xx

"Dreams"–Fleetwood Mac

"Desire"–Cannons

"Love Song"–311

"Here's to the Night"–Eve 6

"Feels Like Summer"–Childish Gambino

"The Chemicals Between Us"–Bush

"when the party's over"–Billie Eilish

"Please Don't Go"–Double You

"Sorry"–Halsey

"APT"–Rose & Bruno Mars

"Wish You Were Here"–Incubus

"Love Like Ghosts"–Lord Huron

"Love Will Tear Us Apart"–The Cure

Chapter One

Now

Avery

I roll my luggage into my Scottsdale penthouse apartment. The click of my high heels on the hardwood floors greets me whenever I come in. The smell of leather and spice warms my insides, signaling I've entered solitude.

I've never given much thought to how I'd spend my future. I'm not one to plot and plan and prefer to be left alone. I enjoy lying amongst my books and pieces of artwork.

It's not that I don't like people. I do. I'm a flight attendant, and that is a large part of the job, but truthfully, there are only a handful of people I can tolerate for long periods. They are my three best friends and sometimes the guy I'm casually dating, Dave. But even Dave isn't allowed to stay over, and I never stay at his place even after over a year of being romantically involved.

Both of my parents unexpectedly died in a car accident when I was seventeen. I didn't know them well. They spent most of my childhood traveling overseas with my father's IT company. I was raised by Maye, my nanny since I was six, and the other staff members on my parents' payroll. That was my life, and I've inadvertently curated the same level of solitude now as an adult.

My phone buzzes inside my bag. I shut and locked the door behind me, then unzipped my travel bag and slipped it out.

Piper: I'll be in town next Sunday! Happy hour at The Poppy?

Bailey: I'm so excited to see you. I'm in!

Lina: I'll be there. I'm ready to hug you, Piper Moon.

I tap out a quick reply to my best friends.

Me: Can't wait to see you!

I'm closer to them than I have been to anyone else my entire life. Bailey and I met in college, and then we met Lina and Piper in flight attendant school. We've been flying together for the same airline since we left school.

I glance at the time and notice how late it is. Dave is taking me out to dinner tonight. In his message, he said to dress nice. He always has something up his sleeve.

I flip on the lights and hit the remote to open the curtains with a panoramic view of downtown. They slowly open and display the spotted lights of the city. My hometown. The place I returned to as soon as I had the chance. I love this place. I'm never fucking leaving.

Since I wasn't yet eighteen years old when my parents passed, I had to give up my entire life in Phoenix and move to a small Northern California coastal town with my aunt Helen. The icing on an already horrible cake was that my inheritance wasn't going to be released to me until I reached a specific age. And once I reached that age, which was eighteen, I would only get small installments. The second came at twenty-one, then twenty-five, with the final and total amount at thirty.

I take the first step on the spiral staircase that leads to the loft area, holding my luggage in one hand while gripping the metal railing with the other. When I get to the open floor plan with my bed, dresser, and mounted TV, I breathe a sigh of relief that I am home. Rolling my bags to the side, I head straight for the shower.

In the middle of soaping up my hair, my phone vibrates. Drying my hand first, I swipe it off the counter.

"Hey, how was your trip?" Dave's voice is low on the other end.

Dave and I met when I had a dental emergency, but my dentist was out of town. He was on call that weekend and offered to see me in one of his offices on a Saturday afternoon.

He drove in a small red sports car and hopped out in jeans, a white T-shirt, and dark sunglasses. I was attracted to him right away.

Over the last year and a half, we've dated casually. During those first few months, we both agreed that this was just for fun. I'd call Dave when I was lonely or had no one to go to dinner with, and then it morphed into us having weekends away together. We're friends who sleep together and spend time together, but the spark is nonexistent. It's more of a friendship, and the occasional hookup isn't bad—he gets the job done.

"It was good. I'm in the shower. Can I call you back?"

"Don't forget I'm taking you out tonight," he reminds me as if I'd forgotten.

Water drips down my arm. "Yeah, at eight, right?"

"That was the plan, but I'm actually at your place now. Buzz me in."

Irritation creeps up my back. Dave said *eight*. I'm not ready to be social yet. I clamp my eyes shut. I need to relax. He's just being nice.

"Okay, give me a minute to get dressed."

"Alright, I'll be down here waiting."

After tossing my phone back on the counter, I shave my legs and get out. It only takes me another ten minutes to slip on a nice red dress and high heels and put on a little makeup. *Shit!* I forgot Dave was still downstairs waiting for me. He doesn't need to come up now since I'm ready to go.

Me: Headed down.

Dave the Dentist: Finally. I thought you had forgotten about me again.

I chuckle nervously, typing out a response. He acts like it happens frequently. It does happen often, but what does he expect? I live in my own head half the time.

Me: HaHa.

I swipe my clutch off the top of my dresser and fly down the stairs. I'm pushing through the double doors on the ground floor and straight out of the building in no time. Dave is standing off the side, with annoyance written on his face. I'm always late, and he hates it.

"You could have just buzzed me in," he deadpans as I loop my arm through his. He's wearing a white collared shirt, dress pants, and more cologne than usual.

"Sorry!" I rush out—a loss of breath from sprinting down the hallway in heels.

"I'm used to it."

I curl my lip at him, but suddenly, my scowl turns into surprise when I see a limo pull up in front of us.

"What is this, Dave?"

"It's a limo," he says. "I thought that was obvious."

"I know it's a limo." I watch as he opens the door for me. "What is it doing here? With us?"

He gestures for me to get in. "It's a surprise."

Weary and unsure, I oblique and slide into the back seat. "Alright."

Dave jogs around to the other side and joins me. "I know you don't like surprises. But you'll love this one."

Dave's love language is acts of service. And I don't mean back rubs or foreplay that focuses on me—he likes to buy things and have things bought for him. I would appreciate the gestures more if they were authentic, but his usual acts of grandeur are meant to stroke his ego.

"You know, you don't have to *buy* me." I playfully smirk.

"I know you have enough money of your own. But I want to remind you of what I can give you. And maybe, at some point, we'll be able to share it all."

Share it all—what does that mean?

The limo pulls up to the back of a tall office building in the

Arts District. A gust of warm May air whips past me as the car door opens. When I step out, that same desert breeze moves through my hair. Dave comes around the other side and presses a gentle hand on the small of my back.

Glancing upward, my eyes scan each floor comprising dark windows, except for the top floor. The yellow glow of the lights and the tables nestled toward the window make me recognize this is a restaurant—and I think I know which one it is.

I turn to Dave. "Saguaro and Wren?"

His smile beams with confidence and a subtle hint of smugness. He knows who he is and what he's capable of and will never give up the opportunity to flaunt the privilege he was born into.

"Yeah, the most exclusive restaurant in the valley," he tells me.

The elevator door opens to a hostess stand.

"Welcome. We've been expecting you, Dr. Stoll." The hostess with the high blonde ponytail greets us.

He's had decades-long connections in the city. The Stoll family owns a large group of dental offices across the valley. His two siblings, father and mother, are all dentists and work out of the prospective offices.

I drag my eyes around the top-floor restaurant and along the floor-to-ceiling 360-degree views. The lights from downtown Phoenix and the low glow from the teacup table lamps are the only lights in this dim space. It's dreamy and romantic.

"We're happy to be here," Dave says as we both watch the hostess grab two leather menus.

"Right this way." She smiles, gesturing for us to follow her. We both fall into step behind as she weaves through the empty tables in this oddly vacant restaurant. *Why is there no one else here?* This restaurant is one of the best in town and is typically fully booked months in advance.

I began putting all the pieces together as we approached the candlelight table covered in red rose petals.

"This is perfect, thank you," Dave compliments, walking over to pull out my chair.

My throat runs dry while I try to swallow the formed cotton ball. *Oh fuck.* My eyes roll over the deserted space, and one more time, a group of staff members lined up by the kitchen door with broad smiles. Then, I find the hostesses, three young girls giggling behind the stand. *Oh my god.* When my focus circles back around to Dave, he kneels before me.

I gasp. Panic zips up my back. *He's going to propose!*

"Avery?" My name rolls off his tongue with confidence and ownership.

"Mhmm?" is all I manage to say as my heart pounds inside my chest. I can barely form words.

"I would wait until after dinner to do this, but I knew if I didn't do it now, then I wouldn't be able to enjoy my food," he tells me. I bite back a chuckle but let him continue. "It's only been a little more than a year, and I know we started as some casual thing, but I also know that you want more." *Do I?* "I'm getting to that age where I'd like to settle down. I need someone to come to events with me, support the boards I'm on, and play nice with the other wives."

This proposal is in true Dave fashion.

"Okay." I nod, fighting the urge to speak because this sounds more like a contractual thing than anything else.

Then Dave slips out a small black velvet box from his front pocket. "This is custom made," he quickly says before uttering those four words with life-changing power. "So, Avery Thomas." He clears his throat. "Will you marry me and become part of the Stoll family?"

A sharp ringing in my ears is all I hear as everything around me goes silent. The light clinking of dishes in the kitchen disappears. The sound of my own breath echoes inside my skull as if underwater.

I should marry Dave. And I believe with all my heart he'll provide me with a safe and secure life. We'll continue to be friends, occasionally hooking up for mediocre sex, who would be living together. We'll rarely fight, he'll agree with most things I say, and we'll live happily ever after in mundane marital bliss. But I know things could be better—I've had better. But I'll never have a love like that again. I've accepted it.

But the moment the word "Sure" comes out of my mouth, I don't get flashes of plans for my dream wedding or fantasies of a future with him. The only image that flashes through my mind is of someone else's, reminding me of a secret I've kept for eight years.

I'm already married.

Chapter Two

THEN

Avery

It's not that I've never loved the beach. I have, but moving to a small beach town from a large city in the desert isn't something I ever imagined I'd be doing.

Filled with conflicting emotions, I walk into my aunt's small sea foam-green beachside cottage.

"I hope you feel at home here, Avery." Her voice is sweet as she takes my luggage to one of the two bedrooms in the home. My aunt Helen is a single, middle-aged, self-proclaimed beach bum. She lives alone, does what she wants, and has a group of friends who are the same way. Never getting married or having children, she enjoys her freedom—until now.

I follow her down the short hallway with the sound of ocean waves rolling in and out along the surf surrounding me. This is the new soundtrack to my life. "Thank you."

Rolling my suitcases to the corner of the room, she quickly cranks the lever on the slatted windows, closing them. "The water can be loud sometimes."

I glance around the tiny bedroom. A queen-size bed rests

against one of the windows, and a white vertical dresser with a seashell-shaped mirror is on the back wall.

"It's fine," I say.

She tucks a corkscrew curl of her grey hair behind her ear. "I'm so sorry you're going through this."

Shrugging my shoulders, I try to brush it off. This is a common phrase I've heard often since losing my parents only a month and a half prior. I should be more upset, but I'm not. The only term to describe my emotions at this time is apathetic. *How can I feel nothing? Aren't I supposed to be sad?*

"I'm glad you're here. It's no secret your dad and I weren't close, but I wished I'd gotten to know you better." She shuffles her feet, unsure of how to address her estranged relationship with her brother. "These horrible circumstances have forced us together, but I hope we can try to connect in the process."

I swallow hard while a single tear falls from my eyes. "Thank you, Aunt Helen. I appreciate you doing this for me."

"Oh, honey, there was no question in my mind when I got the call that I wanted you to live with me," she says, sweetly cupping my face.

I close my eyes and pull my lips to the side, forming a half smile. *Maybe I won't have to pretend to be upset around her.* It's been a constant theater act since the accident, with me as the main character. Accepting heartfelt condolences from my parents' employees, friends, and business partners, I played the part of the grieving daughter. I carefully constructed this cozy childhood filled with warmth and laughter, which could be further from the truth.

"Well, I'm going to let you be to get settled." She glances

around the room one more time. "This is all you brought?"

"Yeah, that's all I brought," I repeat her words, somewhat embarrassed by my lack of connection to the items I once owned.

Uncomfortable silence.

My parents' lawyer organized the estate sale, which sold out in a weekend. All of my things were included. I had no desire to keep anything but my clothes and shoes—even those I dumped most of. I've never been attached to material items, and my parents never kept anything from childhood. Two properties, a boat, and their investments were all put into the trust, with me as the beneficiary. My mother's precious jewelry and family heirlooms are now in a safe deposit box, along with other things I have no desire to access anytime soon.

"Okay, sweetie," she says, changing the subject. "We have the cutest little downtown area with surf shops and stores. So, if you need anything, just let me know, and we can head into town whenever you want."

"Okay, thank you," I say, carefully sitting on the edge of the bed.

"A couple of my girlfriends and I are going down to the beach for a little bonfire and dinner if you want to come. If not, I'll bring food back here if you're more comfortable."

Hanging out with my aunt's middle-aged friends is the last thing I want to do right now. I'm numb, yet a few tears still drizzle down my cheeks. I can't quite figure out what they represent, though.

I want to be left alone.

"I think I'm just going to stay here tonight." I force a weak smile. "Thanks, though."

"Alright. We'll be sitting outside in front of my friend Sherry's cottage. She's only two houses down to the right," Helen explains, pointing behind her. "I'll bring you back food in a bit."

I give her a quick nod. Then she gently shuts the door and finally grants me the solitude I've been deprived of for over a month.

Falling back onto the thick down comforter, my body molds into the softness of the mattress. I stare at the ceiling without a thought in mind. Should I be worried if I'm not falling on the floor crying hysterically by losing my parents or if I were gutted by facing an unknown future without them, but I'm not. *Is there something wrong with me?*

I should be missing them, but I don't. This situation feels no different than my life was before they got into their accident. I rarely spent time with my parents because they traveled often. As I grew up, I began to prefer it to be that way.

The humid sea air sticks my long hair to the sides of my damp cheeks. *Why the hell doesn't she have a ceiling fan here?* I sigh and place a palm on my belly, still facing the low light blue ceiling of my aunt's beach cottage—my home for the next four months until I head back to Arizona for college in the fall.

Rolling onto my side, I get a better view of the bedroom. It is cute, simple, but comforting at the same time. Even with the windows shut, I can still hear the faint sound of the waves outside. I inhale the salty sea air, and suddenly, a sense of warmth washes over me. It's shockingly calming.

I pop off the bed and beeline right for the attached bathroom. My eyes bounce from one seashell decoration to another.

I chuckle at the stereotypical beachy theme. I take in the individually painted shells lining the walls and breathe in the light scent of coconut—*my favorite smell.*

Bending over the sink, I let my head hang low.

"Fuck," I whisper under my breath. Then I turn on my faucet and splash cold water on my face. Glancing up, I barely recognize my solemn expression. My long, straight, dark hair fans my back and shoulders, and my hazel eyes look greener in the dim light. The few freckles on the bridge of my nose have become more visible as the little makeup I had on has since come off.

I need to get out of here. I suddenly feel claustrophobic.

I push off the sink, slide on my sandals, and leave the room. Heading down the hall, I see no sign of my aunt. She has probably already headed out to the beach with her friends. I notice the propped-open double-pocket doors when I enter the small living room.

Taking it as an invitation to walk outside, I step from the indoor rug and directly onto the wooden deck. The breeze whips through my hair. Pushing it aside, I capture the beauty of the water and the pastel-colored cottages that line up and down the beach for miles.

Two houses down, I spot Helen with a group of people sitting in lounge chairs. Her smile is wide, reminding me of my dad's—the few times I witnessed it. They're joyfully chatting under the orange hue of a sunset.

My stomach grumbling breaks me from my stare. I should walk over there and introduce myself to her friends and neighbors. Since I will stay here for the summer, I want to know who they all are.

I blow out an audible breath and head down the three steps onto the sand.

"Hi, sweetie," Helen greets me as I approach the group. "Are you hungry?"

"I am," I say, slightly nervous.

I watch as she drags an extra chair through the sand. "This is my niece, Avery, who I've been telling you about," she introduces me to the group.

A short woman with bleach-blonde hair waves from her chair. "I'm Sandy."

Two more people introduce themselves, but I don't hear them because a loud buzzing whips past my ear. Simultaneously, I catch sight of a dark shadow coming directly toward me. A sharp pain hits the left side of my face. I lose my balance, and instantly, I'm knocked into the warm, unforgiving sand.

"Oh my god!" I hear Helen gasp.

"Is she okay?" A woman's voice I don't recognize.

Flashing lights dot the darkness on the inside of my eyelids. My cheek is throbbing with pain. My arm flies up to protect the ache on my skin, but a steady hand stops it. Fingers gently wrap around my wrist.

"Don't touch it," the smooth yet commanding male voice instructs. I listen, releasing my muscles. "I'll take her back to your place to get some ice."

"What happened?" My eyes flutter open just as I'm hoisted into what feels to be moist, bare skin.

"Alright. Thanks, Jasper. I'll call Dr. Waverly to see if he can come by to give her a quick once over."

"I'm okay," I mumble, a little dizzy.

"I'm going to grab you some ice anyway." His breath is labored. My left eye barely opens through the pain. I keep them closed, but I know we've entered the house since the sound of the waves is muffled. "I'm going to sit you up on the couch."

I nod. The man, who smells of suntan lotion and a hint of sweat, gently sets me down. Letting my back rest against the cushioned armrest, I'm slightly propped up.

I peel open my eyes, one at a time, then blink them a few times until his face comes into focus. Staring back at me is a pair of large brown eyes and a head full of tousled dark brown hair attached to a shirtless guy.

Fuuuck.

"Hi," he whispers, kneeling on the floor before me.

My stomach flips. I'm suddenly aware of how I might look. "Hi."

"I'm Jasper." He pushes a few loose hairs away from my eyes. "Are you alright?"

His tanned, misted skin makes my mouth dry, trapping a ball of air in my throat. I struggle for a minute to speak. "I'm—um, I'm Avery."

"Helen's niece," he says like he already knows. *He did know which house to bring me back to.*

"Yes."

"Are you okay?" He pauses. "Avery?"

I wince. "The side of my face is on fire."

"Sorry about that," he softly apologizes, climbing to his feet and walking to the refrigerator. "It was me who accidentally hit you with that volleyball."

What the hell kind of luck is this? The first day I get here,

I'm on the direct path of a rouge volleyball—which happens to belong to an incredibly attractive surfer who looks my age. *How fucking embarrassing.*

"Here." He hands me an ice pack before sitting beside me on the couch. *Will he put on a shirt?* How am I supposed to have a casual conversation with him when I can only focus on those golden pecks and that white shell necklace dangling from his neck?

"How do you know my aunt?" I ask, recalling her use of his name on the beach.

"She is *friends* with my dad." Then he glances down, blushing a little.

My eyebrows snap together, wondering why he'd be shy about his dad's friendship—*oh.* "Are they—?"

"Yes." He nods. "They're friends who spend a lot of time fucking each other."

I laugh. And not just a light giggle, but a deep roaring laugh from within. "Wow. Okay. Go, Aunt Helen."

He smiles. His eyes dart to the floor before meeting mine again. "If you're staying here for the summer, you'll get used to their late-night *hangouts.*"

"Good to know," I quip, my cheeks burning. Resting the ice pack on my knee, I bounce it nervously.

Jasper removes it from my hand and returns it to my cheekbone. The chill forces a breath. "You'll want to leave it on a little longer," he says, leaning closer. "The ice will help with any bruising."

He's only a few inches from my face. I was never good with math and have had a tutor since middle school, but I bet there are less than four inches between our lips.

"Thank you," I whisper.

"How are you doing, sweetie?" Helen barges into the house with two friends close behind her, breaking the tension between Jasper and me.

Jasper backs away and stands up. "I grabbed Avery some ice."

The way he says my name, drawing out each syllable to savor, makes my heart beat faster.

"I'm fine, I promise," I reassure her with a smile.

She frowns. "On your first day here too."

"It's usually not that violent on our little strip of the beach." Her blonde friend adds sympathetically.

"I spoke with Dr. Waverly, and he said that he's sure you're fine as long as your pupils dilate and you can walk in a straight line," she rushes out with a worried tone.

I rise from the couch. "I promise, I'm totally fine."

Helen glances over at Jasper. "Thanks for bringing her back."

"No problem." His eyes flicker to mine. A bolt of electricity shoots up my spine.

Jasper turns to walk out, but I'm still reeling from our moment. Not sure if I should say bye to him or not. *Why wouldn't I?* That would be weird if I didn't. "It was nice meeting you!"

He smiles at me from over his shoulder while running a hand through his messy hair. "I'm sure I'll see you around."

And that was it. That's all it took for me to become intrigued by him—his confident go-with-the-flow attitude and messy surfer hair.

Chapter Three

Then

Jasper

"I can't believe you hit her in the face," Riley spats, straddling his surfboard while we wait for another wave to break. Easton and Bodhi went into Joe's to grab a fish taco. Those fuckers haven't stopped giving me a hard time since last week when my rogue volleyball came into a direct collision with Helen's niece's face.

The event unfolded in slow motion as I ran at full speed through the thick sand and over to her.

"I was annoyed our game was interrupted," I puff.

"We were for sure going to lose the game to those bastards from Shadow Falls anyway," Riley replies, shaking out his wet hair. "But I can't let you live down how shitty that spike was."

"It was an accident," I repeat for the hundredth time this week.

"Sure," Riley retorts. "And you didn't look that annoyed when you carried her into Helen's house. Like some knight in shining fucking armor."

My heart skidded to a halt when my eyes fell on her dark

brown hair and tiny freckles on the bridge of her nose. It's true, I wasn't bothered any longer. I was pleasantly surprised at how that situation worked out for me.

"I hit her in the face." My palms flip into the air. "What else was I supposed to do?"

"I'm just saying, dude." His voice drawls out, letting me know I won't be living this one down for a while.

"Fuck you," I reply. We both share a laugh. With my legs draped over either side of my board, I lift myself with locked arms and glance over my shoulder for the wave. "The water's too calm today."

"I saw her yesterday at Shore's Bikinis." He smirks, ignoring my attempt to change the subject.

My ears perk up. "Was she shopping?"

He licks his lips, and suddenly, I don't like the look on my friend's face. "She was working there."

Did she get a job already? Interesting. "Do you know much about her?"

"I don't. You're interested, aren't you?"

A smile slipped, and finally, I decided to give in to Riley's harassment. "She's fucking hot."

"Totally."

"I only spoke to her for a few minutes when I took her back to Helen's house, but there's this intense deepness to her that I find fucking sexy."

"She has this gothic princess vibe." He beams. *I still don't like that look.*

"Nothing like the girls here in town."

"Aren't your dad and Helen still hooking up?" he says, more

of an observation than a question. "That's a good excuse to hang out with her niece."

I shrug. "They are, and that's not a bad idea."

Riley stretches his arms, cracking his knuckles. "Duke's the man. He's going to be single forever."

My father hasn't been in a real relationship since my mom died when I was young. They were childhood sweethearts, and both grew up in Coconut Grove. Sometimes, the thought of not knowing her causes me deep sadness. Growing up, I tried so hard to remember things about her. I'd use pictures to help create memories that I don't have.

What I do remember, though, was how hard it was on my dad. Since then, he's had a string of hookups where none stayed long—until Helen. She's independent and supportive, and she accepts my dad for being the distant man he is.

"I don't think he wants anyone in this town. He grew up with all of them, just as we did," I say.

"But he liked Helen because she was an outsider," he states, assuming that's why they've stayed in their *relationship* for as long as they have. "She's not a permanent fixture in this place like we all are."

Bodhi and Easton are waving us down from the shore. Tenting my eyes to get a better look, I notice they're both holding cardboard boxes, probably filled with tacos.

Riley cups his hands around his mouth. "We're coming!"

"I'm starving," I say, flipping onto my stomach.

Riley does the same, and we both paddle to shore.

"It was about this time yesterday when she was working." He smirks, not even using her name. He knows I'm still thinking about her. "Wanna head over there?"

Hell fucking yes.

"Why not?" I roll my shoulders, trying to play it off.

"These are from Joe." Bodhi handed me a basket with three fish tacos in it. Joe is the owner of Joe's Taco Shack. He, my dad, and Bodhi's mom went to high school together. As most of us in this town, our families go way back.

"Thanks. I'm starving," I say, snatching the food.

"Jasper and I were thinking about going down to the boardwalk," Riley tells them.

Easton cocks a brow in my direction. "Dude, you hate the boardwalk."

"Remember that girl I hit with the volleyball last weekend? Helen's niece?" I begin with my mouth full.

Bodhi and Easton both nod.

"Apparently, she works at Shore's." Riley slaps my shoulder, interjecting before I have the chance to continue. "And Jasper here might have a thing for her."

"Looks like we're going to the boardwalk then!" Bodhi exclaims, then turns and starts walking toward the promenade.

"Let's fucking go," I call out, ready to see her again.

It's only a ten-minute drive down the coast toward the other end of town. The guys and I immediately head over to the small shops.

"It's busy today," Riley observes, flipping his sunglasses over his eyes.

"I know," I agree, scanning the crowds. I think of all the missed sales my dad's surf shop is missing out on, not being located on this end of the shore. I told my dad we needed to relocate the shop a few years ago, but he refuses to give up his coveted spot on the south end of town. We're flanked by two luxury resorts and are just a short drive from many high-end businesses.

The four of us walk side by side down the boardwalk, where we've spent our childhood weekends, high school afternoons, and late nights. I lower my sunglasses to block the bright sun of this late afternoon summer day while simultaneously avoiding bumping shoulders with the tourists on the narrow sidewalk.

"Hey!" Easton calls out to a group of girls about our age standing outside a cafe. They all look over and smile, sipping drinks out of hollowed coconuts. *Tourists love those.*

"Let's talk to them," Riley suggests, pivoting in their direction.

"Yeah, buddy!" Bodhi nudges my arm. "Let's go."

I have no interest in those girls. My mind is hyperfocused on getting to know the one I hit in the face with the volleyball. I haven't stopped thinking about her vibrant green eyes and intense stare. This is my chance to see her again while I'm brave enough. I need to act on this impulse because it might not come again.

"I'll catch you guys later," I say, waving them off.

Easton pauses. "Are you still going to talk to Helen's niece?"

I nod. "I have my mind set on it now. Why not?"

"Good luck, man!" I hear Riley reply behind me. He's already approaching the group of girls. I feel better without the baggage of having my friends anyway. They would have made the situation more awkward.

When I get to the entrance to Shore's Bikinis, I don't go in immediately. Instead, I peer through the windows to see if I can spot her. After one quick sweep of the small shop, I spot her. Avery is standing in the corner of the store with a black sundress on. She's wearing the only black clothing in the entire store. I feel my lip curl into a half smile. The strings of what appears to be a matching black bathing suit top peek through the thin straps of her dress. Her long dark hair rests down to the middle of her back.

I catch myself drooling at the sight of her. *She's fucking gorgeous. I can't talk to her, what am I thinking?*

Just then, I see Francesca and a few of her friends walk into the store. I jerk my head back, hiding behind a large bush. Fuck. I hope she didn't see me. She just graduated from my high school and has been trying to get with me since her freshman year. I hoped she would attend school out of state, but I guess not. Her dad owns a hotel in town, and she likes to flaunt their family's money every chance she gets.

How could she think anyone would find that attractive? Only tourists and college guys are on spring break because that's all she seems to hook up with.

I watch as she struts right up to Avery. She glances back at the other two girls with her eyes lowered and a devious smile. The three of them say something and then start laughing, but the look on Avery's face doesn't seem like she finds whatever was said funny. A protective surge shoots up my spine, compelling me to step in.

Against my better judgment, I yank the handle on the door and strode in. Adrenaline is pumping through my veins, knowing that Francesca is acting like the pretentious snob she is.

As I approach the group of girls, I hear one of them comment about the *lack of color* Avery is wearing and that the *only reason she got this job is because of her aunt Helen*.

God, I hate Francesca. I walk right up to Avery and slide my arm around her neck. "Hey, babe. When are you off?"

Avery looks up at me with her eyes wide. "Um, hi."

I smile at her, then look over at Francesca.

"Hey, Jasper." She gives me a fake greeting. "Do you two know each other?"

I turn to Avery, appreciating being so close to her. *Of course, I take advantage of the situation.* "We do."

Avery's eyes bore into mine while her eyebrows furrowed with confusion.

"Oh."

"We're dating." I smirk but keep my tone steady with confidence. "This is Avery."

She turns her nose up in the air. "Yeah, we've met."

"Good," I reply sarcastically, then turn back to the beautiful girl under my arm, who still looks perplexed. "What time are you off?"

Avery rubs her lips together as her cheeks flush red. She *is* attracted to me. *Hell yes!*

"In twenty minutes, actually." She smiles.

My eyes remain locked on hers. "Do you want to meet me on the beach when you're done?"

"Sure," she answers with a nod.

"Okay, well, see you around, Jasper," Francesca mumbles before leaving the store. I assume she was quickly followed by her friends. I barely notice she's gone, and when I do, I realize I asked

Avery to meet me for both the benefit of pissing off Francesca, but also for me.

I slowly remove my arm from around Avery's shoulder. "Awesome."

When I stepped back, she was not the only one flushed.

Embarrassed, I play it cool, running a hand through my hair. "Okay, well, see you around."

Without waiting for her response, I turn on my heels and power walk out of the store with the tips of my ears burning all the way out. Although choking at the last minute, that could not have gone better.

I take a seat on the bench outside the store. I'm not waiting long because Avery walks out exactly twenty minutes later.

My heart pounds in my chest. I smile, nervous but excited. I try to make eye contact, but she keeps her head down and continues to walk toward the parking lot.

Did she not think I was serious?

Popping off the bench, I jog over to her. "Hey, where are you going?"

"Home," she replies as if I should already know.

"I thought we were meeting down on the beach?"

She stops walking and turns to face me. "You were serious?"

We had a moment—or so I thought. Now I feel self-conscience. I'm such an idiot.

"Yes." I wipe the beads of sweat from my forehead and suck in a deep breath. *I can't punk out.* "Do you want to take a walk along the beach with me?"

Her eyes lower. "It's sunset. Which means it's almost dark, and I don't know you."

I chuckle, then extend my arm for her to grab my hand. "Come on." Avery hesitates. Her green eyes fall to the ground, then back up to me. "I don't bite, I promise."

"Okay," she agrees, then cautiously slips her hand into mine. Her hand is small and soft and feels good.

With the sounds of the surf in front of us and the chatter from the boardwalk behind us, I lead her through the sand toward the water. Not thinking any of this through, I struggle with what to say. *Should I make small talk?* I want to get to know her, but she makes me nervous.

"So, you work at Shore's?" I ask, immediately turning my head away to curse at myself for such a stupid question.

Avery nods. "I wanted to get a job for the summer."

"You're only here until August, right?"

I briefly heard from Helen about how her niece was coming to stay with her because her parents died.

"Yeah, then I head back to Arizona for college." Her fingers twitch inside my hand, but she doesn't pull them away. "I'm sure you know I'm here because my parents died."

"I do."

"And you haven't asked me about it yet?"

I shake my head. "Nope."

"Why?"

"If you wanted to tell me, you would."

"Oh." Avery chews on her bottom lip, looking deep in thought or just trying to explain to herself that I'm not here to judge her. "Okay."

"So, you *wanted* to work?" I tease, gesturing for Avery and me to walk around a family building a massive sandcastle.

She coyly tucks a few loose strands of hair behind her ear, giving in my attempt to change the conversation. "What else should I do in a town where I know no one?"

"You could have just hung out at the beach all summer and enjoyed a little vacation before you go back to school," I say.

"Last time I was on the beach, I was knocked in the face by a volleyball," she quips.

She's flirting with me.

I laugh. "Yeah, sorry about that."

"It's alright." She looks down, smiling. "Thanks for the ice."

"No problem."

We're still holding hands. Should I let go? I only held my hand for her to follow me, but now I don't want to let go.

"So, do you have a job?" she asks.

I smile while we slowly walk along the shore. The sun sets over the horizon, and the light rays create a yellow hue, making it impossible for me to stop staring at her.

Whenever she catches me, we both look away.

"I work at my dad's surf shop," I tell her proudly. "I also teach surf lessons to tourists."

She rakes a hand through her windblown hair. "That's really cool. Do you like it?"

"I love it. When my dad retires, my plan is to take over. I'd also like to buy a few beach properties out here to fix up and rent out." Without realizing it, my thumb caresses the insides of her palm.

"A man with a plan," she teases. "Thanks for stepping in with those girls earlier."

I gently kick the sand at my feet, keeping my focus on the

ground. I get a little flutter of butterflies when she thanks me, and for a brief moment, I don't know what to say in return. "You're welcome."

"You don't have to be nice to me just because I'm Helen's niece."

Is that what she thinks? Should I admit to her I find her energy intoxicating and her personality intriguing? Not to mention how beautiful she is?

I can't say any of those things.

I stop walking and turn to face her with a slight smile on my face. "That's not why I did that."

Her eyes blink rapidly. "Then why did you?"

"For one thing, Francesca is an awful person." I pause, capturing her gaze in mine. "And for the second thing, I think you're absolutely beautiful."

Under the dusk sky, I can see Avery's cheeks turn three different shades of red.

"You do?"

She's blushing. She likes me too. I nod. "Yeah."

Now what to do with that information, I don't know.

Chapter Four

Now

Avery

My back hits the door. I mold into the material like a part of the wood. Staring down at the enormous diamond on my finger, panic courses through my veins, pulsing at a rate more powerful than it had earlier. Holding every emotion in for the last three and a half hours was pure torture. I have to marry Dave, so of course, I accepted his proposal.

I don't love Dave, so that means he won't hurt me. If he were ever to leave, have an affair, or become distant one day, I know my heart will be forever safe inside my chest.

"I need a fucking divorce," I whisper to myself inside the secure walls of my apartment.

It's been eight years since Jasper and I ran off together to get married. I had just turned eighteen, and he was turning twenty that fall. We knew nothing about love. Spending a summer under the sun, between the waves. I lived in my bikini just as much as I lived for him. I was utterly captivated by him.

We promised to spend every waking moment together for the rest of our lives. We were inseparable, devoting ourselves to one another, living in pure bliss of young love. Soon, I'd learn better because who finds their soulmate when they're that young anyway?

The summer that changed my entire life. I gave him my heart, and he shattered it into a million pieces. I've never given it to another since—and I never will. Unable to feel that deeply again, I've succumbed to the fate of marrying someone I'm not entirely in love with.

Flipping over my hand, which now carries a rock that could sink the Titanic, I stare at the black ink of the infinity symbol on my wrist. I have to say goodbye to him, especially now more than ever. A single tear falls onto the tattoo. The symbol of love that has meant just as much to me as the person I got it for.

My legs are weak and a little shaky. I slide onto the floor while unintentionally slipping the thousand-dollar designer heels off my feet. I need to speak with my three best friends. They'll know what to do. They know all about Jasper but do not know that we've been married since I was eighteen.

Clawing at my purse, now feeling an urgency to release my secret, I take out my phone and text them in our group chat.

Me: Hey, babes, I've got some heavy stuff to discuss. Are you free to come over to my house? I know it's late, but it's important.

Lina: Are you okay?

Me: Yes, I'm fine. But I'll need to talk to you three in person.

Lina: Say no more. I'm on my way.

Piper: Thank God Jack and I are in town. I wouldn't have wanted to be away for this. It sounds big.

Bailey: Of course. Be right over there. Piper, do you want me to pick up your preggo ass?

Lina: Haha.

Piper: Obviously. Avery, you had better have snacks. It's time for my second dinner.

I laugh. I love them so much. My best friends. My sisters.

Me: I'll make you some breakfast.

Bailey: Mmm breakfast is my favorite.

Me: I know it is.

Lina: I'll just have a smoothie.

When I tell my friends what I'm about to say, they'll need more than a smoothie and breakfast to help digest the news. Poor Piper won't be able to have a drink either. Glancing over at my fully stocked wine fridge and then quickly at the whiskey on the counter, I mentally prepare myself for what I'm about to tell them.

Me: See you all soon.

I peel myself off the hardwood floors, wipe my eyes, and deeply breathe. I haven't told anyone I've been secretly married, and I have no idea how to begin the conversation.

I walk into the kitchen, take out an old-fashioned glass, flip off the top to my favorite bourbon, and pour slightly more than I usually would. The first sip travels through my body, blanketing me with heat and comfort.

Shockingly, another tear slips out. Jasper's emotional hold on me after all these years is infuriating. I have to let him go. I have to let *us* go.

I stand in my kitchen for an unclear amount of time, filtering through memories of getting hit with that fucking volleyball. Little did I know that summer changed the person I was, and not just because I lost my parents—but because that man changed my brain chemistry.

The building buzzer downstairs goes off. I sprint to my double front doors and let the girls in.

Lina barges through and immediately finds the glass of whiskey on the counter in the kitchen. "Damn, you've already started?" She walks over, takes a sip, and grimaces. "I don't know how you drink this shit."

"I don't know how you drink those dirty martinis," I playfully retort.

"Touché." She places her hand on her hip. "Bailey and Piper were right behind me."

"You look so tan from your trip," I say.

Lina gives me a coy smile. "Bora Bora, baby. And I'm surprised I got any sun at all. Carter and I spent most of the time in our little over-water hut." She pauses, running her tongue along her teeth. "We fucked everywhere."

I laugh. "I'm not surprised!"

Just then, Bailey and Piper walk in, wearing workout clothes similar to Lina's. "Alright, it's ten o'clock at night, and you're dressed like you just returned from a fancy dinner. What gives?" Piper comments.

"Should we sit down?" I say, gesturing over to the couch.

Bailey's eyes narrow. "I have known you for a long time, and you're never this formal. Your text got me worried, but your demeanor is unsettling."

Bailey knows me too well. We lived together for four years in college and then again while I was attending flight attendant school. Lina and Piper have concerned expressions.

"Look, I'm safe. But this is a secret that I've been keeping for a long time, and I'm finally ready to tell you guys."

Without a word, all three of my friends slowly enter the living area.

"Wait, I was promised breakfast." Piper frowns, bringing her legs up and tucking them to the side.

Bailey laughs. "We'll make your food, but we must hear this first."

"Okay, but don't forget I'm growing a human over here," Piper says.

"We know," Lina whispers, resting her head on Piper's shoulder. "Spill it, Avery."

I sit on the edge of the couch, leaving some distance between me and my friends. I try to gather my thoughts mentally from the words before they hit the air, but the silence is deafening.

"Dave proposed to me tonight." Sucking in a heavy breath, I prepare to release the secret that I've kept safely inside my heart for years. "But I'm already married."

The color drains from Bailey's face. "Wait, what?"

Piper's jaw drops. "I'm sorry. Did I hear you—"

"What?" Lina interrupts, her pupils dilating.

"I know you'll have many questions, but I need to get this out first." Rubbing my sweaty palms along the tops of my legs, I take their silence as my cue to begin. "You guys know my parents passed away when I was seventeen, and I moved to Coconut Grove with my aunt Helen until I started college, right?"

Bailey chews on her lip, and both Lina and Piper slowly nod. I know they're all fighting back unhinged reactions, but they'll need to fight their urges longer.

Squeezing my eyes shut, I continue, "So, Jasper and I got married that summer—" Bailey opens her mouth to speak, but I bring one finger to her lips, silencing her. "We've never actually divorced either." Cocking my head to the side, I wait for their flurry of reactions and questions, but all three of them remain quiet. "Okay, I'm finished."

Bailey glances at Piper, and then Piper's eyes dart over to Lina's.

Lina smashes her lips together and then makes a popping sound while separating them. "Alright, so that's a lot of information."

"I need a drink." Bailey lifts off the couch and heads for the kitchen. She pulls the cork out of the wine, brings it to her mouth, and takes a swig directly from the bottle.

Piper, now the more level-headed one, surprisingly smiles at me. “Well, um, so can we get into how you *actually* got married and kept it a secret from everyone for years?”

I sigh, feeling the weight of keeping this from my friends for so long. “It’s a very long and emotional story, but the most important thing is that it was hard to keep from you guys.”

Bailey stands in my kitchen with a bottle of wine in one hand and her eyes as wide as saucers. “I can’t believe you kept this from us.” She pauses. “*From me.*”

I nod. “I’m sorry. You know how I am about opening up.”

“Hyperindependence is not always a good thing, Avery,” Lina adds thoughtfully. “I’ve heard it’s a trauma response.”

Piper pauses, gliding her hand over her growing belly. “We can spend time grilling Avery at a different time.” She shoots me a side-eye, telling me she’s not going to let me get away without a better explanation. “The important thing to address right now is why are you two still married?”

“Dave the Dentist proposed?” Lina laughs, interrupting my train of thought and breaking the intensity of the situation.

I roll my eyes. “Yes, he did.”

Lina chuckles under her breath, stifling a laugh.

I jerk my head around. “Seriously?”

She senses my frustration and calms her amusement. “I’m sorry. You know we think he’s a nice guy, but is he for *you*?”

I roll my eyes again, more drastically this time, and flip my hair in her direction. “He’s a good match for me. I’m not willing to discuss that with you all right now.”

“Fair enough. But the question still stands,” Bailey asks,

gripping the neck of the bottle in one hand. "Why didn't you and Jasper ever divorce?"

I stare at the floor with my mind completely blank. I'm still unsure. I don't know how to answer her question, so I respond in the most honest way I can. "I don't know."

"What do you mean you *don't know*?" Piper challenges.

Lina arches a brow. "This is why." Then she grabs my wrist and flips it around. "She's still in love with him."

"I forgot about your tattoo." Piper rests her chin on her palm.

I jerk my hand away and stand. "I get that you guys want to go all therapy session on me, but I just need to talk this out."

Lina walks over to Bailey, removes the wine bottle from her hand, and takes a drink. "Sorry, Avery. We get it."

"What do you need right now? Advice or love?" Piper asks sympathetically.

I exhale. "Thank you. I have every intention of marrying Dave. But I need to fly to Coconut Grove to see Jasper. I need a divorce."

Piper grimaces. "Are you even ready for that?"

"You haven't seen him in what, like seven years or so?" Bailey adds.

"Eight," I mutter.

Lina's back behind me. She rubs my shoulder comfortingly. "Do you want me to go with you?"

I shake my head. "This is something I need to do by myself," I say, then bend and rest my hands on my knees. "I'm just incredibly nervous about it."

Bailey rests a warm hand on my back, too, just as a glass of whiskey comes into my view. I take it from her hand and gulp the rest of the two ounces.

Piper shuffles over and places her comforting hand on my back as well. "We'll be here for you, whatever you need."

"You're *really* going to marry Dave the Dentist?" Lina smirks. Bailey, Piper, and I all shoot Lina with the same side-eye. "Okay, okay, one thing at a time. No matter what, you need that divorce."

"And you both have never tried to contact each other this whole time?" Bailey asks, trying to make sense in her own head why Jasper and I would have let this go on for so long.

I shrug my shoulders. "I've never been ready to face him, I guess. It was easier to pretend like it never happened."

Lina nods. "I get that. Especially since it seems he hasn't initiated anything either."

"Yeah. I don't know if that makes it better or worse?" Bailey gnaws on her lip nervously.

My head hurts. I have a plan and know I must do it as soon as possible. Thank goodness I have saved quite a bit of vacation time.

"Thank you." I smile, grabbing Lina and Piper's hands while Bailey wraps her arms around me. "Now, let's make some breakfast."

"Yes, queen!" Piper chants, pulling away to clap excitedly.

"And then we need to figure out how we can get you a divorce," Lina calls out, grabbing my laptop and taking a seat at the bar. "It shouldn't be that hard, right?"

Piper scrunches her nose, straining to get into the chair next to Lina. "Don't forget, she needs a place to stay too."

I remove a pan from the cupboard while Bailey grabs eggs and cheese from the refrigerator. "You know, we could run the world, right?"

Lina glances up from the top of my computer. "Obviously."

Bailey and I cook breakfast at almost midnight while Lina and Piper take care of my travel arrangements.

Thank god for these women.

Chapter Five

Now

Jasper

I lean back in my chair, pinching a quarter between my thumb and index finger. Giving it a quick spin, I watch as the silver disc rotates on my desk. Lost in thought, the warm summer air brings the repeated heaviness of what I once had and lost.

"Jasper?" I hear Gail, my assistant, say my name over the top of my computer.

I dart my eyes to hers just as the quarter hits the floor. "Yes?"

She clutches a stack of manilla folders against her chest with a frown. "The start of summer is always hard for you," she says softly.

I rub my lips together, giving her a subtle nod in agreement.

The corners of her eyes wrinkle more than they usually are. "How long has it been now?"

"Eight years."

Gail's eyebrow knit. "And you haven't thought about trying to find her?"

I've thought about it every single day for those first few years. But with every painstaking year that passed, it got easier to accept that things would never happen again between us. A fleeting love that you read about in books or see in sappy romance movies. The reality was much different.

"Of course, I have."

It took a long time to accept, but with grief, the mind finds a way to push through. I had to realize that the woman I was unequivocally in love with, the woman I married at nineteen years old, who would have been the mother to my future children, no longer wanted me.

"And?" She lowers her thick glasses.

"She left me, Gail," I say, stiffening my posture. I'm unsure if it's harder hearing those words uttered in the comfort of my own skull or reverberating through my ears. Either way, they both feel shitty. Avery was clear about what she wanted and *didn't* want in her life, and it sure wasn't me. Letting her go was the hardest thing I've ever done, but I knew it was what she truly wanted.

Gail lets out a deep sigh and glances around the room before turning her eyes back on me, wondering if she should continue pressing or let it go. "Well, okay then. How's Melanie?"

"Fine," I say, shuffling a few planning and zoning documents around my desk. I need to work on these approvals as soon as I can. The last few days have weighed on me.

"Just fine?" She curls a lip in shock or disbelief. I'm not sure.

Melanie and I have had this casual thing for the last few months. She moved to town last December to help with her sister's clothing store and never left.

I shrug. "I mean. She's nice."

Gail shakes her head, laughing. "You are unbelievable, Jasper."

"What?" I ask, even though the distaste in Gail's tone is always apparent. She hasn't liked Melanie since meeting her at an event at City Hall last spring. Gail says she's *power hungry and craves the attention associated with being with the mayor*. If that's true, the joke is on her because she's not getting anywhere with me.

"You are the mayor of a touristy beach town. It's like every young woman's dream," she trails on.

"Your point?" I accept her flattery but brush off the comment. "Don't you have kids whose love lives you can meddle in?"

"I do, but they're not as fun." She warmly smiles.

"Aren't I the lucky one," I quip.

"You brought this on yourself!" she teases.

Gail is the same age as my mother would have been. She was our accountant at my dad's shop for years. When I became mayor, I knew she had to come. Taking on the title of assistant from accountant took a lot of convincing and a pay raise. But let's be honest, she runs this place.

"I did, didn't I?" I laugh.

"Don't forget, you must attend the opening of Easton's new coffee shop this evening," she reminds me. Easton is my best friend. I wouldn't have forgotten.

"I know. He's been blowing up my phone about this second location for months," I say, clicking on a random email.

"He's so excited," Gail mutters. "I'm close to finalizing the last-minute paperwork for Coconut Grove Days. I'll keep you updated." She turns on her heels to leave my office, then quickly flips her neck around. "Are you going to take Melanie then?"

When I was a teenager, I never struggled with girls. Now, at twenty-eight years old, I'm struggling with maintaining long-term relationships.

"She'll probably be there. She's at all my events, but I'm not *taking* her like a date if that's what you're asking," I answer, giving Gail a side-eye for her good-hearted overstepping.

Gail smiles, raising her eyebrows. "Just checking!"

"Thank you for your concern, but again, it's unnecessary."

Gail turns to leave my office but quickly whips her head around once again. "Oh, and I must leave early today, if you don't mind. Devin is flying into town with his new girlfriend this afternoon."

"I bet you're excited to see him," I say, keeping my head down and skimming the documents in front of me. "And this is the first time meeting your son's girlfriend, right?"

"Yes!" she replies excitedly. "I spent yesterday evening cooking."

"Have fun visiting with them this weekend," I say, jumping to a new task of glancing through my emails. I can't stay focused.

I stare at these unanswered emails, none of which need to be addressed immediately. I feel my eyes gloss over. My mind is blank. This time of the year rips me apart. The pain never subsides, and the hole in my soul remains unfilled.

I wipe my hands down my face in exasperation with myself. *How can I let her get to me after all these goddamn years?*

"I'm taking a personal day," I yell through the open double doors of my office.

Gail pops her head in, a sympathetic expression on her face. "I figured."

I nod, then log off my computer and grab my things. The beach is the only place I can go on this day that makes me feel better.

I'm already itching to hit the waves after the short drive from town to my small beach house. I walk in, strip off my clothes, and slip on shorts. Heading straight for the back patio, I grab my surfboard, ready to clear my head. The minute my bare feet hit the warm sand, I feel calm.

"Successful grand opening," I compliment, approaching the bustling restaurant with a satisfied smile. I love seeing Coconut Grove flourish with new businesses.

"It definitely helps having my best friend as the mayor." Easton pats me on the shoulder while we walk into his coffee shop after the ribbon-cutting ceremony.

I shrug it off. "You say that all the time, but I have to attend events like this all over town, you know that."

"I'm just saying." He leads me to a table by the window, quickly glancing at the line backing up at the order counter. "Everyone thought we were these troubled, parentless surf boys who were going nowhere in life." His palms come up to move through the air. "And look at us now."

I nod. "Look at us."

"Yeah. Me, opening my second coffee shop. You, the fucking mayor? Riley and Bodhi ..." he trails off.

One of the servers brings over a coffee and a slice of banana bread and sets it down in front of me. "It's on the house, Mayor Collins," she says coyly.

"You can call me Jasper," I tell her.

The server's eyes bounce over to Easton, then back to mine. "Jasper." Her tone is bashful and unsure. She bows awkwardly, then skips away.

I cock a brow. "What the hell was that?"

"Yeah." He laughs. "I told her she needed to address you formally."

I roll my eyes, taking a sip of coffee. "You're an asshole, you know that. Hazing your new employee is fucked up."

"It's not my fault that you're the most laid-back mayor," he says. "Who prefers everyone to call him by his first name."

"If you ever left this small town, I'm sure you'd realize it's more common than you think," I quip, teasing my best friend while knowing he has spent his entire life here with no intention of ever leaving.

I guess the same can be said of myself.

Suddenly, Easton's expression takes an empathetic form. "How are you holding up lately?"

I bend my leg over my knee and lean back in the wooden chair. "Why does everyone keep asking me that?"

"Because we're your friends, and we care about you," he says. "Your anniversary is coming up soon, isn't it?"

"July twenty-eighth."

"We used to live for summertime." Easton makes eye contact with one of the servers, then points at the table behind us, alerting her they're waiting for the check. Then he turns back to me. "Now, it's lost all its joy."

I shrug, scoffing at his observation. "We still surf and eat tacos together like when we were kids, so I don't know what you feel changed that much."

"Don't treat me like a random person who hasn't known you your whole life. I was there that summer. And I have been around ever since."

I swallow hard and sigh. *My best friend is right, but why has it been so hard for me to admit? Am I ashamed that I still let her get to me after all these years?*

Easton and I quickly plaster on fake smiles, waving to a group of patrons entering the coffee shop.

"This time of the year has been hard for you ever since she left."

He's not going to let me off the hook without acknowledging something. "It's strange how one summer changed every other that has come after." I sigh. "It was three months, for fuck's sake."

"When are you going to move on?" he asks.

"I have no idea," I tell him. I hope that one year, when the tides turn and the warm breeze rolls in, I won't be reminded of the dull ache in the pit of my stomach—the emptiness and longing for what could have been.

"Maybe you won't." He leans forward, resting his elbows on the table. Easton is the only one out of my three best friends with whom I can have these conversations.

"What do you mean?"

"When you know, *you* know," he counters.

I rub the back of my neck, then crack it a few times, chasing relief from the last bit of tension that wasn't taken care of earlier this afternoon. "Well, it doesn't matter now. I need to move on."

"Have you been able to hit the waves at all?"

I nod. "Yeah, I took a half day and spent the rest of the afternoon on the water." I shrug. "It helped a little."

"I loved Avery, you know that, but I also want to see you happy."

"I am happy. I have a conference to attend at the end of the month, and a woman from the Orange County Chamber of Commerce caught my eye last fall," I begin to explain, anticipating the next phase of this conversation will be me moving on from Avery. I need to truly put myself out there with someone else. "I was thinking about asking her out."

"Okay, this is a good start." His hand flies up in front of us. "That would be long distance, but I guess that's better than nothing."

"I'm not sure if you're trying to hype me up or insult me."

Easton folds his arms across his chest. "Both."

"I would expect nothing less."

"You guys are still legally married, right?"

My eyes dart around the room, and I feel insecure about how casually he drops that information. "Yeah."

"It's been eight years." He raises and grips the back of the chair. "Maybe it's finally time for that divorce."

"Maybe that's what's preventing me from moving on," I say, mirroring his position. "What if it's like a subconscious thing preventing me from, you know, forgetting about her?"

"I don't think it's about forgetting. I think it's more about just making peace with it," Easton says.

Does peace mean acceptance? Am I at a place of acceptance yet? I'm not sure.

Chapter Six

Now

Avery

The bright sun and crisp, familiar ocean air remind me of where I am. Not every beach smells the same, but this one gives off a scent of home—but also heartbreak and suffocation. The window is down, causing the wind to whip through my long hair.

I forgot how aggressive the breeze is out here.

I pull my rental car into the short, steep driveway of the beach bungalow I'm renting for the next few days. I suspect closing this chapter of my life will be difficult, so I took some time from work to face it.

Piper apologized when she booked this location for me because it's just a short distance down the shore from Jasper's dad's house and my aunt Helen's. I preferred to keep my distance by staying somewhere in town, but they were all booked. Summertime is a popular time for tourists.

The one-bedroom, light blue cottage with white shutters looks inviting—a perfect place for a beachside getaway. The whole town is like that. But beneath the allure of seaside living is the pain I've felt since I left so many summers ago.

Removing my luggage from the trunk, I keep my eyes down, hoping my aunt isn't somewhere on the beach. We've kept in contact here and there since I left for college, but she reminded me of Jasper because I didn't know her well before I met him. I lost parts of myself that summer, and the reminder of it has been too painful.

The distance has hurt Helen, but it was essential to my emotional health. I thought of what I'd say to her about my sudden appearance on the plane ride. She needs to know why I never returned to visit and why I had to stay away. Deep down, I know she understands why.

I didn't tell her I was coming back to town for fear I'd change my mind. I suppose it would be easier to do this electronically, through mail, or by my lawyers, but I need to face this part of my life to move on.

The instant the door swings open, I get hit with the familiar moist air that comes from living on the water. The place is cuter than the pictures. It has a small living room off to the side, a quaint coastal-themed kitchen, and a short hallway with only a bathroom and bedroom.

I roll my suitcases into the bedroom, then quickly peek around, heading back into the living room to text the girls.

Me: I just got in. The place is super cute.

Lina: Christian said you guys landed a while ago. I was just about to text you.

Christian is a friend of ours. He and her boyfriend, Carter, are both pilots for our airline.

Me: The perks of knowing everyone in the airline industry.

Piper: Haha, Lina. I'm glad you like the place. Again, I'm sorry that it's not more private.

Me: It's fine. I just appreciate you handling it for me.

Bailey: What's your plan after you get settled?

I take a deep breath, then tap out a response.

Me: I'm going to head to my aunt's house to see if she knows where Jasper is.

Lina: You're not wasting any time, are you?

Me: My emotions can't afford to spend any more time here than is absolutely necessary.

Piper: Good luck! Keep us updated.

Bailey: We'll try to leave you alone for the next few days, but please check in.

Me: Of course I will. Love you, babes.

After a quick shower, I throw on a sundress and sandals, then head out the back door. Walking a short distance down the shore, I quickly eye Helen's little cottage. My stomach flips with every step I take. The familiar sounds of the surf rolling in and out, the warm breeze, and the low buzz of summer insects bring me right back to that time.

Swallowing hard, I gather my wits, then knock on my aunt's door.

"Avery!" she exclaims, falling into me with a full hug. "Oh, honey, it's so good to see you!"

I wrap my arms around her. Our embrace feels good, maybe even strengthening. "It's good to see you too."

Clutching my shoulders, she pulls back to look at me. "This is such a wonderful surprise."

"Can I come in?" I gesture behind her.

"Oh, sorry, yes!" She steps aside. "Of course."

I walk into the adorably small space. Not much has changed in the years since I've been here. I smile to myself with her familiar comfort, but within that same breath, a forced gulp surfaces. These memories are more intense than I thought they'd be.

Squeezing my eyes shut, I sit on the white linen couch while my aunt hurries into the kitchen.

"I'll grab you some lemonade," she calls out.

"Thank you," I say, tucking my sweaty hands underneath my legs.

A brief moment later, she returns with two light blue plastic cups and a pitcher of lemonade. I remove one from the tray while she settles into the spot across from me—her sun-kissed cheeks and tangled, sandy blonde hair warm my heart. *I've missed her.*

"I'm so excited to see you, but your unannounced visit worries me." Helen sips her drink. "Is everything alright?"

Rubbing my fingers along the condensation of the cup, I avoid eye contact. I have to tell her Jasper and I are still legally married, and then quickly follow it up with the fact that I'm now engaged to another man. I practiced these sentences endless times on the trip out here, but now I can't find the words.

"I'm okay, and everything is alright—"

She lets out an audible breath. "Oh, thank goodness. How is work?"

I quickly regroup to think about work instead, relieving some of my anxiousness. "Work is really good. I love flying."

My aunt smiles softly. "That's great to hear, dear. I've always been so proud of you for attending college and making a career for yourself instead of just living off your parents' inheritance."

"Thank you." I nod, then bite my lip. "I'm actually here for a reason, though." I pause, waiting for her to interrupt, but she doesn't, so I continue. "You know it was hard for me when Jasper and I broke up."

Helen's expression falls with empathy. If anyone knows how difficult that time was on me, it's her. "I know it was."

A vivid memory flashes across my mind like a streak of lightning. "And the other thing too."

Her comforting hand finds the top of my knee. "Oh yes, honey."

"Well, I'm here because the guy I've been dating for the last year proposed to me last weekend."

She pops up. "Oh heavens! That's wonderful. Congratulations!" But when I don't mirror her excitement, she chews on her lip and slowly sits back down.

"Jasper and I never got our marriage annulled or got divorced."

The color drains from her face and her body stills. Her eyes dart around the room. "We might need something stronger than this, love."

"Do you have any whiskey?"

Helen arches a brow. "Good call, I'll grab the hard stuff."

I thread a shaky hand through my hair as clinking glasses echo from the kitchen.

"Okay, so spill it." She hands me a shot-sized amount of amber-colored liquid in a glass.

I breathe in the warm scent of the bourbon before I continue. "He was my everything, and I thought we would be together forever."

Helen leans in, bringing her warm hand back to my knee. "I know."

"Life has been complicated for me since then." The heaviness in my heart intensifies when my words travel through the space between us.

"Why didn't you tell me you two were still married?" She winces, swallowing down a sip. "Why hasn't Jasper told me? I see him all the time. He's the fucking mayor. You'd think it would have come out at some point."

My heart stops. *Wait. What?* "Did you just say he's the *mayor*?"

"I guess we are a small town, so no one ever knew. And he's dated—" Her face shows panic as she halts conversation with herself.

I'm not naïve enough to think he has dated anyone in the last eight years—hell, he probably has a live-in girlfriend by now. Maybe even has a kid—or *kids. Oh my god, I'm going to be sick.* I force down the bile, inching up the back of my throat.

Refocusing my eyes on the soft pile rug at my feet. "It's fine, Aunt Helen. I know he's been with other people." I straighten my posture. "I'm over him. I was over him a long time ago."

She smiles sympathetically, but I know behind her kind gesture, she doesn't believe me. "I know that break up was hard for you, especially after losing your parents just a few months earlier."

"It's fine now. I promise. It was a long time ago." I roll my thumb over the divots on the glass. "But you said he's the mayor now?"

"He is. It's crazy to imagine, right? But he isn't that troubled surfer kid he once was." Her face brightens. "It's only been a little over a year since he was elected, and he's done incredible things for the businesses in the town."

I'm shocked. That's the last thing I expected him to be. I imagined I'd find him without a job, surfing all day and living in a little shore house. I'm surprised at the airy feeling in my chest at the thought.

"That's, uh, great to hear," I say, taking a slightly larger drink this time. "Is *he* married?"

"No, but that's probably because you two still are." She smirks, trying to lighten the mood.

"Oh yeah. Of course." I run my tongue along my teeth, knowing that time is of the essence right now. "I have our divorce papers in my bag. I figured I should do this in person."

"I understand." She crosses one leg over the other, more relaxed than she was when we first sat down. "Are you staying with someone close, or would you like to stay here?"

Of course, she's worried about me. Not overly affectionate, but warm enough to make me feel safe and secure.

"I'm staying in a rental just down the beach." I gesture behind me.

"Oh, you're close?" Her eyes light up. "That's the Hannah family's house, I think."

"Yeah, I think so." I shrug, assuming she's right because Piper had booked it for me. "It's a cute spot."

"Are you planning on seeing Jasper today?"

Her question is typical in nature, and yes, that was the plan the whole time, but it still hits me at the core like I'm just realizing it. I need to shut the fucking door on this chapter of my life. I'm ready to be done. This hold he's had on me for years must be broken. I'm desperate to be free of it.

I clear my throat. "Yes, I'd love to handle it as soon as possible."

"I understand," she says, nodding vigorously.

A text comes through from Dave.

"One moment." I glance down and can't help but laugh that I still have him saved in my phone as *Dave the Dentist.* If the girls knew, they'd never let me live it down.

Dave the Dentist: I have back-to-back appointments for the rest of the day, so I won't be able to answer if you call me.

Me: Okay. I made it here safely.

Dave the Dentist: I figured. Remind me why you needed to go to that small town anyway.

Me: There are just a few things I have to take care of, and that's all. And I wanted to tell my aunt in person about our engagement.

Dave the Dentist: You're probably miserable. I hate little towns like that. Good luck.

Irritation zips up my spine. Despite the heartache this town caused, I created the best memories of my life here. It's a cozy little beach town, and it would make for an unforgettable vacation under different circumstances.

Glancing back up at my aunt, she has a puzzled look on her face. "Your fiancé?"

"Yes. Dave." I rub my lips together, then set the phone back on the glass table.

"You don't sparkle like a woman newly engaged," she mumbles under her breath.

"I need a divorce, Aunt Helen."

Her lungs suck in an audible breath like she can feel the weight on my chest. "I know, dear."

Rolling my shoulders back, I straighten my posture. "Where can I find him?"

"His office is downtown. It's a weekday, so I'm sure he'll still be there."

I chug the last bit of bourbon before rising to my feet. "Thank you. I'll come back to visit before I leave town," I reassure her. With a silent smile, I grab my purse and head toward the front door.

"I'll be here." Her words are upbeat, but the slight frown tells me she's either worried or sad. Neither of which I can think about right now. As I close the door behind me, I promise myself to do a better job at keeping my aunt in my life.

The warm sand sprays the back of my legs as I trudge through it toward my rented beach house. I take the steps two at a time, going in through the patio door. With determination and adrenaline pumping through my veins, I swipe the manilla envelope from my bag, tuck it under my arm, and leave through the front door this time.

My mind is blank, driving down the small streets of this coastal town. Even with the subtle changes in town, I can still spot most of the original surf shops and restaurants here. It doesn't take me long to reach City Hall.

A small one-story building with a white exterior and light blue trim around the edges, it could not be more quaint and fucking adorable. As I pull into the parking lot, my heart hammers, and my palms sweat. *Can I do this?* With shaky hands, I pull into a parking space next to a sign that says "Mayor."

To my side sits a black BMW sedan with dark-tinted windows.

Oh my god, he's here.

"You can do this, Avery. Be strong," I mutter, taking a few weighted breaths. I grab my bag from the passenger seat and exit the car. I consider leaving at least two more times on the walk up the short rose-bush-lined walkway. Two antique surfboards don both sides of the entrance.

I can fucking do this. I yank on the door, and a gust of cool air hits me when I take my first step inside. An older lady with tortoiseshell glasses tips her head from beyond her desk.

"Can I help you?" she drawls.

I swallow the growing cotton ball in my throat. "I'm here to see Jas—the mayor."

"Is he expecting you?"

I shake my head, my eyes darting down the long hallway to my left.

"I'm sorry, but the mayor only sees people who have scheduled meetings with him," she dismisses me and returns to her work.

I raise my tippy toes, leaning over her desk until I'm only a few inches from her face. "He'll want to see me."

Shocked by my forward gestures, her eyebrows snap together. She looks like she will challenge me but doesn't, so she lifts from her chair. "Can I tell him your name?"

"Tell him Mrs. Collins is here to see him."

"Um, okay, Miss." She pauses, confusion sweeping across her face. "One moment."

This is it.

Chapter Seven

Now

Jasper

"Of course, Gerald. I'm sure it's going to be a fantastic event." I lean back in my chair, tucking the phone into the crook of my neck. "Let me know if anyone at the chamber needs help from our office."

"You're the best, Jasper. Thanks," he says. Just then, Gail scampers through the French doors of my office. Her face is flushed.

"We'll talk soon. Take care." I abruptly end the call, sensing Gail's flustered demeanor. "You look like you've seen a ghost."

"There's someone here to see you." She pauses to take a breath. "Harper, the new receptionist, said that the woman told her." She pauses again with her arms bent while she twiddles her thumbs. "Her name is Mrs. Collins.

My heart stops. "I'm sorry, what?"

Gail cranes her neck, looking over her shoulder and down the hall. "She said her name is *Mrs. Collins.*"

I blink a few times, flipping through the possibilities of who this could be because there's no way it's Avery—*not after eight years.* I bet it's someone messing with me.

"Okay, well, send her in then."

Gail nods nervously. "If you need anything, Sheriff Wyatt is still in a meeting in the conference room."

I chuckle. "No one's going to hurt me. It's probably just a joke."

"I don't know, Jasper. I was watching Dateline last night—"

Raising my palm to the air, I silence another one of her many true crime recaps. "I'll be fine."

"Alright." She huffs, then swiftly exits my office.

I focus back to the never-ending tasks of things to complete before the annual Coconut Grove Days event this weekend, when I hear shuffling on the floor and a light creak of my office doors closing.

"I need a divorce."

I feel my eyes widen, straining the top lids. Glaring at the unopened email at the top of my list, frozen in place and scared to look up.

A voice that I haven't heard in years but one I will never forget. *Am I hearing things?* My throat runs dry—my heart pounds in my chest. I lift from my chair without looking up. If it is her and she thinks she can just come here without a *hello* or *how are you* then she has another thing coming.

"I need a divorce," the voice repeats, firmer this time.

It takes less than a single second for my eyes to meet hers—those gorgeous hazel-green sparklers. I feel a smirk pull at the corners of my mouth as soon as I notice her annoyance. "I almost didn't recognize you with your clothes on."

"I'm surprised you own more than board shorts and a shell

necklace," she quips.

I slide my hands into the pockets of my jeans. "That's not the only surprise I can give you, Arizona."

"Alright, Jasper," she says, crossing her arms at her chest. "You know what I'm here for." Avery is still feisty. I'm not surprised at how much joy it still brings me to piss her off.

"Nice to see you too, *wife.*" I walk around my desk until I'm in front of her. She's wearing a light blue sundress that hugs every curve—the same curves I've had my hands and mouth all over.

Damn, she looks good. I bet she still tastes the same.

Avery backs away, placing a hand on her hip. "I'm not here to play."

"I think I can change your mind." I smile widely, showing my teeth.

"Seriously?"

I lean against the desk with my legs crossed at my ankles, trying to seem casual and unbothered, even though my insides jump excitedly. "You want a divorce *now*?"

Her eyes dart away, then back to me. "Yes."

"I have an extremely busy week ahead of me."

Avery's hand flies up in front of us. "You're making excuses."

"You can't just come back into my life after nothing for years and expect me to drop what I'm doing to give you what you want."

"It's not what you want too?" A flippant response, which concerns me if she really is serious. "Don't you want to move on with your life? I'm sure you have a girlfriend—or many you'd like to put a ring on."

"Jealous?"

"Of course, that's what you'd say."

"How about this?" I attempt to harden my expression to seem more serious, even though I know she can see through it. "We'll discuss it after this week is over. I have the Coconut Days event happening." I pause to wave at Gail through the glass in the doors. "Let's have my assistant check my schedule."

Avery's mouth drops. "What?"

Gail slips through the door behind Avery. "Yes, Jasper?"

"Can you check my schedule for the beginning of next week, to see if I'm open for an hour-long meeting with Mrs. Collins?"

Gail smiles but is unsure of what's going on. "Sure."

Glancing back at Avery, I make sure she sees the smug expression on my face.

Her lips are set in a hard line, and her arms are crossed tight at her chest. "Dammit, Jasper. Why do you have to make everything so difficult?"

"That's what I do."

"I flew all the way out here to close this chapter and now you're brushing me off?"

Pushing away from the desk, I return to my chair. "You didn't have to fly out here. These things can be done electronically now."

"I have tried to contact you!"

"When?" I bite back. She did it once, about a year after she left. I wasn't ready to give up, so I ripped the papers and threw them into the trash.

She rolls her eyes. "You know when."

"Maybe." I cross my leg over the other.

"Don't you want to move on?"

Suddenly, my phone vibrates. *Perfect timing.* "I have to get this."

Her eyes grow wide. "Are you fucking kidding me right now?"

Raising the phone to my ear, I hold a finger up to her. "Gail will see you out," I say, waving at my assistant again.

"Jasper," she warns, her voice low with frustration.

I do want to see her again. She can't leave town yet. Not until I get my closure.

"Leave your number with Gail, and I'll call you."

"Fine." She lowers her eyes, flexing her posture. "If you don't, I'll be back."

"Mayor Collins," I answer the call, then quickly hit the mute button. "Considering how well that worked for me last time, I doubt it." *I know she will, and I hope she does.*

Avery's mouth is pulled to the side, the outline of her plump red lips turns white. "Asshole."

"Love you, too, wife," I call out in a low voice as she stomps out of my office.

As soon as I'm alone, I hang up the phone. It was just a telemarketer, but oddly, this time, I'm grateful it was a call like that.

I jog around my desk to shut the doors, then scan the hallway for any sign of her. She's gone. There are so many different emotions colliding into one another inside me. I've always hoped I'd see Avery again, but I also knew she'd probably have moved on. I haven't pursued a divorce, and I'm not sure why. *Maybe because the thought of hope is too much to lose? Or maybe not having some type of connection to her feels incomprehensible.*

I spend an unclear amount of time staring at my computer screen, contemplating life if I am to lose her again.

Gail pops her head in. "Was that Avery? Like *the* Avery?"

I nod.

She scrunches her nose. "What's she doing here?"

Letting out an audible sigh, I shrug my shoulders.

"You don't know what she wants?"

"I do."

Silence.

She rests a hand on my wooded desk, cocking a hip. "But you're not going to tell me, are you?"

I glance over with a side-eye. "Nope."

"Well, you're no fun." She huffs.

"It's not what you think."

"Maybe you should invite her to the Coconut Grove Days?"

"I don't think she's in town for pleasure," I mumble under my breath.

"It's worth a try," she replies in typical Gail fashion—kind, sweet and optimistic.

I shrug my shoulders.

"Okay, I can take a hint," she says before leaving my office and closing the door behind her.

My heart never slowed for the remainder of the afternoon.

Walking to my car, I scroll through my phone, searching for Avery's number. It was surreal putting it in after Gail read it off to me before I left. As soon as I heard the first three numbers, I recited the rest in my head. I've had it memorized for years. I figured she'd have changed it, but she didn't.

Is it too soon to call her? I can't let her know I'm anxious to speak with her. Maybe I can chalk it up to being respectful of her time. No, she'll never believe that. *Ugh.* I wipe a palm down my face and hit send on the number that's been tattooed on the back of my eyelids for most of my adult life.

"Jasper," she says my name in a breathy tone as if she's relieved to hear from me but annoyed by it simultaneously.

"Don't act like you're not happy by my call. I know you've been waiting for me all day," I quip, keeping my voice low.

"You'd love that, wouldn't you?" She sneers.

"What are you doing?" I ask, starting my car.

She pauses before answering. "My takeout just arrived, so I'm sitting on the deck eating dinner."

"Are you staying with Helen?"

"I'm not, but oddly enough, just down the way from her house in a vacation rental," Avery replies.

While taking the last left into my driveway, it quickly dawns on me Avery might be staying at the Hannah family's beach house. They spend the summers in Seattle and rent out the small bungalow while they're away.

"Isn't that the Hannah family beach house?" I ask, walking inside and heading straight for the bay windows toward the water.

"Yeah, I guess so."

As if fate couldn't have planned it better, my new place is exactly three houses down from the Hannahs—which means less than a two-minute walk from Avery right now. Opening my balcony doors, I stare down the beach at the row of cottages and bungalows, letting my eyes land on hers. I can see the lights on, but I can't make out if she's on the back deck or not.

I bite back a satisfied smile. "Where did you get takeout from?"

She sighs. "Did you just call me to chat?"

Getting comfortable in one of the chairs on my lower-level deck, I prepare to keep her on the phone as long as possible. The sound of the waves is now amplified through the phone because we're both listening to the same ones.

"I haven't decided yet." Propping my feet up on the opposite chair, I smile at her annoyance. "I'm the mayor, you know, so I have a personal interest in all the businesses in this town."

"Yes, I realize that." Her words are tight. *She's smiling.* "Are we going to talk about a divorce?"

I'm not going to make this easy on her, but I am surprised at how fast she got back to the topic of divorce. I might have to save this little game for another day. "I have another call coming in. I'll contact you tomorrow."

"Jasper!" she exclaims.

"I promise. I'll call you in the morning," I tell her, then end the call. I glance over at her cottage to notice the light is now out. She's pissed.

Now that I feel like I've done my part for the day and stalled her attempt to leave town so soon, I can focus on what I plan on doing to ensure she stays. *Do I want her to stay?* I do, but in what context? She left me once, and I'm pretty confident she'll do it again.

I lift off the chair, close the doors, and head inside to make myself dinner. Walking through my three-story beach house, I imagine what it would be like to have someone to share it with, but the solitude of being alone is hard to let go of. Avery extinguished those dreams long ago. By now, we'd have a child with whom to run through these halls. I'd teach him or her how to surf and raise them in this small coastal town I love so much.

Chapter Eight

THEN

Avery

I thought getting a job would help me make friends, but the last two weeks have done nothing to further that cause. When my aunt Helen mentioned her friend Mel was hiring for her sought-after bikini store on the boardwalk, I jumped at the chance. Staying cooped up inside my bedroom was not something I wanted to do for the next three months.

It's a benefit that Helen knows almost everyone in town, but that also comes with the bonus of local catty girls, who conveniently found and sniffed me out in this small town. I assumed I'd left that sort of behavior in high school. Of course, the ones out here in Coconut Grove have found me. They sense I'm different. Girls like that always do.

I know it.

"So, how's it going?" Cassie is one of the employees here at the bikini shop and the only other girl my age who doesn't seem to pick up on my insecurities. She's been ...not overly friendly, but kind. I'm not sure if it's genuine or just curiosity on her part.

"Fine," I say, shrugging my shoulders.

Cassie cocks a brow. "Sorry, Francesca's a bitch."

"I really don't care." I keep my focus trained on the box of new sandals in front of me.

"Francesca has been trying to get a job here for a while, as most of the girls in town do," she tells me like it's some type of consolation for the way she acts.

"I don't get what's so special about it. It's *literally* just a bathing suit store." I roll my eyes.

"It's a hot spot around here."

"So it seems." I stand in front of the mirror with another black sundress over my bikini. I'm not like these blonde, bubbly beach girls who surround this town like the plague. I feel like a black fly in a glass of chardonnay.

"Only three months," I whisper to myself, subconsciously counting down until I can return to Arizona for college.

"I saw you the other night after work with Jasper Collins." Cassie bends over the counter of the cash wrap, continuing to speak even though I'm disengaging.

"Yes," I respond vaguely, moving on from the sandals to the new palm tree swimwear line.

She squints her eyes, lowering her head to meet mine. "Avery, I feel like you have more to say."

My blush deceives me, creating a burn on my cheeks. I can't hide the flutters in my chest at the mention of him. She's the closest thing I have to a *friend* right now. I might as well gush to her.

I drop the hanger and turn. "What do you want to know?"

"What were you guys doing?" Cassie's eyes grow wide, and a grin forms on her face. "Are you into him? Your aunt and his dad have had this thing for years," she trails off.

"I don't know. Um ..." I suck in a deep breath. "He pretended to be my boyfriend a few days ago when Francesca and her friends were being bitchy to me and then asked if I wanted to meet on the beach after work. So, we did."

"Jasper is ridiculously hot. And he like never dates anyone seriously. Not even when we were all in high school," she shares with me. I can't lie. Her information about him makes me happy.

I chew on the side of my cheek. "You went to school with him?"

"Yeah, he and my brother were friends. I think he's about a year or so older than us."

"Helen mentioned that he's going to take over his dad's surf shop, and that's why he decided not to leave for college last year," I recall.

"Yeah. It's insanely successful too. He's inheriting a gold mine," she says, gliding her tongue along her pearly white teeth.

I nod, more interested in what she says than ever. "Interesting. He doesn't seem like someone who has a lot of money."

"It's just him and his dad. They're both beach bums." She laughs again. "Living the life, I guess."

"He's modest," I mumble with a smile.

I respect that. I have no plans on telling anyone in this small town how much I'm worth. I'm not making that same mistake again. Growing up, people were just friends with me for my money. It's not worth the fake friendships they used to be when I was younger.

She takes my silence as a cue to continue. "If my family had that much money, I wouldn't want to go to school either." She chuckles, flipping her hair back.

It's funny because I want nothing more than to do the complete opposite.

"Avery, your raw juice is ready!" Helen's voice is muffled from the kitchen. She juices twice a day and insists I drink at least one.

I finish changing out of my bikini from work and quickly slip into a pair of drawstring pants and a tank top. Heading down the hallway, the sea breeze from the open balcony doors dusts my face with a light mist. *I could get used to this.* The ocean is the best part of this town.

"Do you remember Jasper?" my aunt asks, handing me a cup of green liquid. I grimace, weary of what's in it.

"Yeah," I casually answer, sipping my drink. Of course, I remember Jasper—the sexy, dark-haired surfer who knocked me out with a volleyball and whom I also had a long walk on the beach at sunset with the other night. *I definitely fucking remember him.*

She leans against the counter. "Well, his dad and I are ..." An uncertain looks sweeps across her face. "Friends."

I roll my eyes, chuckling. "You mean you two are hooking up?"

Helen blushes. "Um, yes."

"You don't have to be embarrassed. I get it." I wink. "You're a single lady. You should be able to play with whatever men you want."

"Oh my god, Avery!" She laughs and tosses a napkin at me. "Stop it!"

I laugh, catching it and throwing it aside. "Anyway, so what about him?"

"They're coming over for dinner tonight." Her grin is wide. "I hope that's okay."

Flutters fill my stomach at the thought of seeing Jasper again. My hand hasn't been the same since being tucked safely into his, only a few nights ago. "Of course, I don't mind."

"Are you sure? I want to give you as much space as you need," she says thoughtfully, reaching her hand over to rest on top of mine.

"It's fine. Thanks for asking."

Helen gives me her back, turning on the sink to rinse out the juicer. "We'll be eating outside, so please don't feel pressured to join us if you're not up to it." Her kindness is refreshing.

"No, I don't mind. Thank you for being understanding, though."

"Of course." She smiles, then walks over to the fridge. Helen's eyes dart around the shelves for a few minutes. "I was thinking we could barbecue, make a salad and some fruit."

I shrug. "That sounds great, but aren't you a vegetarian?"

"Oh, honey, we'll have black bean burgers," she assures me, then closes the door and pulls out her phone, seemingly to make a list of items we'll need. "Duke makes the best grilled watermelon too."

"Grilled watermelon?"

Her eyebrows bounce with excitement. "It's good. You should try it."

"I don't know, maybe." I catch sight of the clock on the wall. Realizing what time it is, my posture straightens. *It's almost dinnertime.* "Wait, what time are they coming over?"

She continues puttering around in the kitchen, going back and forth between cleaning the juicer and the fridge. "They'll be here any minute."

Oh no! I look sweaty and tired from work. The last time Jasper saw me after work, I was embarrassed about my appearance. Thank god the sun was setting when we spent time on the beach.

"I'm going to freshen up really quick," I stutter before bolting back down the hallway to my bedroom. I fluff my hair a few times, touch up my makeup, and then head into the adjoining bathroom to brush my teeth. My nervous appearance apparent in the mirror. *What am I doing?* I'm only here for the summer. I can't get myself hung up on my guy—that may or *may not* be into me.

Suddenly, I hear the light vibrations of voices outside my door. *They're here.* I let out a heavy breath and then leave the room.

"Hey, Avery." Jasper's voice zips up my spine as I round the corner into the living room. He's sitting on the couch with one arm propped behind him. Heat scorches my cheeks. Does he own any other clothes besides board shorts and T-shirts?

Fuck, he's hot.

"Hi." My voice shakes.

Helen and his dad, Duke, walk out of the kitchen. "This is my niece, Avery," she says, introducing me to Jasper's dad.

He gives me a warm smile and extends his arm. "It's so good finally meeting you. I've heard wonderful things from Helen and my son."

Jasper talks about me? My eyes fly over to Jasper, now with his leg bent and his ankle resting on the opposite knee. He's unbothered and simply smiles at me.

"It's great to meet you as well." I shake his hand.

"Avery, my sweet, you are in for a treat tonight because I make the best black bean burgers." Duke clasps his hands together. "And my son decided to join us tonight, so I'm sure he can keep you company while we cook."

No wonder Helen likes Duke. His energy is infectious. "Fabulous."

A few short hours later, Jasper and I are sitting in the sand under a tree, watching the sunset for the night. "Dinner was a lot better than I expected it to be."

"Eating healthy is simple when fresh produce is easy to come by," he says.

"Are you teasing me about coming from a landlocked state?"

"Those were your words, not mine," he retorts, shooting me a smirk.

"Funny."

Jasper leans back onto his elbows. "How was work today?"

"It was good, I guess," I say, brushing hair away from my face.

"You don't need me to pretend to be your boyfriend and scare off the mean girls again, do you?" he jokes.

I dip my head down, trying to hide my cheeks' redness. "No, that won't be necessary."

His eyebrows raise. "Are you sure? I don't mind."

"I'm used to girls like that." The phrase slips out of my mouth, and I instantly regret admitting it.

"What do you mean?"

I slap the sand off my linen pants, keeping my head low. "It's nothing."

Jasper leans forward, now resting his arms on bent knees. He turns his head, capturing my eyes in his. "Tell me."

I briefly pause before speaking. "I grew up more well off than the average kid, let's just say that." Rapidly blinking, I look away. "I was often used for my parents' money."

He nods. "Interesting."

"What do you mean by *interesting*?"

"Nothing." He scoots closer to me. "Then who was there for you when your parents died?"

A little forward of him to ask such a personal question, but I go with it. I can hardly admit to myself I've had no real friends, so why not a guy who I barely know?

"No one."

"Really?" He keeps his voice low, but it's impossible to hide the shock it's laced with.

Maybe if I tell him the truth that I never needed anyone anyway, then he'll drop the conversation, and everything will make sense why I've never had real friendships either. Or I could lay it all on the table, but admitting that I prefer to spend my time alone?

"I've never had any real friends." I pull my lip to the side, a little embarrassed about my submission, but whatever.

"I find that hard to believe." He smiles, then nudges my shoulder with his.

"I prefer to spend my time alone." I look away, avoiding the impending scrutiny for being different.

"But you're so friendly."

"Again, funny," I say.

"I am, aren't I?" His smile grows wider. The dull hue from the sunset casts a shadow across his perfectly sculpted chest. "I bet you're funny too."

"If you like dry humor?" I quip.

Jasper scoots closer to me once again, my leg is now flush with his. "I like whatever type of humor you have." *What does he mean by that?*

My breath hitches. "Maybe it's not just humor, maybe it's that I find being around people draining."

"I respect that. I'll try not to drain you ..." From the corner of my eye, I see his arm come up to the side of my face. His fingertips graze my cheek before he tucks a few loose strands of hair behind my ear. "If you'll let me be around you more."

I swallow cotton. My eyes locked on his. My mind goes blank, so I say the first thing that pops up. "The wind is going to loosen it again."

The side of his mouth quirks up. "Then I'll just have to keep brushing it away."

"Thank you," I whisper.

Our lips are less than a couple of inches away from one another, and I can't help but part mine with the anticipation of him kissing me. Jasper leans closer. The tips of our noses touch. I tilt my head to the side, letting my eyes fall closed, but the feeling of having his plump lips on mine doesn't come. Instead, I feel a light dusting off his breath. "What are you doing tomorrow?"

I pull back, licking my lips. Thoughts of confusion swirl around my thoughts. *Oh my god.* He wasn't going to kiss me. With my chest in a tight grip, I force out a response. "I don't work, so nothing."

His Cheshire smile lights me up inside. "Good. I'll be by your house around nine am."

I'm getting his signals wrong, but I will see him again in the morning. This doesn't make what just happened seem too much like an embarrassment. He just wants to be my friend—probably because his dad is fucking my aunt? I can live with that. Having another friend might make the summer go by faster.

"What are we going to do?" I ask.

"You'll see," he tells me, rising to his feet. "Make sure you're wearing a bathing suit. And don't worry, we don't have to talk much. We can just enjoy the energy if you want."

"Okay?" I look up at him, unsure of what I've just agreed to. I'm anxious, but also excited.

"Awesome." He starts walking away. *Wait. What?*

"Wait!" I climb to my feet. "Energy? What are you talking about?"

"Don't worry. It's good for your soul," he dismisses me with confidence.

My palms meet the air between us as the distance grows larger. "You're not going to tell me what we're going to do?"

Jasper looks over his shoulder. That sharp smile could cut glass. "Nope."

Maybe this summer won't be so bad after all.

Chapter Nine

THEN

Avery

I had butterflies in my stomach the entire night. I wish sleep was enough to calm their erratic flying, but it wasn't. I woke up earlier than usual, read a few chapters in a romance novel, and then had breakfast and a green smoothie with Helen. My nerves jump excitedly while I stand at the sink, rinsing my cup.

Twisting my arm in the warm water, I think of what Jasper could have planned for us this morning. An extra bit of daydreaming is sprinkled in because of how he reacted to me opening up to him yesterday. The absence of judgment or the typical expression of aversion left me feeling light and possibly even weightless.

A pointed knock on the door startles me from my steam-filled, lustrous state. I flip the water off and grab the dish towel to wipe my hands.

"Hey, Jasper." I hear my aunt greet him from the other room.

"Good morning, Helen."

I peek around the corner and spot him leaning against the side of the door with his hands firmly in the pockets of his shorts.

God, he looks good.

"What can I do for you?" She opens the door wider, allowing him to step inside. "Is your dad okay?"

"Yeah, everything is fine. I'm here for Avery," he says as I walk over, a smile beaming from ear to ear.

"Oh." A surprised look flashes on my aunt's face. Her eyes bounce from me to Jasper. "Okay."

"Hi." My voice hits the air with a firm tightness from biting back the uncontained grin.

"Hi, Avery." He smiles, and my knees go weak.

Helen steps back, letting me walk in front of her. "What, uh," she stammers. "What are you guys going to do today?"

Glancing at Jasper, I shrug my shoulders. He still hasn't told me yet.

"I'm just going to show Avery around the town." His voice is smooth.

Helen's eyebrow raises. "Oh, that's nice of you. When will you be back?"

"I don't know." He winks at her playfully. "I'm kidding. Before dinner."

Helen sucks in a deep breath, seemingly confused about whether she should be more curious or not. "Alright," she says, aggressively nodding. "I have a few errands today. Just text me if you need anything."

"I will," I say, slipping past her and out the door.

"Bye, Helen." Jasper waves her off while we both step off the patio and onto the sand.

"Have fun," she calls out, but her tone is low.

When we get closer to the break, I turn to Jasper. "I think

Helen was a little shocked we're hanging out."

He chuckles. "Probably."

Sitting halfway between Helen and his dad's houses, I notice the two surfboards in the shade. They're propped against the two large trees we sat under last night.

Oh no. Jasper's not expecting me to surf with him, is he? Shit. I can't surf. I'm going to make a fool out of myself.

"Wait." I stop, placing a hand out in front of us. My palm lands directly on the warm moistness of his skin. *Fuck.* Blushing, I yank it away. "Sorry."

"It's okay," he says, flipping his longer top hair away from his eyes. *Who would have thought surf guys would be so hot?*

"We're not going into the water with those, are we?" I point to the boards in front of us—one more weathered than the other.

He laughs. "That is what you do with surfboards."

"I know that," I say. "I meant, you're not expecting me to ride one, are you?"

Jasper walks over and runs his hand along the smooth, firm foam. "Yes. I'm going to give you lessons."

"Who said I wanted a surf lesson?" I scratch my head, playfully giving him a smirk but second-guessing every choice I've made this morning.

"You can't live here, on the beach"—he licks his bottom lips—"hanging out with me and not knowing how to surf."

"We're hanging out now?"

"Do you want us to hang out?"

Tapping my finger on my chin, I glance up at the sky, then back to Jasper. "Let me think."

"It's going to be like that, is it?"

I rub my lips together, staring back at him. "I think it is."

"So, Arizona ..." He takes a few slow steps toward me. "Can you swim at least?"

Did he just call me Arizona like it was an insult?

"Of course I can swim." I cross my arms at my chest, cocking a hip out. "We have pools in the desert, you know."

"Okay, good." His sly smile lights up my insides. Then, suddenly, the breath is knocked out of me. I'm lifted into the air and thrown over Jasper's shoulder. The pressure makes my stomach spasm, bringing out a full belly laugh.

I'm barely able to squeak words before he runs full speed into the ocean. "Jasper!"

"Hope you can swim!" he yells, diving us both into a low wave. We're sucked under the water. I quickly plug my nose and try curbing my laughter so my nostrils don't fill with salt water. Jasper's stronghold on my waist never loosens while he pulls me into him right as we both break the surface.

"What the hell?" Laughing hysterically, I wipe the water and snot from my face while simultaneously pushing my hair back. "If you wanted me to swim with you, you could have just asked."

"Will you swim with me?" Under the water, I feel his other arm wrap one of my legs around his waist. I let him move my body as he wishes, enjoying the gentle control. Then, I bring my other leg around to match. Our bodies are flush.

"Alright."

His broad, dark eyes flare as they bore into mine. "Let me teach you how to surf."

The intensity forces a hard swallow and a slight curve of my upper lip. Damn, it's hard to be this close to him and not kiss his wet lips. "If you really want to."

"People pay up to a hundred and fifty dollars for lessons from me." His gaze falls to my mouth, and the light dusting of his breath tickles my lips. "For only an hour. And I'm offering them to you for free."

"When you put it that way," I whisper, keeping my focus away from the only thought in my mind. "Do you have room in your schedule?"

Jasper's thumb caresses the skin of my outer thigh while his other hand cups my ass cheek, clutching me like he's afraid I'll get carried away by a wave. "I have room for *you*."

"Okay." I smile, my cheeks burning. "Let's get started." I gesture toward the beach, immediately regretting agreeing to embarrass myself. If this is what it takes to spend more time with him, so be it.

"Wait," he says, his eyes following back to my lips. They tingle under his intense stare. Jasper tilts his head to the side and brings his mouth to mine. My eyes close. When we connect, a shock wave travels up my spine, causing my hips to arch forward and rub against his length. His kisses are soft and intimate. I melt into him. His tongue darts out to run along the seam before I open to let him in. He moves with purpose, exploring my mouth. The spots on the backs of my eyelids increase with euphoria. I swing my arms around his neck, urging him into me and craving more. But he slowly pulls back, resting his forehead on mine. "I want to spend more time with you."

With my eyes still shut, I rub the tip of my nose across his. "We will be, you're giving me lessons, right?"

"I want more than this," he smoothly demands, softly kissing the corners of my mouth and tracing along my jawline.

I smile, my heart skipping every other beat. Thank god he's gripping me tightly because I would have been carried away by a wave. "I would like that too."

Clutching my hips, he urges me further into him, rubbing his hardness against my throbbing core. There are only a few pieces of thin fabric between us, and it would be so easy to push it all aside and take him in. But I've never slept with anyone before, and I'm not going to lose my virginity in the ocean of all places.

"Ready to surf?" His demeanor returns to playful as if he picked up on my hesitation with our close contact.

"Let's do it."

"Awesome." Jasper releases his hold around my waist and slips his hand into mine. He pulls me along as we both swim toward the shore. Soaked, we both trudge through the sand and under the tree.

"The water is a bit chilly this morning," I comment through chattering teeth.

He laughs. "The waters of the Pacific Ocean are not as warm as the Indian Ocean but are a close second."

Giggling, I lean over to shake out my wet hair. "Is that so?"

He smiles confidently. "Yes, it also has the largest heat reservoir, which helps the top layers of the water stay warmer."

"Of course you would know that."

He shoots me a quick smile, showing all his teeth. "I love the ocean."

"I can tell."

"Okay, now down to business." His expression turns into a playful firmness. "Let's start with the basics."

Squinting in his direction, I block the sun with my hand to get a better view of him as he speaks. "I'm listening."

Jasper lifts the more weathered surfboard from the top. Pointing with his other hand, he meets my eyes. "This is a surfboard."

I roll my eyes and laugh. "I know what it is."

"You are from the desert, so I shouldn't assume."

Blushing, I look away. "If you're going to poke fun at me all day, then I'm out. I'd rather go eat tacos."

Jasper's arm hooks around me. He pulls me into his wet chest. It's warm and inviting. "Alright. Alright."

"Let's move on," I play.

"Okay," he agrees. "Let me show you something," he says, slowly rotating my body so I'm facing the crystal blue waters. "See that?"

Staring into the open ocean and a clear blue sky, I'm confused about what I'm supposed to be looking at. But I don't want him to tease me anymore. He's having way too much fun with it. I nod and agree. "Yes."

From behind, he leans in, his lips grazing my ear lobe. "That's called the ocean," he whispers.

Oh my god. I belly laugh and push away from him. "Jasper! I know what the ocean is!"

Laughter bubbles up from inside him. It's the best sound I've ever heard. A perfect, authentic, and raw emotion. And at this moment, all the loneliness of my life before slowly fades away.

Chapter Ten

THEN

Jasper

My mind struggles to stay focused on the new merchandise as Easton and I unload the recent shipment. I have been giving Avery surf lessons every chance I get. We hang out multiple times a day, with me sometimes squeezing her in between my paid sessions.

She's unlike anyone I've ever met—raw and self-aware. It's intoxicating.

"Jasper." Easton arches a brow, confused. "Volcom can't go with Billabong."

Startled, I look down to see I've mixed two branded T-shirts. "Oh yeah, I know."

"Distracted today?" Easton tosses a box of newly licensed products on the floor.

I push one of the rolling-back stock shelves. "Nah, I'm fine."

"Hmm, well, how do you explain getting the schedule wrong this morning? Or trying to start a team when we already had our meeting on Monday?" he points out.

I scoff him off, climbing to the told shelf. "I'm fine."

"Or what about how you forgot your call with the payroll company before lunch?" he continues with confidence and a stupid grin.

"Simple mistakes. Not a big deal."

"I've been working here since before it was *legal* for me to be working." He chuckles. "And I've never seen you mess up anything."

Easton has been hanging around my dad's shop since we were kids. It didn't take long for my dad to give us little tasks around the place. In exchange, he'd let Easton shop whenever he wanted. His dad left when he was young, so it was just him and his mom. She worked long hours and struggled to afford things for them. He spent a lot of time at my house and at the shop.

"Nah, I'm good," I say in a last attempt to dismiss my best friend. I don't want to admit I can't stop thinking about Avery. He'll tease me about it.

I wonder what she's doing tonight. We'd made plans to see each other every night this past week, but yesterday, I was back-to-back with lessons, and I forgot to check in with her.

"Also, I've never seen you absently mix brands either."

"I'm fine, dude. Back off," I say, throwing a balled packaging at him.

"It's Arizona, isn't it?" He smirks.

I place a stack of board shorts on the last rack, ready to give in. "Fine. It is."

He laughs. "I figured. You've been spending a lot of time with her lately."

My body heats, thinking about how intense our make out sessions have become on the beach under the trees. "I've been giving her lessons."

"For free," Easton states with a chuckle. He pokes his head out from behind one of the rolling racks. "Or maybe she's paying you in other ways."

"Fuck you, man. Avery's not like that," I say. I would love to go further, but she's apprehensive, and I'd never want her to feel pressured.

"Maybe she's a virgin," he says, more serious this time.

"Who's a virgin?" My dad walks into the back. Usually, we hear his flip-flops turning the corner, but we don't this time.

"It doesn't matter," I tell him.

"Whoa, Duke. Are those socks and shoes?" Easton pokes fun at my dad.

"Yeah, Dad. Where are you going?"

Walking past us and into his office, I catch a quick roll of his eyes. "I do own other types of shoes besides flip-flops."

I crinkle my nose, unsure if I believe him. "Do you, though?"

"I'm going to require proof," Easton says, following me into my dad's office.

Annoyed with us giving him shit, he turns in his chair and sticks his foot into the air. "Here."

Easton leans against the wall, crossing his arms at his chest. "One pair means nothing."

My dad twists back around to face his computer. "Don't you two have work to do?"

"Yes, since I'm the one carrying all the weight today," Easton jokingly spats at my expense.

"Have you had a lot of lessons? I didn't see any on the schedule." My dad lowers his glasses.

I shake my head, walk over, and slump into my chair parallel to my dad's. "Don't deflect. Where are you going in those shoes?"

"I'm hiking with Helen in a bit."

Easton's eyes fly over to mine. I flip him off. *If my dad is going hiking with her aunt, that will mean Avery will be alone.* Glancing at the schedule, I quickly scan to see who's working this afternoon. Now, I want to leave early so that I can see Avery.

"Speaking of Helen." My dad turns to face me fully. "I've noticed you hanging out with her niece, Avery, a lot lately."

"I'm giving her surf lessons." I pause. Easton crosses his arms at his chest, expecting me to say more. "And I'm kind of into her."

My dad's eyebrows raise. "You are?"

I nod.

"She's a cute girl, Jasper. But isn't she going back to Arizona for college in the fall?" he says like I haven't thought about it a million times since I hit her with that volleyball.

I enjoy being around her, and I refuse to let it steal the joy I feel now. And for someone like me who has battled depression for the last few years, it's energizing being around someone I don't have to mask.

"I know. It's extremely casual," I lie. There is nothing casual about how infatuated I've become with her.

The bell to the shop door chimes. Easton heads onto the floor to help the two employees already there.

My dad sighs like he does when he's about to tell me something I don't want to hear. He leans forward and bends one leg over the other. "I would hate for you to get too involved and trigger an episode when she leaves."

He's seen me through some rough times these last few years. I can't remember the first time I realized what I was going through was *depression*. The first time my body turned itself off, I felt confused and alone. I wondered why I was hit with this sort of numbness that I couldn't shake. It was an overpowering and painful sensation that came out of nowhere.

"Thanks, but it will be fine."

"You've said that before," he softly argues.

"I know, but I'm learning to deal with it," I say, rotating to give him back, hoping to drop this conversion.

"Are you still taking a break from your meds?" my dad asks as if I'm a child. I get a flash of irritation because I'm not a child anymore.

"I am." I rise from my seat. He's not going to let this go that easily. I slap a hand on his shoulder. "Look, the meds will always be there. If I feel like losing control, I can start them up again."

He sighs. "I don't think it's a good idea to go off and on medication like that, Son."

"I understand your concern, but I got it," I say reassuringly. My dad's one of my best friends—I can't lose my cool.

I recently stopped taking the medication because I wanted to prove that I could handle it myself. Being chained to a bottle for the rest of my life is daunting and not something I'm going to do unless I have no other options.

Being able to pacify my dad this time doesn't feel like a success. He'll bring it up again like he always does.

A short time later, I'm sitting at my desk sending over a contract for an artist we commissioned to create custom boards for the store. Easton is in the stockroom adjacent to the offices. I overhear him briefing a few employees about what has to be done during their shifts tonight.

I glance at the clock for the third time in ten minutes. I'm anxious to see Avery, but I must finish this before leaving.

Easton suddenly walks into the room. "How long are you staying today?" he asks, rolling his chair over.

"I'm leaving as soon as I get this contract sent over."

His face beams. "That's for the artist, isn't it?"

I hit send, then turn to face him, clasping my hands together on the back of my head. "Fuck yeah."

I'm proud of this business deal because it's the first one I've developed, negotiated, and coordinated.

"Dude, it's going to be so sick to have him here," he says.

I close my laptop and then slide it into my backpack. "I know, I'm stoked."

"You leaving already?" He gestures toward the door.

"Just sent it over. I'm out of here."

"Going to see Arizona?" he asks, knowing my answer already.

I smile proudly. "I am."

Easton folds his arms across his chest, leaning back in his office chair. "Good for you."

"See you tomorrow morning out on the water," I toss over my shoulder before heading out.

"I'll be there."

By the time I get to Helen's house, I'm jumping out of my skin to see her. I can't wait to touch her, hold her, and dive my tongue down her throat.

"Hey, Jasper," Avery answers with a tight little skirt, crop top, and hair thrown into a high ponytail. Fuck.

I slide my arms around her waist, urging her into me. "I missed you."

"I missed you too," she says, threading her hands through my hair. "I thought we wouldn't hang out until late tonight."

"Well." I lightly kissed the tip of her nose. "I didn't want to wait that long." Whispering, I trace the outline of her lips and down her jaw. I feel every accelerating inhale and exhale of her sharp breath against me.

"Helen's not here," she tells me, sliding her hands into the front of my shorts. Her smooth skin is heavenly. My length grows into her small hand, begging to be stroked more.

"I know. She's with my dad." Avery tightens her grip. I gasp, craving to be inside of her finally.

She stares up at me, a smile playing on her lips. "Want to go to my room?"

"Of course."

Avery loosens her grip on me while sliding her other hand into mine and leading me down the hallway. I'm hot on her heels, buzzing with a wild desire. She's everything to me. I've become completely obsessed.

When we get to the doorframe of her bedroom, she turns. Possibly wanting to say something, but I don't give her the chance. I'm on fire, and I can't contain it any longer.

I slide a palm along her cheek and grip her on the back of the head, bringing her lips to mine.

"I want to taste you," I murmur into the warmth of her mouth. *That's right, I'm going to do this.*

She pulls back, her eyes wide with shock. "You do?"

"Lift your skirt," I gently command.

She falls to the side of the bed. "I'm nervous."

I don't care. It's frustrating to wait for her to be ready, but I will as long as she needs me to. But that doesn't mean, in the meantime, I can't do all the other dirty things that I want to do to her.

I fall to my knees. "I don't think you understand. I want to kiss you more."

"We are kissing," she says, blushing. Her hair is tousled around her face.

I take a few loose strands and twirl them around my finger while shaking my head silently.

"No?"

My mouth waters with a desperate need. Something I've wanted to do since the moment I saw her in that tiny bikini on the beach. I can go without sex for a while, but I'm about to fuck her with the next best thing—*my tongue.*

"I want to kiss you down there." I gesture between her legs.

The color drains from her face, but I go feral the second I see her nipples harden through her thin T-shirt. "Lift your skirt."

"I, um—" Her breathing picks up.

"We don't have to do this if you don't want to, but I have a feeling you're going to like it." Giving her a chance to change her mind, I lean back on my bent legs.

To my utter joy, she nods and lies back but still frozen in place. *She's letting me, but she's nervous.*

Bringing my fingertips to the inside of her thighs, I glide them along her creamy skin, spreading her knees apart one at a time.

"Oh, Jasper," she moans. I'm sure in anticipation.

"Lay back and enjoy, Arizona." I move up her skirt, inch by inch. "I've heard it's a nice place to visit." I lower myself closer, pushing away the tiny triangle fabric of her panties to expose her. *Fuck, she's beautiful.* I can't wait to devour her and spend the rest of the night here. "But I have no plans on just visiting because I'm about to live down there for fucking eternity," I say, then take one long lick across the seam of her core.

Avery gasps. "Ohh."

She's all mine.

Chapter Eleven

Now

Avery

The moment I saw Jasper, my heart sank. All those unresolved emotions I've kept repressed for years shot back to the surface. It was overwhelming and impossible for me to keep a level head during our exchange. I'm not surprised he gave me a hard time about the divorce—that's what Jasper does. I figured I'd need to stay the weekend.

Despite the low buzz of nervous energy, I did sleep well. There's something calming about returning here and sleeping to the sound of crashing waves outside my window. It's what I'd imagine someone going back to their childhood home would be like—the emotions of the good times—and the bad.

I had groceries delivered yesterday, but I'm restless and need to leave the house. I can't sit around. I need to do something.

As I got up, showered, and dressed, I fought the urge to call Jasper. For more reasons than one, I did not need to initiate contact. Last night, when he called, I played it off as if I was frustrated, but the truth is, it was nice to hear his voice again. The smooth, comforting tone brought me hurdling back to those warm summer nights lying under our favorite tree in the sand.

Determined to find a restaurant without connection to me or my past here in Coconut Grove, I scoured through Google and luckily found one just down the street.

I throw on some workout clothes and hop into the car. It only takes me a few minutes to arrive at the quaint little cafe. It's a small white structure with a traditional thatching roof and outside seating. People are scattered around the entrance, waiting for tables. A familiar breeze whips past me as I pull on the double doors. *I should have called ahead.*

"Hello, welcome to the Coffee Hut and Cafe."

"Can I—" I see a guy in my peripheral. Before I get a double take, he pushes open the swing doors and disappears into the back kitchen. I shrug it off. It's probably just a coincidence. "My apologies. Can I place a to-go order?"

"Avery?" I hear my name said from behind me.

Oh no. I only lived here for a few months, years ago. I'd hoped I wouldn't run into anyone I knew.

I slowly turned around to see that it was someone I knew who darted into the kitchen just a second earlier. *One of Jasper's best friends.* "Easton?"

He jumps over to the low counter at the coffee bar, and before I realize it, I'm pulled into a full-body hug. A little stiff and unsure, I lightly pat his back with a friendly greeting.

"How the hell are you?" He pulls back, moving me to arm's length away.

I smile but am uncomfortable and don't know how to act. The last time I saw Easton, he came to my aunt's house to talk to me before I left for Arizona. "I'm doing well. How are you?"

"Great! This is my cafe." He gestures around him at the packed tables. "Can I get you anything? It's on the house."

I run a nervous hand through my windblown hair. "That's very kind of you, but it's unnecessary."

He leads me to a spot at the end of the coffee bar. "I insist. Please."

Easton was my favorite of Jasper's friends—a good guy with a kind heart. I nod, getting comfortable on the stool. "Alright."

"We can get you anything. Just name it," he says, waving over a server.

"Scrambled eggs?"

"Carrie, can you get her the wakeboard special with scrambled eggs?" he tells one of the servers.

She smiles in my direction. "Of course."

When the blonde woman escapes into the kitchen to start my order, Easton turns back to me. "So, what are you in town for?"

"Business," I say, wary of having this conversation in public.

He scratches his chin, lowering his eyes. "Does Jasper know you're here?"

I bite the side of my lip and filter through several responses ranging from vague to highly detailed accounts of the last twenty-four hours. "He does."

"And?" He leans in close. "Have you seen him yet?"

"I have."

His eyes flicker around the restaurant a few times. "You don't want to tell me, do you?"

My head falls back, and I let out a heavy sigh. "I went to his office yesterday. Which was interesting because he's the mayor now."

Easton crosses his arms and leans over the counter. “I know, right? Crazy to think that happened, but he’s doing really well.”

“I can see that.”

“That doesn’t explain why you’re back,” he presses.

I’m going to give in. Easton can talk Jasper into giving me what I need, so we can both move on with our lives. Jasper’s blowing me off just to piss me off.

I straighten my shoulders and look him in the eyes. “I’m engaged to someone else, and I need him to give me a divorce.”

“Shit, you two are still married?” He arches a brow, but a little smirk is hiding within his smile, telling me he already knew that.

I roll my eyes, picking at the cardboard sleeve on my coffee cup. “Don’t act like you didn’t know.”

“I mean …” Chuckling, he lifts his palms to face upward. “What do you expect? He’s my best friend.”

I release, letting a tight laugh slip through. “I get it, Easton.”

He grabs a towel behind the counter and wipes the espresso machine. “How was the look on his face?”

“You know, he tried to play it cool like my sudden appearance didn’t faze him, but I could tell by the look in his eyes that he was shocked to see me,” I explain.

“That’s hilarious. I’m kind of hurt he didn’t tell me about it,” Easton jokes.

I glance around the bustling restaurant. “He’s probably been too busy avoiding me.”

“Damn, look at the size of that thing!” a younger server exclaims as she emerges from the kitchen holding my to-go bag. She’s referring to the giant rock on my left finger. Proudly, I raise my hand for her to get a better look. She quickly sets down the bag and grabs my hand. "Easton, did you see this thing?"

"I saw it," he responds, keeping his eyes locked on mine. Jasper is his best friend, and I'm sure this stings a little.

"Thank you," I say to her.

"What did he say when you asked him for the divorce?" He picks up our conversation.

"He basically blew me off."

A sly smile inches across Easton's face. "I would have guessed."

"What's that supposed to mean?" I ask, frustrated. "Doesn't he want to move on with his life?"

"You'd think so? But I'm not always sure I understand what goes on in his head. I do know that he's going to make you work for it."

I roll my eyes, slipping my arm through the loops in the brow bag. "I'm going to go before the food gets cold. Nice seeing you, Easton. Thanks for breakfast."

Now, I'm not only starving and in need of more coffee, but I'm actually wondering if it's too early for whiskey. I need to head back to the beach house and regroup. I'm sure the girls will give me some advice.

"It was good seeing you, too, Arizona." He forces a smile. "How long will you be in town for?"

Grinning, I pop off the stool. "As long as it takes for Jasper to give me a divorce."

I'm halfway through my food when I finally message the girls.

Me: Another day in paradise and another day without a divorce.

Bailey: I'm glad you texted us. We were all trying to give you space.

Piper: It's only been one day. Give it some time. What happened?

Lina: Sorry to hear there's no divorce, but also not sorry.

Lina will say she's not a hopeless romantic, but secretly, she's always rooting for love.

Me: Oh, Lina. It's not like that.

Lina: Keep telling yourself that every time you look at that infinity tattoo on your wrist.

Bailey: Tell us how it's going.

Me: He basically avoided the topic altogether.

Me: Then, this morning, I ran into one of his best friends, who mentioned that he was not surprised that Jasper was avoiding it.

Piper: Because he still loves you.

Lina: YEP.

Me: You guys are so far from the truth. I'm engaged to Dave. Jasper and I had our shot, and it ended horribly.

Bailey: I don't know. If he's pushing you off, maybe he isn't ready to give you up yet.

Me: He gave me up a long time ago.

Piper: Maybe it just wasn't your time.

My friends are not helping the situation. Jasper and I were over years ago, and even though the flame he ignited within me will never entirely go out, I know there is no future with us. This chapter needs to close.

Me: I'm texting you all for help, and all you're doing is making things worse. lol

Piper: Okay, okay. We're sorry. How about changing up your approach?

Bailey: That's not a bad idea.

Me: I did go in a little aggressive yesterday.

Lina: Try again with a different tone.

I slump down into the soft cushions on the couch and tap out a response because they might be on to something.

Me: Okay, see, this is the type of advice I'm looking for. Thanks.

Lina: Haha. Took us a minute to catch on!

Bailey: Get it, girl.

Piper: Good luck.

If Jasper is going to make this hard on me, I can't approach him with the mindset that he's changed, because even though he's sitting behind that big desk as mayor, he's still the same surfer guy who lived in board shorts and ate way too many fish tacos. I need to play his game like I used to.

Armed with a new view of how to get what I want, I scroll through my phone and click on a phone number I haven't called in years. With each ring, the knot in my throat gets bigger until I hear his voice on the other end.

My skin breaks out in chills, just like it did when he called last night—a physiological response to him I have no control over.

"Avery."

Picking at the button on my pants, I suck in a weighted breath. *Be strong.*

"How are you?" I ask in an even tone even though I'm buzzing with nerves.

"I'm good. How did you sleep last night?'

"I slept well, thank you. You?"

"Good. Come out to your balcony," he gently demands.

I think for a second before rising to my feet and walking to the door. Then, out in the distance, I see him holding up his surfboard with his phone to his ear. Clicking my tongue, a smile pulls at my lips. "Are you spying on me?"

"No, I was just out for a morning swim."

I open the door, slowly walk to the balcony's edge, and lean over. "You still go out every morning?"

"Only when I can. It still clears my head," he says.

"Working helps me clear my head."

He runs a hand through his wet hair. "And what is work for you?"

Sighing, I rest my hand on my chin. "I'm a flight attendant."

"That fits."

"What's that supposed to mean?"

"You like to run away." His tone is light, but there's a dark truth behind it.

"That's not nice." I play it off, switching the phone to my other ear. "What about you? You're not working today?"

He shakes his head. "Everyone is off to prepare for the Coconut Grove Days this weekend."

I flashback to the only other time I attended this event. *That night. His truck. Everything that followed.* I was out of my mind in love. And in way over my head for how young I was.

"I remember that event," I say fondly.

"I've made some changes, but it still happens every year." *Silence.* "Do you remember that night?" he asks, his voice low. I barely hear it over the waves.

I blush. I can still feel the way his body commanded mine. The warmth of his breath on my lips. The connection of him being inside of me. A feeling I haven't experienced since being with Jasper.

"I do."

"So do I."

Panic zips up my spine. With all the heady sensations, it's also followed by anguish. This conversation is taking a turn in a very personal direction. "Aren't you hot standing out there?"

"No, I'm used to it."

"So, what are you doing for the rest of the day?" I ask, keeping the subject away from the painful direction it was going. "Besides hanging out outside of my rental."

He chuckles. "I was surfing. It's not my fault you chose to stay only three houses down from mine."

Slightly embarrassed by my attempt at sarcasm, I stomp my foot, frustrated that I let the girls get into my head. He doesn't still have feelings for me.

"I had no idea where it was. My friend booked it for me." I make sure to emphasize that I didn't consciously do it.

"What are *you* doing later?" he asks, ignoring my last comment.

"Uh." Caught off guard, I stumble over my words. "Um, nothing." *Waiting for you to sign my divorce papers.*

"I have to get over to the town square to help with setup," he tells me. Then I see him wave in my direction, walking down the beach with his surfboard tucked under his arm. "But I'd love to show you something later, if you're up for it?"

He wants to show me something? I don't think I trust myself alone with him. We'll end up fucking or getting into a fight. Neither of which will lead to getting these divorce papers signed.

I sigh, watching as he trudges through the sand toward his

house. “I don’t think so.”

“Come on,” he pushes. “Maybe if you give me what I want, I’ll give you what you want.” *Classic Jasper.*

I roll my eyes, but my stomach flutters. “Okay, well, bye,” I blurt out, hurrying off the phone.

“Wait … Avery?”

“Yeah, I’ll go. It’s fine.”

“Good.”

“Okay, bye.”

“Wait …”

I huff. “Yes?”

“I know after all this time, you’ve been with other men, but nothing has made me sleep better at night than knowing I had you first.” He drops those words with pride.

I’m speechless.

“See you at four,” he states before ending the call.

Dammit.

Chapter Twelve

THEN

Avery

My eyes bore into the tiny surfboard hands on the clock on the far side of the store. Four o'clock can't come soon enough. Nine more minutes until I see Jasper. My stomach flutters, and my hands sweat with anticipation of touching him. We don't make plans to see each other anymore, it's become something we now both understand. But today, as I'm riding this high of life, I also carry a weight.

Today is, *was*, my mother's birthday.

"Anxious?" Cassie smacks her gum, smirking at me.

"Maybe."

"I'd be anxious, too, if I got to hook up with a guy like Jasper Collins," she playfully quips, climbing onto the ladder to change the sale sign.

Her comment reminds me that Jasper and I haven't had sex. It's not that I don't want to, because hell, I want to more than anything. I'm worried about the feelings that come when a girl loses her virginity. Jasper and I are having fun right now, and it's great.

What if when he finds out that I've never had sex, he freaks out? What if he doesn't want to see me anymore because of the pressure that might put on him? On the other hand, I could give myself to him, and then everything intensifies. Or worse, what if it's harder for me to leave for college?

Today, being my mother's birthday, I wonder what it would be like if my mom was still around to give me advice. But with that same fleeting thought comes the reality of who my mother was and how I barely knew her. I can't remember a single birthday we spent together.

Why aren't I more upset about losing my parents? Maybe my soul matches the clothes I wear—dark and ominous like the girls in elementary school used to say? I push that thought aside. I'm too old to think like that anymore.

"Yeah, I guess." I shrug off her comment, not wanting to share more.

"Catch!" Cassie tries to toss me the old signage, but it floats down, making it hard to grab. "So, you're here until you move to college, right?"

"Yeah, at the end of August." I clasp the thick paper with two hands. "I'm excited."

"You don't think it will be hard for you to return to Arizona after your parents pass?" she asks, concerned. Sure, it would be difficult for anyone to lose their parents unexpectedly, but I didn't grow up in a typical household. I need to seem upset. I can't tell her that I barely knew my mother and father and that they were little more than strangers to me most of my life. That would open up many questions I don't have the energy or time to answer.

"It's my home and all I know." I sigh. "Besides, the college I'm attending is a few hours north of Phoenix anyway."

She nods with a warm smile. "That's good."

I glance up at the clock one more time. "Two minutes," I whisper, then turn back to Cassie. "I'm heading out."

"Okay, cool," she says, descending from the ladder. "Do you work tomorrow?"

I grab my purse from underneath the counter. Swinging it over my shoulder, I quickly type out my employee number on the computer and clock out. "I don't, but I work Sunday, though."

"Me too. Day shift?"

"Yep, see you then," I call out, sprinting toward the door.

When I exit the store, the bright sun hits my eyes, and my sandals step onto the bustling boardwalk. I lower my sunglasses, scouring the crowds to find Jasper.

"Arizona!" Jasper waves from a few yards away. He's wearing board shorts and a shark tooth necklace around his neck without a shirt. His hair is wet as if he just got out of the water.

"Hey!" I shout to him. Bouncing on the balls of my feet and run over. At full speed, I come crashing into his warm, sticky chest. He laughs, catching me as I wrap my legs around his waist.

"I missed you," Jasper says, burying his face in my hair. Goose bumps span the back of my neck.

"I missed you too." I giggle, peppering the side of his face with kisses. He tastes salty from either sweat or the ocean. But I know Jasper. He lives on this water, so it's most likely from that.

He clutches my hips, holding me tight. "How was your day?"

"Good," I say, hopping down. "Better now."

Jasper dips to press a soft kiss on my lips.

"Way better now," I mumble.

He pulls back, smiling. "What do you say we skip lessons today and hang out at the beach?"

"Isn't that what we do every day?" I tease, scrunching my nose.

He laughs and swings an arm around me. "That's true, but I was thinking we could grab some takeout and make a little fire." He urges me closer while we walk along the shore as the sun sets. "Pick up a few blankets and have dinner under our tree."

I rub my lips together, swallowing the sheer number of butterflies inside me.

"That sounds perfect," I say. Keeping my head down, watching the sand kick up from underneath my feet, I realize this is what girls in school used to talk about—these types of feelings with guys. I had to travel to an entirely different state to find it—to experience it. Guys in high school tried to pursue me before, but I've never been interested in them.

Especially not like this.

"Cool. I'll call Joe to place a taco order. Then we'll stop at my house for blankets and matches," he tells me the plans.

I nod and go along with it.

Jasper walks me to my car, and we quickly kiss goodbye, with plans to meet back at the beach in an hour. I freshen up at home and check in with Helen. We have a brief conversation about my day, where I tell her I'll be with Jasper for the evening. She smiles and tells me to be safe. Having a family member to check in with is not something I'm used to, but it feels good. *Is this how other kids grew up?*

By the time Jasper and I meet back on the beach under our favorite tree, he has the fire already going and to-go containers with our tacos in the middle. I catch my breath with a gasp. Romantic and utterly perfect.

"Hey, you," I coo while walking over, clutching the extra blankets close to my chest.

Jasper steps over one of the blankets on the ground and slides both palms along my cheeks. His fingers thread through my hair, pushing the strands away from my face. "You look beautiful."

My eyes stare into his dark eyes. "Thank you."

"I got you chicken tacos," he says, gesturing behind him.

Breathing in his scent, I smile weakly. "Thank you." I open my mouth to take a bite when I sense Jasper staring.

"Is everything okay?" he asks, concerned.

"Yeah," I quickly dismiss, brushing off his question.

His eyes narrow. "Are you sure? You seem off."

How could he pick up on something like that? We've been with each other for all of five minutes?

I nod, moisture bubbles in my armpits, nervous from being put on the spot. "Yes, I'm fine. Everything is fine."

Jasper returns his taco to the paper wrapper next to him then turns to me. "I can feel something is on your mind." He leans in, rubbing a thumb across my lower lip. "You can talk to me."

He's not going to let this go until I tell him. I sigh. "It's my mother's birthday today."

With a sharp rise of his chest. "Oh no. I'm sorry."

I shake off his comment. *I'm done pretending to be sad.* "Thanks, but I'm alright."

"You've mentioned that you didn't have a close relationship

with your parents—" he begins, but I interrupt.

"I know what you're going to say, that you're sorry for me, and it's okay to be sad. But that's not the problem, Jasper."

He clasps his hands together over bent knees. "What is the problem then?"

I clear my throat, buying time to think of a response that won't make me look heartless. "The problem is that I don't feel much of anything."

"What do you mean?" he asks.

My eyes dart around the beach, searching for the words I don't have, looking for a way to explain my lack of love toward my parents. I can't let that portion of my truth ever hit the air. *Or can I?*

"I didn't really know my parents." A slow tear rolls down the side of my cheek. "They spent most of my life traveling all over the world with my dad's company. They were in love and obsessed with each other. There was no room for a child in their world."

"I'm so sorry you had to go through that. And I'm sure that every single emotion you're having or not having is warranted," he says.

"I feel like a broken person. Who doesn't mourn the loss of their parents? Who doesn't miss their dead mother on her birthday?" My voice cracks with desperation. I've held much of my true feelings inside for a long time.

Suddenly, Jasper's two fingers are on my chin. He angles my face toward his with a light pinch and a gentle tug. His pupils are large, with an intense stare that hits every part of me. "You are not broken."

My stomach spasms, forcing an audible breath to escape. "Then why does it feel like that?"

"Because you've never had anyone to remind you of how special you are. About how you are the most perfect but complex person in the world," he says, then brings his lips to mine. "Your feelings are yours, and you do not need to defend or justify them to anyone."

"Thank you," I whisper.

Jasper and I lay on our backs, staring at the night sky. Safely tucked into his arm, I imagine what life would be like if I could do this every day. The waves roll in and out in the background—the sounds, the smells—everything in this moment. A potent sense of belonging washes over me.

"Jasper!" A guy's voice comes from my left. It's familiar, but I don't know who it is until I'm getting hammered by two more. Easton, Bodhi, and Riley run right toward us. All three guys throw themselves onto the ground and into the blanket between Jasper and me.

"What the fuck, you assholes," Jasper scolds, shoving Riley to the side.

Easton playfully hooks an arm around me. "Well, this looks romantic. Where was our invite?"

"You didn't get one," Jasper snaps.

Riley smiles down at me, which tells me that their playful

nature is not something new between them. If I continue to spend time with Jasper, I have to accept that he's a package deal. Despite them being a little annoying at times, I like them. I didn't grow up with siblings. Being included in their tight friend circle is nice.

"We're headed over to the cove for a beach party. You guys in?" Easton says.

Jasper opens his mouth to answer, but I interject. Slipping my hand into his, I answer, "Yeah." Jasper's head whips around. His brow arched with surprise. "I don't mind going."

"Are you sure? We don't have to let them pressure us," Jasper reassures me, throwing the guys a side-eye.

"We're not pressuring her to have a good time, man," Bodhi rebuttals.

I smile at Jasper, fluttering my eyelashes a few times. "It'll be fun."

"Are you sure?" He dips his head low, not believing that I'd want to hang out with them.

"She said yes, dude. Let's go!" Easton playfully rests a hand on Jasper's shoulder.

The five of us take the ten-minute walk down the beach. No one even mentioned driving our cars, which is interesting because that's the first thought that crossed my mind. People walk everywhere around here. The weather is wonderful, and unlike Phoenix, where everyone hibernates in the summer, in Coconut Grove, much of the town's life is spent outdoors.

It doesn't take long before the music drowns out the sounds of the waves, and a bonfire lights up the clear night sky.

While walking closely and with my hand comfortably inside

Jasper's, he leans in and whispers, "We can stay for as long or short as you'd like."

The warmth from his breath on my temple causes goose bumps to span the skin of my neck. I tilt my head, meeting his soft lips with mine. He kisses me.

"Thank you, I'll let you know," I mutter into his mouth. We both released as our group approached a larger group of people chatting, drinking, and listening to music.

A few people say hello to us as we get closer to the group.

"Are you all drinking?" a blonde guy asks. Dressed identically to the rest of the guys on the beach in board shorts and lacking a shirt, he stands in front of two light blue coolers. A few more were stacked behind him.

"Clark, this is my girlfriend, Avery." Jasper wraps an arm around my shoulders, pulling me closer. *Marking his territory, I guess?*

"Hi," I say. That's the first time I've heard Jasper refer to me as his girlfriend. *Is that what I am now? Oh my god.* I'm his girlfriend. He's my boyfriend—this tall, dark-haired, toned, tanned, incredibly hot guy. I curl close, letting myself fall victim to his possessive move.

"Nice to meet you, doll. What would you like?" Clark's voice is smooth and friendly.

"What do you have?" I ask, a little nervous. I only went to a few parties in high school. Most of the time, the "friends" I thought I had were only the more popular kids wanting to use my parents' boat on the lake. I fell for it until the second semester of my junior year.

"Clark is going to own a bar in town one day. He can make

any drink you can think of and never comes to a shore party unprepared," Jasper says.

Clark smiles and holds his arm out, presenting the inside contents of the coolers. My palms sweat. I have no idea what type of alcohol any of this is—let alone what is needed to make certain drinks.

Jasper picks up on my confusion, speaking before I have the chance. "We'll take an old-fashioned."

Biting my lip, I glance up at him.

He winks. "You'll like it."

"Okay, you got it!" Clark says. Giving us his back, he grabs a plastic cup from a reusable grocery bag and plucks an orange from one of the coolers behind him. While Clark works on whatever type of version of this drink he can make with the limited resources he has with him, I turn to Jasper.

"That was embarrassing," I whisper.

He flashes his pearly white teeth. "No worries, Arizona. I've got your back."

I know that now.

Chapter Thirteen

THEN

Jasper

I wasn't surprised when Avery was confused about what she wanted to drink. She doesn't strike me as the type of girl who parties or goes out a lot. The little she has shared about her life made me even more infatuated with her.

It's heartbreaking to think about how Avery grew up relatively alone—isolated from her parents in a big house and never having authentic friends. My mother passed away when I was young, but I've always been incredibly close with my dad. I've had the comfort of living in this small town my whole life and growing up with the same group of friends I've had since I was a kid—which she hasn't had the luxury of.

I will keep her forever. She's mine now. And as long as she continues to choose me, she'll never know a day without love.

"You want to sit over there?" I point to a more secluded spot on the sand, away from the rest of the people. Clutching her drink in one hand, she nods and follows me.

"How do you like it?" I ask, bending to sit in the sand. Facing the dark, endless ocean, from the corner of my eye, I see Avery lower next to me. The outsides of our legs touch, causing a spark to shoot up the inside of my thigh and straight into my dick. I adjust myself, so standing at attention isn't completely obvious.

"Surprisingly, I like it a lot." She giggles. "The first couple of sips burned on the way down, but the more I drink it, the smoother it gets."

Leaning in, I run the backs of my knuckles against her cheek. "Good. I knew you would."

"So, you've known these people most of your life?" she asks, rubbing the condensation on the side of her plastic cup.

"Not all of them, but most."

"I wish I knew what that was like," she trails off, lost in thought.

"Avery," I mumble her name before lowering to nibble her bottom lip. She closes her eyes and smiles. "You have it now."

"What do you mean?" She gently bites me back. *I love it.*

"Whatever I have is yours."

She pulls away, her eyes bouncing between mine.

"You don't have to feel like an outsider. Coconut Grove is your home now."

Her expression falls. "For the rest of the summer."

I refuse to think about that right now. Lost in a fog, I enjoy every moment of getting to know her. My days consist of Avery and thoughts of only her. I can't let my mind go there. I'm not prepared for the spiral of darkness that will follow.

"Let's not think about that now," I say, swallowing what we both are thinking.

"You're right," she agrees, taking a generous swig of her

whiskey and polishing it off.

My eyes follow the drop of amber liquid rolling over her lip and down her chin. I take my thumb and wipe it away. "It's going to be that sort of night, huh?"

"Nah, I'm a horrible drunk," she says, biting the same lip my finger just grazed. "I'm just tired now."

"Tired?"

"Maybe we can get out of here?" The corner of her mouth quirks up.

"I'd rather be cuddling in your bed anyway," I say.

"Yes."

"Besides being tired, I noticed you're in a better mood," I say, lifting to stand in front of her. I hold out my hands.

Avery slides her hands into mine, and I hoist her to her feet. "Thanks to you."

"I did nothing," I reply.

"Sometimes all people need is someone to just sit and listen to them." She wraps her arms around my shoulders, her fingers moving to the nape of my neck. "Security based in a silent trust."

The tightening in my chest deepens. "You get me more than anyone else ever has."

God, I'd love more than anything to make love to her. It's fucking brutal to feel this intense connection without being able to strengthen it. But I need Avery to come to me when she's ready. She's a thinker—always in her own head—and won't do things unless she wants to. I love that about her. Calculated like the sea and, at times, chaotic but always knows which way to go.

That's why I asked her multiple times about attending tonight's party. I never want her to feel like she's not in control.

Because when it comes to us, I'm secure in what we have.

"And you get me," she mumbles, resting her head against my chest.

I squeeze her tight. "Do you want me to take you home?"

She angles her head up, glancing around the beach, then turns her half-open eyes to mine. "I wish for infinity nights like these. Every night spent on the beach under the stars."

Fuck, I'm obsessed with her. "Infinity nights it is."

Avery's focus falls to my lips, then darts back up. "We should probably head back."

"You got it, Arizona."

She rotates in my arms and faces the black sea before us. The endless Pacific Ocean that goes on for thousands of miles.

"Thank you."

My front is flush with her back, and I know she can feel me grow bigger between us. *Do I pull away? Or do I let her see how bad I want to be with her?*

"Come with me."

"Of course." I thread my fingers through her silky hair. "I wouldn't let you walk alone."

"Should we say goodbye to the guys?"

"Nah, I'll see them tomorrow." I chuckle, scoffing at my friends. "Hell, I see them all the damn time."

She laughs. "That's true. Let's go."

With my arm hooked tightly around her shoulders, I keep her close while we walk back to our side of town along the shore.

In what feels like a blink of an eye, we're already back at Helen's beach house. I'm not ready to say goodbye for the night, but she's tired, so I hold in my disappointment about our night ending earlier than I would like.

"Thanks for hanging out with my friends tonight," I say, leaning against the outside of the house.

With her hands linked behind her back, Avery steps into me. "Wait, you're coming in, right?" she confirms coyly. *Hell fucking yes, I want to come in!*

"I would love to come in." I smile and press a kiss on the tip of her nose. I watch as she turns around to unlock the door.

"Good, I hoped you knew I was serious." She flashes a smile while blushing.

Following her up the steps, I take each one casually, trying not to let on how stoked I am to stay with her.

Avery leads me through the quiet, unlit house and down the hall to her bedroom. Taking care not to make a noise that would disturb Helen, we slip into her room. Avery quietly locks the door behind us.

I can barely make out the outline of her as she crosses over her bed to turn on a small lamp on her nightstand. She removes her shirt and switches it for a white tank top. Then drops her pants, replacing them with Northern Arizona University sweats. *The college she's going to.*

A pit in my stomach reminds me our time is limited.

"I don't think Helen heard us." Avery climbs onto her bed.

I slip off my shoes, remove my shorts and get into bed with her. "Probably not."

"I don't think she'd care too much if she knew you were sleeping over anyway."

I raise my arm, letting her cuddle into me. "You turn eighteen in two weeks anyway."

"That's true."

"What do you want for your birthday?" I ask.

"Hmm." She scratches her head. "I'm not sure. Nothing."

"That's not going to happen," I say, kissing the top of her head. "There must be something you want."

"I want to remember this summer forever." Her voice is small, but heeds something so much larger.

"You will, Arizona," I say. "If I have anything to do with it."

Another silent beat passes before she speaks. "How many tattoos do you have?"

"Eight," I answer. Avery traces the outline of the small pieces of art on my arm. Her delicate fingers cause my skin to break out in chills.

"I'd love to be brave enough to get one at some point." She scoots a little lower, getting more snuggled under my arm.

I hold her close, fighting the heaviness of my eyelids. "You are braver than you think."

"Maybe," she mumbles.

The morning light shines through the shutters, warming the side of my face. My eyes spring open. *I'm still in Avery's bed.* Shit.

I roll over to wake her, but before I do, I take a moment to admire how peaceful she looks. I didn't mean to fall asleep for the entire night. My plan was to sneak out before dawn like I have every other time before. But experiencing the feeling of waking up to her safely in my arms was worth the mistake.

"Avery," I whisper, brushing her hair away from her face.

She stirs a little before slowly opening her eyes. "Jasper?" Then sits straight up in bed. "Oh no. We fell asleep!"

I laugh. "Good morning. And yes, I did."

She palms her face. "Oh no. What will Helen say?"

I shrug. "At this point, it is what it is," I tell her. "She knows we're seeing each other."

Avery nods. "Yeah, you're right."

"It'll be okay." I kiss her forehead. "I'll just walk out casually. Maybe she won't be bothered."

Avery chuckles. She lifts off the bed and grabs an oversized shirt from her drawer.

I slide back on my shorts. When we're both fully dressed, we meet at her door.

"Let's do this." Her face crinkles with nerves. "Maybe this is a good chance for us to tell her that you'll be sleeping over more often, and then it won't have to be a surprise."

"I think that's a good idea." I grab her hand, and we walk out together.

"Good morning, Jasper." Helen's voice is upbeat as Avery and I round the corner into the kitchen. She has two cups in her hands. "I made you a raw juice."

Avery and I exchange a glance. I should be more nervous about being caught by my girlfriend's family walking out of her room, but I've known Helen for a while now, and we have a good relationship.

"Thanks, Helen," I say. Unbothered, I take the cup from her hands.

"I made you one too." She then turns to Avery.

"You don't seem surprised to see Jasper walk out of my bedroom ?" Avery says, climbing onto the high chair at the counter.

"I might not have had my own kids, but I do know what it's like to be eighteen and nineteen years old," she retorts sarcastically.

I chuckle.

"Good morning, Son." My dad's voice booms from behind me. He brings a hand to my shoulder.

"Dad?"

"Have a nice night, you two?" he jokes.

Avery buries her face in her hands. "This is awkward on so many levels."

My dad pours himself a cup of coffee and then slides his arm around Helen's waist. "Shall we have this talk now?"

Leaning against the counter, I fold my arms across my chest. "What are you talking about?"

Helen speaks first. "You're both technically adults." She looks at Avery. "Avery, very soon, and we want you to know we're both comfortable with what's going on. You don't have to feel like you need to sneak in or out."

"Either house," my dad chimes in.

Helen nods and continues, "Yes. But the only thing we want to make sure of is that you're being careful." *Little do they both know, Avery and I haven't had sex yet.*

I catch Avery sucking in a breath. "Of course."

"Obviously," I agree. "Well, this was a great conversation to have first thing in the morning."

My dad and Helen share a laugh, but Avery still looks uncomfortable.

"I'm going to run home and take a shower. I have an early lesson." I kiss Avery on the top of her head. "See you at the shop later, Dad. Bye, Helen."

I sprinted out of the house as quickly as I could. I felt a little guilty about leaving Avery alone with my dad and Helen, but the whole thing was a little weird.

Chapter Fourteen

THEN

Avery

"Are you seeing Jasper today?" Helen asks, handing me a green smoothie.

My cheeks burn through a smile, and my aunt arches an eye in my direction. She *sees* what I'm feeling.

"I am." I throw my bag over my shoulder while taking a small sip of my smoothie. I glance at my phone, but he hasn't texted me yet today. "We're supposed to meet down by the pier. He's been giving me surfing lessons."

She dries a cup with a towel and then places it into the top cupboard. "Lucky you. He's one of the best in town."

"I know." My heart flutters, and my lips tingle, thinking about how lucky we are to get along so well.

I turn to start walking toward the door, but a question crosses my mind. I'm curious to know more about the relationship Helen has with Jasper's dad. Obviously, they have sex, they hang out together, and he spends nights here often. But what do relationships like that mean? They're dating, *but not?*

"What's up with you and Japer's dad?"

"I figured this question would come up at some point." She closes the dishwasher and walks to the counter, resting her elbows on the granite. "What do you want to know?"

"Are you guys fuck buddies or what?" I bluntly ask. Not knowing how else to phrase my question, I get hit with slight regret when I hear my own words.

"Well." She pauses, searching for how to explain this to me. "We are great friends who enjoy spending time together." She sighs. "And who also sleep together."

I nod with a small smile, showing her my appreciation for her opening up to me. "Yeah, I figured that's the nature of it," I quip, climbing onto the bar stool, wanting to discuss further. "But I guess what I'm really asking is if you're okay with it? I mean, are you satisfied with the way things are?"

Helen's face lights up. "Absolutely."

"Interesting," I reply, with another question starting to form.

She continues, anticipating my curiosity for more details. "Look, I'm independent. I've never imagined myself with a husband and a family. I've loved living a simple life by myself. I have a great circle of friends and can do what I want." She grabs her cappuccino from the other side of the counter and continues, "He gives me what I need, and I give him what he needs. It works for both of us, and I can't imagine a more perfect situation."

My young, almost eighteen-year-old mind attempts to make sense of this lifestyle, but one thing is clear—I am intrigued by her power and self-confidence. Helen is living her life the way she wants, and it blows my mind.

"That's incredible," I mutter, unable to find a better word to describe it. I've never thought much about my future, but I've assumed I'd end up living alone.

"It's important to live your life the way you want. Lean into things that bring you joy and push away from the things that don't," she says. "What Duke and I are doing is unconventional, but it works for us, and that's all that matters."

I smile. "I've never met anyone like you, Aunt Helen."

"And you never will, dear." She winks. "How about we talk about you?"

"What about me?" I ask.

Helen flips her salt-soaked hair to one side. "I also have a good understanding of what's going on with you and Jasper, but I want to hear it from you."

"Yes." My face flushes. "What would you like to know?"

She sets her cup down and crosses her arms at her chest nervously. "I'm not sure what your mom has talked to you about or what type of open communication you've had with her," she begins. *Oh fuck, I know where this conversation is going.*

I put my hand out in front of me. "My mother and I never had those conversations, but I'm not naïve. I know to be careful."

"Duke brought it up the other morning, which was a total Duke thing to do, but we haven't had the chance to speak alone about it yet." Her face takes on a more serious expression. "You're on the pill, aren't you?"

"Yes, I am," I say, even though Jasper and I haven't had sex yet. It's not that I don't want to. I do more than anything, but I fear what will happen afterward.

"Okay. I'm just making sure. You're a grown woman, so I don't want to tell you what to do," she politely reassures me.

"I know, and I appreciate the respect." This talk reminds me that I'm at the end of my pill pack. "Speaking of that, I do need to get a refill from the doctor."

She nods. "Okay, I'll call Dr. Hasbro. She's great, and I'm sure she could get you in this week if all you need is a refill."

"Awesome, Helen," I say, then again glancing down at my phone, realizing I still haven't heard from Jasper—which is unlike him. He texts me first thing in the morning every day. A pit forms inside my stomach, and I get a rush of panic. "Thanks for the chat. I'm going to head to the beach."

"Okay, dear. Will you be around for dinner?"

"I think so. I'll text you."

"Have fun!" I hear her call out behind me as I shut the door.

I pull up to the beach, anxious to see Jasper. I called him twice on my drive over here, but he didn't answer. I try not to get too worried. I'm sure he's out on the water without his phone.

By the time I get to our usual meeting spot, he's nowhere to be found. I scan the handful of surfers riding the waves but don't see *my surfer*. Worry stings the tips of my ears. *Where could he be? Does he not want to see me? Maybe I got the days mixed up, and we're not supposed to meet today.*

The sun shines bright along the horizon. I tent my eyes, continuing to scour the beach for him. Still no Jasper. I slip my phone out one last time to try him.

No answer.

I'm not the type of girlfriend who worries when she doesn't hear from her boyfriend, but the uneasiness in my stomach sends an alarm that something's off. I take one more good look along the beach, then head back toward my car with only one place to go—his house.

If he's not home, I'll try his dad's shop. Confusion plagues me until I arrive at his small bungalow. *I'm sure everything is fine. He's not breaking up with me,* I think while I sprint up the steps to his front door. Anxiously, I knock a few times on his door, but there's no answer. *Goddammit.* I whisper-yell under my breath. I step back and glance at his house, unsure of what I'm looking for. *His room is toward the back, and I wonder if he's sick or needs help.*

I jog around the house to the back and see the window in his bedroom is open. I pull one of the chairs from the patio table, place it against the paneling, and climb on top. Peering in through the crack, my heart sinks as soon as I see Jasper lying on his bed.

Is he sleeping? Is he alright?

I push the window all the way open and slide through. "Jasper," I say, stepping onto the floor. He doesn't move. *What the hell?*

Filled with a mixed bag of emotions and questions, I approach Jasper's bed. He's curled into the side, facing the wall, and looks like he's in a deep sleep. I let out a sigh of profound relief. There wasn't anything wrong. He probably just slept through our lesson.

I kick off my shoes, pull back his comforter, and crawl into his bed. Tucking myself into his back, I inhale his scent, letting it flow through me. He continues to lie still.

"Avery?" Jasper's voice is distant and weak. I don't recognize it.

"Are you okay?" I ask, burying my nose into the creases of his shirt.

He rolls over, facing me. His usually vibrant brown eyes are now a shade lighter. He slides an arm between my legs, hooking me and pulling me into him. My face falls into the warmth underneath his chin.

"I'm alright," he whispers.

I'm still unsettled. A slight anxiousness rests in my mind, wondering if there is more to this story of him being just *alright.*

I run my hand through his hair, then lightly kiss him on his wet lips. "Are you sure?"

"Yeah," he says with an unconvincing smile. This is all he's willing to give me now, so I push my concern aside and cuddle into him.

A dense silence surrounds us. Even the typical sound of the waves in the background is muted. Realizing I had left my water bottle in the car, I decided to get a glass of water from the kitchen.

"I'm going to grab something to drink. Do you want anything?" I ask him.

Without a verbal response, Jasper only shakes his head.

I nod in acknowledgment, then slide off his bed. While walking down the shallow hallway, I hear the door unlock. It must be his dad."Hey, Avery," Duke warmly greets me with bags in his hands.

"Hi, Duke," I respond, going to the kitchen.

He places a few grocery bags on the counter. "How's Jasper?"

I bite my lip and stiffen. I'm unsure how to answer this

question because I hoped Duke would know. "He's in bed."

"Okay." A worried but expectant expression transforms his typical jovial, sun-kissed face. "He'll be fine in a few days."

I can tell by Duke's response, he knows more than he wants to share too. I want to pry, and I fight every urge not to, but I care for Jasper and he's not acting like himself right now.

"Okay," I say, then grab my glass of water and head back to Jasper's bedroom, but my legs stop moving. I need to know what's going.

With my eyes focused on the tan shag carpet beneath my feet, I turn on my heels. "Duke?"

He glances up from behind the door of the refrigerator. "Yeah, sweetie?"

I suck in a breath of courage. "What's going on with him?"

He closes the door and then leans against it. Clicking his tongue, he's thinking about what to tell me—or how. "Has he ever mentioned to you about what he struggles with from time to time?"

My heart squeezes in my chest. "No."

"I don't think he'll be upset with me for telling you," he begins. "Hell, it might help."

"Okay," I say, waiting for him to continue.

"Jasper has depression."

My brain cycles through all the things I've heard or even seen on television about depression. What I do know is that it can be debilitating for the person it affects. Sometimes, it is even to the point where episodes can hit when they least expect it. But I doubt my little knowledge barely even scratches the surface of this condition.

I nod, forcing a weak smile. "Thank you for letting me know."

"Of course." He tips his hat in my direction. "I have to run back to the shop for a bit, but I'll be back later today. Are you staying for dinner?"

"Sure."

"Good. Maybe Helen will want to join us too."

"I'm sure she will," I say.

A million questions flood my mind. *How long has he known he has depression? How can I be there for him? Has he tried medications? I'm sure he has. That's a stupid question.* There will be time for more details later. Right now, all I want to do is to be with him.

By the time I get back to Jasper's room, my heart is full of affection for him but also empathy. I pull back the covers and crawl back into bed with him.

"I spoke with your dad," I tell him softly.

"You did?" he responds, keeping his eyes closed.

"Yes." I slip my hands under his shirt and lightly graze the warm skin on his stomach. "He explained what's going on with you. I want you to know I'm here for whatever you need."

Jasper exhales, hooking an arm around me. "Thank you."

He's here, but his body is stiffer than usual. It's like having a conversation with someone over the phone, and you can tell by their empty responses they're not *actually* listening. It's not that Jasper isn't listening to my words, but his mind is elsewhere—unable to be fully present. A strange disconnection inadvertently causes my insecurities to kick up, even though it has nothing to do with me.

Sliding my arms under his shorts and around his back, I lift my tank top, bringing us skin to skin. I'm touching him, but he's not there. I'm desperate for a connection to him, but there's an invisible block between us. A palpable energy field surrounding him, meant to keep the world—and me—out.

Closing my eyes, I let my body sink into the cushion of his mattress. I will stay here with him as long as he needs me to. I'm physically unable to part with him.

Chapter Fifteen

THEN

Avery

It's my eighteenth birthday today.

"Keep your eyes closed." With his hands on my shoulders, Jasper guides me up a few steps.

"I have a blindfold on." I giggle, covering my eyes with my hands anyway. Never imagining spending my birthday this way, I buzz with excitement from the day I've had.

After celebrating dinner with Helen and Duke, Jasper was quick to whisk me away. The only information he gave me was to pack a bag for one night. We're spending the night away, just Jasper and me.

I've had that just got off a roller coaster feeling since he told me his plans. When I tried to ask where we were going, he kissed my forehead and told me not to worry. I did the exact opposite and have been thinking about it ever since.

"Is this where we're staying for the night?" I ask. He leads me through a set of double doors.

"It's not. I told you we had one stop before that," he tells me, just as a bell on a door chimes. *We're at a store?*

Suddenly, the scent of ink fills my nostrils while a low buzz tickles my ears. I recognize both, but I can't place our location. My mind scrambles to put the pieces together.

"Can I take off the blindfold now?" I ask, my heart pounding against my rib cage.

"Yes." Jasper's voice is full of excitement.

Wasting no time, I rip off the black silk. Shock forces me to suck in a break. *A tattoo shop.* "Am I getting a tattoo?"

"*We.*" Jasper hooks an arm around my shoulders, playfully yanking me into him. He presses a soft kiss on my temple. "We're getting tattoos together."

Oh my god. I've never gotten a tattoo before. I don't think I've ever thought about getting one either.

I drag my eyes across the walls covered with polaroids of happy customers and hand-drawn examples of the type of work they do. It's all beautiful.

My hands sweat with adrenaline. "Are you serious?"

"Yeah, Arizona. Let's do it." He flashes an encouraging smile.

"I don't know if I can do this."

Jasper angles his head toward me. "I think you can if you want to."

Biting my lip, I slowly back away. "I'm scared."

"Don't be. It's an amazing experience."

My eyes bounce from the chairs in the back to the artwork on the walls.

"Look, if you really don't want you, we don't have to," he assures me softly.

"I do. I think I do." I suck in a heavy breath. "But I'm nervous."

"We're getting one together." He rubs my arm in a soothing motion. "I'll be right there with you."

"I don't even know what I'd get," I say, glancing down at his arms covered in ink. "Do you even have room for more?"

His chest rumbles with a chuckle. "Of course I do. My body is a canvas just waiting to be covered."

"Hey, Jasper." One of the artists comes over to greet us at the front. "Is this your girl?"

"Yeah." His eyes flicker. "This is Arizona."

The amount of pride I feel being referred to as *Jasper's girl* is not healthy for my feminism.

"Cool." He extends his hand to me. "I'm Tripp."

I shake it, noticing the elaborate snake coiling around his forearm and down to his wrist. The details are incredible, but look painful. "Good to meet you."

"Do you have a book we can look through for her?" Jasper asks.

"Sure." Tripp slides a thick binder from underneath the glass countertop and lays it in front of me.

I stare at the shop logo printed on the cover. A beat passes before an idea forms. I know what I should get. The image of an infinity symbol is all I can see—the representation of endless nights with Jasper, living in a fantasy under the sun without a care.

"I know," I say gently, pushing away the binder. "An infinity symbol."

Jasper smiles. "I'm going to get one too."

My chest tightens. "Really?"

He nods. "Hell yes. I don't want to ever forget these summer nights."

"Matching tattoos, it is!" Tripp exclaims, clasping his hands together.

I can't explain the surge of adrenaline that takes over my limbs as my bare legs touch the black leather on the chair. Jasper takes the seat to my left.

My entire body is humming. I can barely keep my arm straight.

"Nervous?" Tripp smirks.

I shake my head, then turn my wrist to face upward, my eyes blaze into the fine tip point of the needle. The black sketch now holds the place where a permanent infinity symbol will be. Holding my breath, bile creeps up my throat. *Oh my god, can I do this? How bad is it going to hurt?*

Tripp leans in, hovering his large body over my extended arm. The second the needle pierces my skin, Jasper's hand slides into my opposite hand. I whip my head around to see his warm, comforting eyes staring at me with a fire I've yet to see from him. The powerful flames sear right through me, and suddenly, everything makes sense.

Maybe it's the excitement of doing something new? Perhaps it's the feeling of being alive. Or maybe it's discovering a part of myself I never knew existed.

In my eighteen years, I have never felt more clear about what is happening in my mind and with my body. This isn't just some summer fling. Jasper is unique and different. He looks at me like no one has ever done—not even my own parents.

Jasper got a matching infinity on the inside of his arm, no longer than my pinky finger, and entirely black ink like mine.

"I can't believe I did that." I praise myself for my bravery.

He glances at me from the driver's seat, one hand on the wheel and the other holding mine on top of the center console. "I know. I'm so proud of you. You did amazing."

I stare at the small white bandage covering the tattoo. "It didn't hurt as much as I thought it would."

"Once the initial touch of the needle passes, the rest of it turns into a dull ache."

"Yeah, similar to a sunburn," I say.

"Exactly." He smiles.

We pull onto a dirt road. The only things around me are the darkness of night and the tall trees lining the bumpy drive.

"Where are we?" I ask.

"I want to show you something." His smile is wide, while his eyes fill with excitement. *This must be important.*

"In the middle of nowhere?" I tease, chuckling. Then, before my eyes, the trees clear, opening up a small house on the edge of a cliff. There's no cloud in sight, allowing each star to shine to its brightest.

"Here we are." He shuts off the engine and twists in the seat to face me.

I scan the area. It's pitch-black outside except for the glow of a porch light. "An abandoned beach house?"

Jasper runs the back of his knuckles across my cheek. "I'm buying it."

My mouth drops. I quickly glance at the faded blue paint on the panels of the house and the tiny white picket fence needing more than a few repairs. "You're buying this?"

He nods proudly. "You want to see the inside?"

"Yes."

Jasper jumps out of the car, then sprints to open my door. I step out. With a warm nighttime breeze dusting across my shoulders, I breathe in deeply. The energy between us has shifted, and it is no more apparent than on the car ride to my next surprise destination. The typical playful exchanges are absent. I feel alert, clear-minded, and calm all at once.

Jasper grabs both bags from the back seat.

"Are we staying here?" I swirl my finger in the air.

"Yeah." Again, with a proud smile.

"Is there furniture?" I ask cheekily as he grabs my hand.

Jasper guides me up the short steps and to the white front door. "No." He pauses. "But it will be fine."

When he told me to pack an overnight bag, I knew we'd spend tonight together. And at first, I didn't think much of it. He spends the night with me at Helen's at least three times a week, but this is different.

Confused, my heart is pounding in my chest, but not from nerves. It's pounding from excitement. "Okay."

Jasper swings open the door. The small beach house consists of an empty room with wooden floors and a pile of padding and blankets in the middle. Pillows surround the makeshift bed, and tall white candles line the walls. The sight takes my breath away.

"Jasper," I whisper, taking it all in. Two double doors on the back wall are cracked open, with the crisp breeze from the ocean flowing through.

Jasper places our bags in the corner of the room.

"This place is going to be mine."

"Oh my gosh." Dragging my eyes across each space in this little area, I instantly fall in love. The home is cozy even with all the repairs to be done. To the left, I can barely make out a short hallway with a bedroom and bathroom. Behind us is a small eat-in kitchen. "I love it so much."

"Joe's parents used it as a summer beach house growing up. Then it became a rental, but now that his parents are older and haven't been able to keep up with it, Joe offered to sell it to me." He rushes out like he's been keeping this bottled up for too long. "I plan to live in it while renovating, then use it as a rental later."

"You are incredible, Jasper Collins." I slowly walk over to him and slide my hands around his waist. "Do you know that?"

He cups my face, his deep brown eyes bounce between mine. "Happy birthday, Arizona."

"Thank you," I say quietly.

"Will you stay here with me tonight?" He leans in and kisses the corner of my mouth but doesn't pull back right away.

My eyelids fall closed. I melt into him, letting my front become flush with his. "Of course."

Chapter Sixteen

THEN

Avery

My body trembles with nerves. I'm about to give myself to Jasper. I don't know if he knows yet, but he might suspect.

"I have to tell you something," I begin, a lump lodged in my throat.

He creates a trail of wet kisses from the side of my mouth, along my jaw, and down the sensitive skin on my neck. I break out in goose bumps. "What is it?"

"I've—" I take in a deep breath, mustering up the courage to tell him. "I've never had sex before."

Jasper lifts his head, bringing his flared eyes to meet mine. "You're a ...?

I nod, rubbing my lips together, somewhat ashamed.

"Thank you." A subtle smile cracks the corners of his mouth.

"For what?" I ask, confused.

"For choosing me," he mumbles, leaning in to kiss me.

"Oh, Jasper," I moan, eyes falling closed. "You're it for me."

Jasper continues kissing along my jawline, before reaching the flicker of my pulse. He presses a kiss on my pebbled skin, then he lets it linger before lifting to meet my eyes. "Can I show you how much I care for you?"

The hard thuds of my heart vibrate through my ears, and now that's all I can hear. "Okay."

Jasper's eyes darken. Pinching the straps on my dress between two fingers, he gently slides it off my shoulder. Then does the same with the other. My dress slips off, piling on the floor at my feet.

A sharp inhale captures my breath, with my hands at my sides, in only a bra and panties. Not much different than the bikinis I spend my days in, but these feel more intimate.

Jasper's knuckles run along the length of my forearm, grazing my skin with gentle pressure. Without a word, I clasp a string of his shorts and give it a light tug. The tie comes undone.

"Take them off," he commands.

I swallow hard as my fingers find the elastic on his waistband. Giving them one forceful tug, they fall to the floor. Jasper's dick springs free.

I gasp.

"You're shaking." His tone is low and filled with concern.

I nod.

"Oh, Avery," he says tenderly, cupping my face. "We can go as slow as you want."

I nod.

"Come here." Placing one arm under my legs and the other bracing my lower back, he lifts me. As he carries me to the bed, I wrap an arm around his neck and curl into him. Jasper softly lowers to the mattress. Staring at him from a lying position on my back, I drag my eyes over every inch of his toned body—every tattoo, the divots of his toned chest, and his tousled-on-top dark hair. *He is mine.*

Jasper crawls on top of me, a smile playing on his lips. He stops at my core. "You're beautiful."

"Thank you."

He hooks a finger under my panties and slowly inches them down. His warm breath on the inside of my thighs temporarily settles my nerves.

"I'm going to loosen you up a bit." His words hit the outside of my pussy, making it throb with anticipation.

"Uh, okay," I squeak out, unsure what he means by loosening me up, but I do know what he's planning on doing between my legs.

Jasper rubs his nose along the inside of my thigh, slowly licking my bumpy skin. I frantically reach for a pillow, a blanket, or anything to brace myself. He hooks both arms around the back of my knees and, with purpose, scoots me closer. I'm his to mold and manipulate.

"We don't even need to have sex. I could stay down here all day," he mumbles, then darts his tongue out, shooting it directly into my core. I gasp. We've done this before, but knowing what it will lead to makes it all that much better.

With a curve of his tongue and a light touch of his nose, I'm hit in both of the most sensitive areas. He slides in and out, licking every part of me. My legs begin to tremble like aftershocks from an earthquake, but instead, working in reverse because they only gain momentum.

"I need to make you nice and relaxed. I'd never forgive myself if I hurt you," he says, tilting his head to get a better angle.

My fingers find his head. I thread them through the soft, short strands of hair. "You could never hurt me, Jasper."

"We're going to be together forever," he purrs into my core.

The slickness of my arousal coating the inside of my thighs, his tongue laps it up, covering the landscape of my most desired area. I've never had another guy down here, and I hope I never will.

"Ohh," I moan, my eyes roll back. My pussy pulses with a deep intensity as tingles start from within. The pit of my stomach drops like a free fall, causing my back to bow off the bed.

"Come for me, Arizona," he tells me. "I want to have every part of you, in every part of me."

I'm coming. Now recognizing this feeling.

"Oh god!" I grit out. My hands grip the back of his head, moving him in the direction I need, riding his face, not caring at the moment whether he can breathe—desperate to feel it all. An orgasm rolls through my body like a hurricane, wrecking everything in its path.

Jasper releases, raising his head and looking drunk on lust.

Matching his energy, I smile. "You could breathe, couldn't you?"

He wipes his face on the back of his hand and crawls up my torso, leaving a trail of my wetness with his kisses. "It doesn't fucking matter."

I giggle.

"How do you feel?" he asks, resting his body on mine.

"Perfect."

His smirk is wide. He's satisfied with himself. "Good."

"I'm happy I waited to do this with you." My voice cracks through a whisper.

Lying underneath Jasper, our heartbeats are synchronized, and it is something from out of this world. I understand now why I wasn't interested in any other guy. They were self-centered and immature, and I barely breathe the same air as them. I thought I was the issue, but it wasn't me—it's that none of them were Jasper Collins.

He is my person, and I'm so lucky to have found him at only eighteen years old.

"Me too." Jasper's warm, inviting lips meet mine in an all-consuming kiss.

"Are you sure you want to do this?" Jasper's elbows are bent at the sides of my face, and his palms are cupping my cheeks. He hovers over me, caging and locking me in place.

"Yes, more than anything." My eyes dart around the room, unable to focus through the trembling.

"Avery." Jasper angles his head, forcing eye contact. He captures my gaze, leading me back to the center. "Breathe."

Violently shaking, I part my lips to take in a breath of precious air. "Okay."

"Are you ready?"

I lick my lips, then nod. Terrified, excited, and full of adrenaline, I let Jasper's legs spread mine. In one swift motion, Jasper presses a deep kiss onto my lips while entering me with a commanding yet gentle thrust.

"Ohh," I groan. With a light sting and a dull ache, he fills me.

"God, Avery," he grunts, but his body immediately stills.

"You're okay?"

A tear slips from under my eyelid and rolls down my cheek. A million emotions rage through me. "Yes."

Jasper wipes the wetness with his thumb with a smile. "Make sure you talk to me."

He throbs inside a few times before thrusting deeper. Another groan leaves my lips.

Jasper's misted forehead rests against mine. His body moves slowly and thoughtfully, but his pants get louder. "I love you," he whispers.

Oh my god. Another roll of his hips, teasing a sensitive spot at the top of my clit. "I love you too."

With another deep thrust, he pulls back. "You do?"

Smiling up at the millions of emotions written on his face, I answer him. "Yes, I do so much."

With a smile wider than I've seen, Jasper's slow thrusts become more frantic. My hips move in sync with his motions. A mix of pain and pleasure and connectedness travels through my veins like a drug.

A low grunt escapes from the back of my throat, and suddenly, his body stiffens above me. His limbs lock into place. "Fuck. I love you so much."

I kiss his face, wanting to feel every bit of him. "You feel so good."

Jasper releases everything inside me, then falls onto me.

"Oh my god," Jasper labors in a breathy explosion of words. His head, resting on my chest, moves with the sharp rise and fall of my lungs. Cradling him with both arms, our bodies slick with sweat. "I can't lose you."

"You're never going to," I reply wholeheartedly, brushing his hair away from his wet forehead.

Chapter Seventeen

THEN

Jasper

"Did Avery have a good time?" my dad asks as soon as I walk into the office.

I smile to myself, thinking about the awesome night Avery and I had for her birthday. Waking up that next morning after we'd finally had sex was unreal. She is perfect, and I love her so much. I didn't think I could get more protective over her, but I have. I've only slept with a handful of girls before her—none were virgins, but the way Avery's body is made for mine is un-fucking-believable.

"She loved it," I tell him, leaving out the intimacy part, although I'm sure he knows. I slink into my office chair, just returning from an early morning lesson. I haven't seen my dad since Avery's birthday dinner. "I thought she wasn't going to go through with the tattoo, but she did."

"Hmm. Good for her."

"We ended up getting the same ones."

"Tattoos?" he asks.

"Yeah," I tell him, smiling.

"That's great, Son," he says, but there is apprehension behind his words.

I spin back around to him. "Is everything alright?"

He rubs his chin and sighs.

I clasp my hands together to lap and wheel my chair over to him. "What's up, Dad? Something is bothering you."

"Have you both thought about what will happen when she returns to Arizona for college?" He comes right out and forces me to acknowledge that this bubble we're living in won't last forever.

I flex my shoulders with irritation. He's only bringing up the inevitable. I wanted to live in the moment a few weeks ago and not think about how the summer would end, but things have changed between us.

"Arizona is only a couple hours' flight away," I counter.

My dad's eyebrows raise. "Alright, okay, so this is serious."

"I'm in love with her." I look him in the eyes, showing how serious I am about Avery.

"She's a special one, isn't she?" he points out with concern.

I nod with a smile. "Yeah."

"How is the new medication coming along?" He immediately goes into the real reason why he's worried about Avery and me getting so close.

After sinking into another episode two weeks ago, he convinced me to get back on medications. It wasn't the right one.

"I need to try a new one," I admit, knowing I've already stopped taking it. "It makes me feel anxious and gives me insomnia."

"That's a drag. Well, back to the doctor to try another one, then?"

"I know. I'll make an appointment this week," I agree, but I'm pissed.

I'm angry I have to live with this condition. The new medication did give me a small amount of relief. Enough to enjoy Avery's birthday, but I feel the heaviness banging at the back door of my thoughts daily. It's always there, waiting for something to break me down and let it in.

"I took Avery to Joe's beach house," I tell him, lightening the mood.

"Yeah, buddy." He smiles. "And what did she think?"

"She loved it." I fold one leg over the other.

"I'm so proud of you, but still a little hurt that you won't live with me anymore," he teases, tossing a hanger from his desk into the hanger collection bin.

"You'll get over it," I retort. "I can't live with you forever."

"I thought we were going to be roommates for life." He leans over and slaps my knee.

"Look"—I rub my chin—"when you're too old to wipe your own ass, I'll let you move in with me."

"Fuck you," he spits, waving me off and turning back toward his computer.

I spend the rest of the day at the shop, reviewing orders, staff questions, and scheduling. Even though numbness always floats below the surface, it still lingers by late afternoon. I miss Avery.

I finish a few last things and text her that I'm heading out for the day.

Me: What are you up to?

Arizona: I just got off work. Helen and I are having lemonade on the patio.

Me: I'm getting off soon. Do you want to meet me at my house? Or should I come over there?

Arizona: I'll come over to you. I like the way your bed smells.

Me: My sheets smell like you.

Arizona: I like it that way.

Me: Me too.

Me: See you in 30 minutes?

Arizona: I'll be there!

After reading her last text, my dick is already jumping inside my pants. If anything can get rid of this cloud, it's sinking deep into her. She's the light of my life and the only thing keeping these depressive episodes away.

I pull up to my house a short time later. A smile tugs on the corner of my lips when I turn onto the sloped street where her car is already there. Anxiously, I park in the two-car garage and then hop out. By the time I make it to the driveway, she's already walking up.

"Damn, I missed you," I moan, gliding my fingertips along her bare sides. "The loose strings on these bikinis fall off so easily."

She giggles. "I wore it in case you wanted to get in the water."

Yanking her into me, I bury my face in her neck. The smell of her coconut shampoo is heavenly. "You know I always like to get into the water."

She wiggles out of my embrace and slides her hand into mine. "Let's go inside."

"Whatever you want," I say, leading her through the garage door.

"Where is your dad?"

I kick off my shoes while leading her upstairs to my bedroom. "He's at an event at the house next door."

"When will he be back?" she asks coyly, hot on my heels.

I turn to face her, opening my door from behind. "Not until late tonight."

Avery raises her tippy toes, meeting my lips. She nibbles on my bottom lip, and I instantly stand at attention, tenting my board shorts. "I'm going to go to the bathroom." Her eyes dart to my pants. "Be right back."

Damn, I love how she plays. "I'll be waiting."

She skips into the attached bathroom in my bedroom, shutting the door behind her.

My body is heated. I can't wait to be with her again. Hopefully, I won't have to go slow this time. The animalistic urge she brings out of me is new and exciting. I fall onto my bed, eagerly waiting for her to return.

Avery steps out of my bathroom with a sad look on her face.

I feel a deep furrow in my brows. "Are you okay?"

She lets out a deep sigh. "Jasper, I don't want you to think I'm checking in on you or overstepping in any way," she begins, sitting on the side of my bed. *What happened in the bathroom? Did she find something*? I'm clean, and I don't think I left a mess. "But I love you." She avoids eye contact.

"What's wrong?" I press, resting a hand on her bent knee.

"Are you not taking your new medication?"

Fuck. I exhale in frustration. Avery shouldn't worry about that. It's my problem. "That's not something you have to worry about," I reassure her, tucking loose hair in her face behind her ear.

Avery's posture stiffens. "It's my problem too. I care for you and have seen firsthand what happens when you don't take your meds."

I shift myself away, planting both feet on the floor. "I appreciate it, but have it handled."

"Then why haven't you answered my question?" she challenges.

"What question?"

"Are you not taking your medication?" Her tone is clipped this time. She wants an answer and deserves respect enough for me, to be honest. "I found the full bottle in your trash can."

Resting my elbows on my knees, I lay my head in my hands. "I'm not taking it."

"Why?" she asks a little softer.

"I didn't like the way it made me feel," I painfully admit. *God, I hate being this vulnerable*. I'm the one who's supposed to be protecting her, and here I am, an incomplete person.

"But you *like* the way the depression makes you feel?" she retorts, scooting closer.

"No. I fucking hate it. I hate that I have to live with this when so many other people get to go on with their lives without a grey cloud looming over them on a daily basis." I rise to my feet. I'm not prepared to talk to her about my struggles—or anyone for that matter—but I love Avery. I need to be open with her.

She rests her head on my shoulder. "Tell me what it's like."

Wrapping an arm around her, I bring her down on top of me. She tucks herself into the crook under it while we stare at the revolving banana leaf ceiling fan above us.

"You don't want to know."

She faces me fully, her lips set in a hard line, proving she won't let this go easily.

"What do you want to know?" I give in. I envisioned spending the afternoon with fewer clothes, but at least I'm with her.

"Everything." She caresses the side of my stomach with her fingertips. "Anything you're comfortable sharing."

Rubbing my forehead, I try to find the words to begin. *How do I explain to another person what depression is like? Especially if they don't have it themselves.*

"I don't always remember what it feels like when I'm not in it, but I know it's bad." Avery lays still and silent next to me. "Sometimes, there's a trigger, but not always." Running a hand down my face, I struggle with an explanation.

How do I tell her it starts slow, eventually morphing into not wanting to get up in the morning and intrusive thoughts like,

What if I wasn't here? I can't tell anyone those things, let alone Avery. She'd freak out and think I am broken, unworthy of her love. Thoughts like that aren't meant to leave the safety of my head.

"Sometimes you don't even get a warning?" she asks. "How are you supposed to live through it?"

"It's just a part of who I am. I've learned to deal with it," I reply. It's honest and raw but the truth.

My eyes dart around my bedroom, a space that's become a sanctuary during particularly rough episodes. "Most of the time, I can put on a mask with a fake smile and act like nothing is wrong when, on the inside, a powerful war is raging between how long this will last and whether I will ever feel like myself again."

"I had no idea." Her words come out breathy. The painful realization of my flaws is apparent. The last thing I want is for her to pity me, but there's also this belief that if she loves me, she will love all the parts of me—even the darker sides.

"I don't tell people about it, Arizona," I say. The worst part is the heavy feeling of loneliness—being with someone you love but not being able to love them at that moment. "I'm telling you because I love you, but not even the guys know."

"I appreciate you trusting me." Avery nestles her nose into my cheek. "I love you so much and want to be there for you in any way I can."

"Thank you, but depression is an invisible battle which, most of the time, can't be helped by others." I roll over, bringing my arm around the top of her. Lightly pressing into her back, I nudge her closer.

"Do they last a long time?" She sniffs, her nose leaking.

"It depends. Some episodes are worse than others. Sometimes, they bring a physical weight, like being pressed on my chest and shoulders." My body feels the sensation now as I recount some aspects of it. Swallowing a cotton ball in my throat, I attempt to clear it before continuing, "Other times, it's not the physical sensation, but the mental ones that are tough. While pushing through, I wonder if I'll ever get through it or be able to gasp a full breath again. But just as quickly as the wave comes, it moves over me, passing by, and then life is what it should be once again."

Avery props herself on one elbow. With an expression of empathy, she leans over me and kisses me. "I love you. And you are not alone in this," she mumbles into my lips. The love I feel for her is unexpected. I'm only nineteen, and I worry about whether it's typical to have intense feelings toward someone like this.

I bring my free hand to the back of her head and gently push her to deepen our kiss. She falls into me, lifting herself to straddle my torso.

I dart my tongue inside her mouth and swirl it around before diving into the back of her throat, craving to be further inside her. Avery is my lifeline. We remain connected until I feel her giggles rumble inside my chest.

"Jasper!" She laughs, flipping her hair around. I stare into her beautifully hazel-green eyes, which always seem to have more green in them than brown.

"Take your swimsuit off," I growl.

She licks her lips, her cheeks turning crimson. "You didn't say *please.*"

"Please ..." I groan, licking her nose. "Take ..." I bring my mouth to her neck, sucking hard. "Your swimsuit ..." *Bite.* "Off."

Maybe we can turn this afternoon around after all.

Chapter Eighteen

Now

Avery

I spent the entire day pacing back and forth between the living room and the balcony. I thought about walking down to visit Helen, but my thoughts were swirling with heaviness from this town. I can't imagine having to answer the endless questions I'm sure she'll have.

A buzzing sound coming from the kitchen table breaks my stream of unconscious internal ramblings for a moment before they're back once again. I don't know how Coconut Grove managed to sink its warm, beachy claws in me again or how, after so many years, it still has a profound hold. I've tried to make sense of the summer that changed my life, but I haven't been able to.

The insistent buzz continues for an unclear amount of time before I realize it's my phone. Absently swiping it off the counter, I also drop it on the floor. *Shit.*

"Hello," I answer, frazzled and without checking to see who it is first.

A man's voice on the other end of the call startles me. "Hi, babe."

"Hi?" I pause, confused. *Wait.* "Dave!"

"Yeah, of course," he hisses with annoyance.

"How are you?" I bend to sit on the couch, barely missing the edge while scrambling to string a full sentence together—one that does include me calling him *Jasper.*

He pauses before answering. "Fine. Are you alright? You seem a little off."

"I'm fine, just getting settled. That's all."

"Have you spoken to your aunt yet?" he asks. I told Dave I needed to come out here to tell Helen about the engagement in person. He knows I lived with her the summer after my parents passed, but that's the extent of it.

"I did a little." My legs bounce. "I think I'm going to stay the weekend with her," I tell him, anticipating this visit down memory lane is a longer road than I expected.

"Oh, so you won't be back for a few more days?" he clarifies, impatience in his tone.

"No, sorry."

"I have that Dentists of the Valley Association dinner on Saturday. I was hoping you'd be back for that."

My heart is heavy having to lie to him, but I need to do this for myself. "I know. I'm really sorry."

"Why do you need to stay that long with her anyway?"

My eyes lower. "Because she's my aunt, and she meant a lot to me. I'm sure you understand."

"You haven't seen her since I've known you," he quips. *Why is he suddenly arguing about me staying away?* "Don't you think I deserve to spend time with my fiancé the first week after I proposed to her?"

"It's not about you. I need to do this." I stand, feeling defensive. "I'm sure you understand." We've only been casual for the last year and a half. It's not my fault he decided to propose and suddenly wants to claim more stake on me.

"Fine. Do what you have to do." His words come out low with frustration. "Just so you know, I'm pissed you're making me go to this without a date. I thought this was our understanding."

"I get it and I'm sorry," I offer, trying to sympathize with him. "It is what it is."

"Thank you," I say. "I'll call you tomorrow, okay?"

"Fine, Avery," he spits, followed by an abrupt end to the call.

I shrug off Dave's attitude, but guilt about my relationship with Helen hits. I need to spend more time on this short trip. We've spoken here and there over the years, but after how much I was gutted that summer, I didn't want anything to do with this place. She was a reminder of all of it. Maybe one day, I'll give her the explanation she deserves. But first, I need to handle Jasper.

I watch anxiously as the little surfboard-shaped hand on the clock inches toward the four.

Molding myself into the couch, a thought pops into my mind. I glance down at the sundress I'm wearing and the lace-up sandals. *Do I look cute enough? Do I smell good?* I shouldn't care, but I do.

I fly off the couch and sprint down the hall to the bathroom. While giving myself a spritzer of coconut body mist, I take another look in the mirror. A flash catches my eye—Dave's engagement ring. Twisting it in my finger a few times, I make the choice to side it off. I'm confident Jasper knows at this point, but I'm not going to rub it in his face. Whether he's over me or not, it feels disrespectful. I place the ring safely in a ziplock baggie and tuck it into my suitcase. I fluff my hair a few times, and then a light but forceful knock hits the door.

My stomach drops—that intense feeling of riding a roller coaster for the first time. The anticipation, the excitement—*the fear.*

"You can do this, Avery," I whisper to myself. "You are a strong, independent woman with money and a career," I continue to repeat as I shuffle toward the front door.

"You can do it." I open it to see Jasper with a thin cotton shirt, shorts, and Converse like he's still nineteen. *Fuck me.*

"Hi." He smiles, leaning against the door frame.

"Hi."

"Are you ready to go?"

I nod, biting my lip. "Yeah, let me get my purse." He waits patiently on the porch for me to return. "Okay. All set."

Jasper nods and steps aside.

A few minutes later, Jasper and I are driving down the beach in his car. It's not long until he pulls off onto a dirt road.

"We're headed into the middle of nowhere?" I ask, but something about this rural part of town is familiar. *Déjà vu?*

"I guess I should tell you this now," he begins, flashing me a quick side-eye.

I cock my head to the side. "Tell me what?"

"I'm kidnapping you," he states cooly.

A rush of adrenaline zips up my spine. "Funny."

He laughs. "You'll see."

I stare out the window, watching as he turns left out of the forest. A small light blue beach house with a white fence comes into view. *It can't be what I think it is.* He pulls his car around to the side—the open ocean right in front of us and not another house in sight.

"Jasper?" I utter his name in disbelief.

"Look familiar?" he says, opening the car door.

"Oh my god," I mutter as he walks around to my side. I step out and into the tall grass. "Is this—?"

"Yes," he interjects, taking my hand. Jasper leads me down a narrow dirt path lined with green grass. The high blades reach up to my waist.

"It looks different." My eyes land on the yellow beach cruiser resting against the front window on the porch.

"Well, it's had some upgrades in the last few years," he replies. I follow Jasper to the door with my heart in a death grip. "Do you want to go in?"

I smile, my eyes stinging with moisture. "Yeah."

His eyes meet mine. "Okay."

When the door swings open, I can hardly take in a breath. The small cottage is set up exactly how we talked about it. The furniture is blue and white, with island theming throughout.

"Jasper, it's beautiful," I mumble, taking in this space that was once going to be our home. The kitchen is white, with light-colored wood and a small round table sits to the side.

"Remember we talked about how hard it would be to have all the guys over this small place at once?" he recalls, dreamily.

I smile, turning on my heels in the small living space. "I do."

"It turned out well, didn't it?" he boasts, sliding open the large glass doors on the opposite side of the living space. "There are two bedrooms and one bathroom. Want to check out the rest?"

I nod. Jasper clasps my hand with his and leads me into the bathroom first.

Rounding the corner into the bathroom, a chuckle bubbles in my chest. *Pineapples.* "Pineapples?"

"They're your favorite, right?" he says, stepping into me. My back is against the door while Jasper's body crowds me in this small space.

My breath quickens. "You remembered?"

"Of course." His eyes drop to my lips. "And orange is the only color you like outside of black."

A flush creeps up my neck. "You remembered that too?"

"Yes."

My breathing picks up. *Oh no.* "You don't live here anymore, do you?" I ask, quickly breaking the tension.

"No," Jasper replies. Then he backs up and walks away.

I take a minute to control my breathing and slowly follow him. He stands in the living room with his back to me, looking at the water.

"It's beautiful."

"I lived here for a while after you left." *Oh god. Here it comes.* "I fixed it up myself, well, with the help of my dad." He turns to me with his hands inside the front pockets of his shorts. "Now I rent it out to people during tourist season."

I cautiously sit on the soft white fabric of a wicker couch. "Now you live in your dad's house?"

"When he got sick, I bought the house next door to his so I

could be closer." His attitude has become somber. Talking about us and his dad can't be easy. It isn't for me.

"My aunt said he passed a few years ago." My voice cracks with sadness. I haven't seen Duke in years. He was an incredible guy and Jasper's best friend. I can only imagine how hard the loss was on him.

"Yeah. It was rough."

"How did you do?" I ask, wondering about his depression. Maybe it is out of line, but it feels natural.

He raises his eyebrows. "You mean with my depression?"

"Yeah, but I understand if you don't want to talk to me about it. Bad habits die hard, you know?" I avoid his gaze, feeling ashamed that I brought it up. It's not my place. "I shouldn't have asked."

Jasper sits beside me on the couch, his leg barely rubbing against mine. "It's okay, Avery. I don't mind talking about it."

"Okay."

"It was hard. But I've been on medication for the last few years, and things have been stable." His lips part, and he continues, "I haven't had a bad episode since I lost him three years ago."

My stomach twists with a pang of regret. "I'm sorry I wasn't here."

He shakes his head sympathetically. "Don't be."

"I wasn't around for Helen either," I reply, hanging my head low. "I know it was hard on her."

Jasper's firm touch finds my chin. Pinching it, he lifts my face, capturing my eyes. "You needed to do what was important to you."

My lips tingle with the memory of having his mouth on them. And the flashback of the first night we came here together.

"Thank you." Jasper breaks contact, dropping his focus to the floor. A sly smirk crawls across his face. I catch it, and it forces me to blush. He's thinking about something, and I'm dying to know what. "What?"

He shrugs, straightening his posture. "Nothing."

"What are you thinking?" I press, arching a brow.

He gestures toward the set of chairs by the window. "This room."

My cheeks redden. The corners of my mouth quirked up. "Oh, I remember that night."

"I remember that night too." He turns away, but I can tell he's grinning with how tight his voice is.

"I was so nervous," I admit. The night I gave myself to him. Having him for the first time is a vivid experience. And now, reliving that night here with him years later is surreal.

"So was I."

"How? You had been with other women," I quip. My words sound more annoyed than I'd like them to be.

"That didn't matter. You were ..." He pauses. "*You*."

Thick tension fills the air, creating an apron around us. For a brief moment, I'm taken back to that night when nothing mattered except for Jasper and me. The emotions come rushing back, slapping me like an unexpected wave. I panic and quickly stand.

"I should go," I whisper, but I don't want to go.

"You're probably right."

Running my hands along my dress to straighten out the

wrinkles, I catch Jasper staring at me with a look in his eyes that I can never forget. It makes my insides clench. "Are you checking me out?"

"You're still my wife. Can't I appreciate you before you aren't anymore?" he replies, discreetly licking his bottom lip.

That subtle action and his words—wetness pools in my panties. My fucking body is betraying me. When he speaks to me like that, I fall right back into the same safe place of knowing I'm his.

"Is that why you won't sign my papers?" I snap, taking a hard exit out of the heat of our conversation. I can't get caught up in his charm.

"Maybe." His expression turns from playful to firm. "Let's go."

Chapter Nineteen

Now

Jasper

Waking up this morning, I was still reeling from my conversation with Avery yesterday. It's always been so easy with her, and we have slipped back into the comfort of what used to be. I haven't felt that in a long time. But something else has kept me up. It hadn't dawned on me that she could be here asking for a divorce because she's engaged.

I should have expected it, but it didn't shield the literal gut punch when Easton called me yesterday afternoon to tell me she'd been into his café for breakfast that morning, and the *little* planet-sized rock on her finger clearly indicated her true intentions. *How could I have missed that when she showed up in my office that day?*

A light knock on the door.

"Be out in a minute," I call out.

"The new Chamber of Commerce CEO is looking for you." Gail's voice is a loud whisper through the wooden door.

Loosening my tie to take a full breath, I feel relief to be alone.

I grip the cold countertop in the restroom, trying to pull myself together. Public events like these are a part of the job, and I've reveled in them. Chatting with business leaders in the town is one of the best things I get to do, but tonight, my mind is on something else—*someone else.*

"I'm in the bathroom, Gail." I swipe my forehead. "Can I not have five minutes alone?"

When I dropped Avery off at her rented beach house earlier this evening, so much was left unsaid. The moment we shared at my old beach house proved I'm not the only one still battling feelings.

I haven't mentioned her tattoo, but I'm sure she's seen that I still have mine too. I was surprised when she still had it, but then I realized it's not like a name that would be hard to explain to people. It's a simple symbol, meaningless to everyone but us. Knowing she's kept it all these years lights me up. If she wanted to erase our past, that would be the logical first step.

It didn't go unnoticed that she was also missing an engagement ring on her finger. The same place where mine used to be. She took it off on purpose. *Did she not want me to know?*

"You've been in there for almost an hour, Jasper," she counters. "Time to socialize."

I push myself off the counter, blow out a breath, and swing open the door. "I haven't been hiding in there that long," I snap. "And what if I did need privacy? You don't know what I was doing."

Gail leans against the door frame with her arms tightly folded at her chest. "You didn't."

"How do you know?"

"Because if you did, you wouldn't have walked down to another part of the hotel when there are at least three restrooms closer to the conference room."

I cock my head to the side. "Whatever you think."

"I'm your assistant. This is what I do." She smiles with satisfaction.

I slip past her. "Fine."

"She's suddenly come back, and it's getting to you, isn't it?" she asks, but it's more of a statement of accusation.

I stop with my back still facing Gail. "I don't know what you're talking about."

"Jasper," she says with frustration. "You know exactly what I'm talking about."

I squeeze my eyes shut. Of course, Avery being here is getting to me. *How could it not?* She was my first and only love. The day she left ripped my heart out. It's been an open wound since.

My head falls back. I turn to face Gail. "Yes, it is."

"Do you know what she's here for?"

I painfully nod. "I do."

I'm certainly not going to tell Gail why Avery is back in town. That brief mention of her being *Mrs. Collins* when she showed up at my office that day hasn't been brought up again. I'm hoping Gail and the receptionist up front forgot about it entirely.

"What is it?" Her shoulders bounce with confusion.

"I don't want to talk about it." I clear my throat. "We have a lot of history. Let's just leave it at that."

She shakes her head, prepared to pepper me with more questions. "I have known you and your dad for years. I'm aware of your past with Avery, but I feel there's something more you're not telling me."

"You said the new Chamber CEO, Chris, is waiting for me, right?" I dismiss her comment.

"You're not going to tell me, are you?" she huffs.

I turn on my heels and walk back down the hall toward the conference room. "Nope."

I hear a light sigh from her as the distance between us grows. *This is my secret.*

Pulling open the doors, I make a beeline for the bar in the back of the room.

"What can I get for you, Mayor Collins?" the bartender asks.

"I'll take an old-fashioned," I tell him, then turn to scan the room for Chris. It only takes me a second to spot him, and sure enough, he's walking in my direction.

The bartender places the drink on top of a square white napkin. "Here you go."

But before the glass touches the paper, I grab it from his hands, bring it to my lips, and take a large swig.

"Thank you." I set the half-empty drink back on the napkin. "I don't like to drink at work functions. You can toss the rest."

A puzzled look sweeps across his face. "Um, okay."

"Mayor Collins." A man's voice booms behind me. I turn around to see Chris, an older gentleman the board hired as the new CEO of the Chamber of Commerce. He's from Southern California, and the community is excited to have him in our town.

"Chris Hooper," I greet him, extending my arm.

He shakes his hands with enthusiasm. "I'm glad we finally

were able to meet."

"Yes, likewise."

"I've heard about all the incredible things you've done with the town since being elected last year."

"Thank you," I say. "It's my home, so this community means everything to me."

"I'm looking forward to being a part of it." He smiles, raising his glass. I had nothing in my hands, so I grabbed the first drink I saw, which was a water bottle. *Fuck. I'm off my game tonight.*

"Cheers," I say, giving him a quick nod. "Glad you could come to our monthly business owners' mixer."

"Happy to be here," he says, sipping his red wine. "You also own a few properties out here, correct?"

"My dad and I owned a surf shop before he passed," I tell him, a wave of sadness at the thought of my father. "Now, it's just me that owns it."

"Sorry to hear about his loss," he offers. "Will you pass it down to your kids one day?" he asks, possibly thinking he's lightening the mood—an innocent question I've been asked numerous times over the years, but with Avery back in town, it kicks up past trauma in a way it hasn't in some time.

I swallow the threat of emotion and push away the memory of that night. "That has always been the plan."

"I bet." He smiles, oblivious to the battles inside my head.

My phone vibrates in the front pocket of my slacks.

> Arizona: Thanks for taking me to see the beach house today. It's incredible what you did.

My heart skips a beat. *She's texting me.* She's initiated contact this time.

"Excuse me, Chris." I place one finger into the air. "I have to take this."

"Yes, yes." He nods, stepping away.

"We'll talk soon." I smile, then search for the closest door. I sprint through the groups of people chatting about business with cocktails in their hands. Before stepping into the hall, I catch sight of Gail. Her eyes bore into mine, suspicious of where I was going.

Me: Thank you. I had a lot of inspiration.

I tap out a response as soon as I'm in a quiet area.

Arizona: So many memories there.

I smile to myself.

Me: Yes.

Arizona: Was it hard to live there after everything?

Me: Yes. But in some way, it was comforting.

Sitting on a bench in a secluded part of the hall, I savor every moment of her attention.

Arizona: I'm glad.

Me: What are you doing?

Arizona: I'm sitting on the back patio with Helen, listening to the waves.

Me: I'm glad you're spending time with her.

Arizona: Me too.

Me: Are you still coming to the first day of the Coconut Days event tomorrow night?

Arizona: I'm not sure.

Me: Arizona.

Arizona: I'm kidding. Yes, I'm still planning on going.

Gail's head pops out of one of the conference room doors. Her animated wave grabs my attention. I should head back in. We only have another hour left.

Me: I'll see you tomorrow night then.

Arizona: See you tomorrow.

She's the shot of dopamine I need to finish the rest of the night. And by the time tomorrow comes, and it begins to wear off, I'll see her again.

Chapter Twenty

THEN

Avery

Helen and I show up to the Coconut Grove Days late afternoon, ready to listen to live music and snack on amazing treats.

"I'm going to say hi to Joe. His taco booth is on the south side of the vendor row," she says.

This event is significant for the town and attracts thousands of tourists annually. It's a chance for local vendors, artisans, and restaurants to showcase their goods and services. From what I've heard from Jasper and the guys, the event is also like one big party.

"Of course." I nod. "I'm going to Duke's. Jasper said he and Easton would be at their booth."

With one arm around me, she gives me a tight hug. "Okay, honey. Text me if you need money for anything."

I smile at my sweet aunt. I don't need her money, and she knows it. On my birthday two weeks ago, I received the first installment from the inheritance. But her offer means more to me than she realizes. "I'll let you know, but I'm sure I'll be fine."

"Okay. We'll meet up in a little bit." She releases me and begins walking toward Joe's. "Have fun!"

Jasper didn't sleep over last night because his dad needed help making a few custom surfboards for the weekend. They worked late into the night. When he texted me this morning, he mentioned their vendor space is toward the front entrance. As I gaze across each spot, I see familiar restaurants, coffee shops, and even an artist selling beautiful art made from driftwood.

My breath catches when my eyes lock with my other half—*my person*. I play it cool by giving him a quick wave before walking over.

"Arizona!" Easton yells as soon as he sees me.

I'm still a few feet away from the table when Jasper sprints around from the back, clutches my waist, and lifts me into the air.

"I missed you last night." I dip my head between his shoulder and neck while wrapping both legs around him.

With his hands tightly grabbing my ass cheeks, he holds me close. "I fucking missed you too."

I breathe in his salty scent one more time before he releases me. I slide down, then walk over to greet Duke.

"Hey, little lady. Where's your aunt?" he asks, struggling to angle a surfboard away from the direct sun.

"She went over to Joe's," I tell him, sliding my hand into Jasper's.

"Okay. I'm sure she'll stop by later," he mumbles with a convincing tone, more to himself than us. "Social butterfly."

"I'm sure she will." I smile, seeing him worry about my aunt. There is something more between them than just a casual thing.

In the two months I've been here, I've seen a deep love and partnership. It's heartwarming.

Jasper lovingly kisses the top of my head, then brings his dark eyes down to mine. "Want to go grab something to eat?"

"I'd love to." I flutter my lashes.

"Alright, you two are making me sick," Easton spats, kneeling in front of a box of shirts.

Duke arches a brow. "Where do you think you're going? You need to stay here and help us."

Jasper smirks at his dad. "Relax, I'll be back. I promise."

"This is going to be yours one day, and you're not going to be able just to come and go," he calls out as Jasper leads me away.

"I know, Dad," he says over his shoulder, with an arm hooked around my neck.

"I don't mind hanging out at the booth with you guys," I say.

His forehead furrows. "No way, Arizona. You need to experience this event to the full extent."

"What does that even mean?" I giggle.

"It means that you're going to listen to every song that these local mediocre bands have to offer." He pauses, dipping down close. "And try food from every single vendor."

"What?" I laugh. "I can't eat that much food!"

"Well, you're in luck because I'm here to help you." Jasper playfully nuzzles the tip of my nose with his. At the same time, I rise, angling my head to the side to capture his mouth in mine. We both laugh into each other's lips.

"Fuck man, you two," Bodhi comments, walking up with his arm around an unfamiliar brunette woman. "Don't you two have *enough* sex?"

I gaze up into Jasper's eyes, ignoring Bodhi's sarcastic remark. "No, we don't, actually," I retort.

"Would you like more?" Jasper's eyebrow raises. "My truck is only a short distance away."

I coyly tuck a few loose strands of hair behind my ear. "Maybe later."

Bodhi extends his arm, raising his hand in the air. "That's what I'm talking about, keeping my boy here happy!"

I play into him by meeting his palm for a high-five.

Jasper slaps it away. "Okay, enough. We're going to grab a few things to eat and head over toward the stage. You coming?"

"What do you say, baby?" he asks the woman on his arm.

She shrugs. "I guess so. I just have to be back with my family at least by nine."

"Are you visiting?" I ask her, wondering why I haven't seen her with Bodhi before.

"Yeah. We're on vacation here for a family reunion," she says excitedly. "We come every year."

"That sounds fun," I say friendly.

She loudly smacks her lips together, chewing the gum in her mouth. "My mom said when I'm a senior, I don't have to come anymore."

I thought she looked a little young when they walked up together, but now I'm even more curious. "And when will that be? I just graduated this past year."

"Well, next year, I'll be a junior, so I have some time." She turns to Bodhi with butterflies in her eyes. "But if we return here, it might not be such a bad trip."

My brain quickly does the math. She's got to be only sixteen, and I know Bodhi is twenty— a year older than Jasper. I've just turned eighteen, but there's a big difference in two years. I wonder if Bodhi knows.

My eyes fly up to take in the expression on his face. *He didn't know.*

"I thought you said you were eighteen?" he accuses, inconspicuously removing his arm.

She pulls her lips to the side and tilts her head upward. "Did I?"

His expression hardens. "Yes."

Jasper clutches my waist, and I know exactly what he's thinking. He's never going to let Bodhi live this down. I can feel the laughter bubbly from inside his chest as Bodhi's face drains of color.

"Oh, oops." She giggles. "It doesn't matter anyway, right?"

"Yeah, it kind of does." Bodhi scratches the top of his head.

"Well," Jasper says, breaking the awkward tension. "Bodhi, let's head over to the stage." Then he turns to the brunette. "It was nice meeting you. I hope you enjoy yourself in Coconut Grove, but at this time, we're going to go our separate ways."

I rub my lips together, holding in an eruption of laughter.

She lifts her upper lip with disgust. "Oh, alright."

"Don't forget to check out all the local vendors while you're here!" Jasper tosses over his shoulder while the three of us walk away. *Always looking out for the town.*

"Okay, so in my defense, I did not know she was that young." Bodhi grabs complimentary blankets from the event staff booth before we get to the open field.

Jasper shoots him a side-eye, grabbing one of the large

blankets from Bodhi's hands. I follow the two of them toward the middle of the grass. Jasper shakes it out and lays it flat. Bodhi does the same with his.

"You didn't mess around with her, did you?" I grimace, kneeling next to Jasper. He lies back and clasps his hands behind his head.

"Hell no," Bodhi answers quickly. "I almost did, though."

Jasper nudges me down. "Only you would try to hook up with a tourist that young."

Bodhi sits with his knees bent, facing the band. "What about Arizona?" He cocks his head in my direction. "She turned eighteen like two weeks ago."

"It's not the same," I tell him, knowing it is similar. "Besides, we didn't hook up until after my birthday."

Bodhi clicks his tongue and slaps Jasper on the shoulder. "Interesting."

"Fuck you, man." Jasper shoves his shoulder, knocking him over.

"My point remains." He laughs. "I'm starving. I'm gonna go see what everyone else is doing." He pops up onto his feet. "They're at your dad's booth, right?"

Jasper covers his face with his baseball cap and answers Bodhi without removing it. "Yeah, I think Easton is still there."

Bodhi rubs the top of my head, messing up my hair. "Cool. Later, Arizona."

"Bye." I shoo him away.

Jasper and I lay on the grass, cuddling and talking while local bands took their turns on the stage. At one point during the evening, Helen came over to say hello and to tell me she'll be at Duke's booth until close. We also saw a few more of Jasper's friends.

A crisp nighttime breeze brings a chill to my bare shoulders. I shake with a shiver.

"Are you cold?" Jasper asks, reaching behind us for another blanket.

"A little bit," I say. I glance around the open field, noticing the vendors beginning to break down their booths as the crowds head toward us for nighttime entertainment.

Jasper wraps the thick fabric around me. "Better?"

"Much," I coo, slipping my hand underneath his shirt and caressing his stomach. He breaks out in goose bumps. "I love spending these nights with you."

Jasper smiles. His eyes blaze into mine while the back of his knuckles glide across my cheek. The sounds of the band and the crowds of people are no match for the pounding inside my chest—it vibrates through my ears. Flutters in the pit of my stomach erupt. This time, I don't have to wait until they pass. Now, I know how to relieve the aches they bring.

"Let's go to your truck," I mumble into his ear, then give his earlobe a sharp nibble.

Jasper's body stiffens. "You got it."

Adrenaline pumps through my veins as we both get to our feet. Jasper folds the blankets over his arm and grabs my hand with the other. I jump on the balls of my feet as we drop it off at one of the event tables and sprint to his truck.

My thighs clench when we reach the parking lot, and his truck comes into view. It's hidden in an unlit spot, away from all the commotion of the event. The first time we had sex was painful, but the last couple of times have been amazing.

As we approach the driver's side door, Jasper reaches out to open it for me. I waste no time climbing in. Crawling across the leather bench seat, I can feel him slide in after me. I'm still on all fours when his arm comes around my side, scooping me up by my stomach. In a full belly laugh, he flips me on my back.

"This is better," he growls, positioning himself on top of me.

"Finally, we're alone," I purr, nipping at his lower lip.

His elbows are bent on either side of my face as his dark eyes flicker into mine. "I love you."

Nothing else in the world matters except for us. No one has ever looked at me with the love that he does—not even my parents. I was treated as a simple fixture in their lives—a piece of furniture that was a part of the house. When I spoke, they didn't look at me. They looked over me. Jasper makes me feel like something. A *real* person worthy of taking up more than just space in the world.

I swallow hard, feeling his length grow in between us. Slipping my hand between us, I slide under the hem of his pants. "I love you too."

He lets out a groan when I wrap my hand around his cock. He dips to kiss me, deep and passionate. As I stroke him, his tongue darts in and out of my mouth, swirling around to taste every part of me.

"Can I take off your panties?" His gentle request is enough to make my inside throb.

"Yes," I mumble into his wet lips.

Jasper's warm hand glides up the outside of my leg, then around to the inside of my thigh and under my sundress. He slowly pushes up the fabric before hooking a finger under the string of my panties. While he inches it down my legs, my core coats with wetness. *Fuck.* These sensations are still new to me and highly overwhelming.

I begin to tremble.

He stops. With one leg free, I open for him, letting him position himself between them. "Are you alright?"

"Yes, I'm perfectly fine," I say, my voice cracking. "These feelings are still new to me."

"I'll go slow again." He smiles into the sensitive skin on my neck.

Do I want him to go slow? The heat building from within is screaming for relief. My eyes fall closed. "No, don't go slow. Please go faster."

He makes eye contact, pausing for a moment. "Are you sure?"

Swallowing hard, I nod.

Suddenly, he grips my ass, yanking me closer into him. Then he lifts and unzips his shorts. His dick springs loose, making my eyes and mouth water. The sight of him is perfect. Heavily breathing, I reach up to cup his face. Bringing him down on top of me, his lips connect with mine right as he thrusts into me.

"Oh," I whimper, reminded of that brief sting.

With his head buried into my strewn hair, he lets a soft groan. Grabbing my leg, he brings it up to my chest, getting deeper. Force travels up my body, causing me to gasp, but he continues to roll his hips.

"Just like that, Avery." His voice is husky and desperate, making me burn.

I arch my back, enjoying both the dull pain and pleasure of it.

I can't imagine having done this before Jasper. *He is everything to me.*

After a few more deep thrusts, I feel his muscles begin to shake. *Oh fuck, he's going to do it.* Preparing myself for the last few pulses, I feel his hand move in between us, then his finger goes right to my clit. On contact, electricity fires off through my body. He massages me in a circular motion and picks up his pace.

"Oh my god," I grit out, my foot kicking the steering wheel.

"Same time," he replies. It takes me a second to realize what he means, but by that time, a tingling sensation bowls over me. My head falls back, and I suck in a breath just as Jasper slams into me one last time.

His entire body goes limp, forcing him to collapse on top of me. I'm out of breath and buzzing all over. Jasper's head rests on my chest. Our bodies are slick with arousal and sweat. It's fucking amazing.

"I want to do that every goddamn day." I giggle uncontrollably with euphoria.

He chuckles into the skin above my nipple that's now half out of the top of my dress.

"As soon as my house closes, I plan to live only on sex and surfing," he says.

His house closes in August.

I leave for college at the end of August.

And with that, the high of summer love has dissipated.

Chapter Twenty-One

Now

Jasper

The excitement of the Coconut Grove Days never fails to amaze me. Tourists flock in to experience the best of our small beachside town. They can sample food and drinks from the best restaurants, listen to live music, and take home fresh produce. For the kids, there are carnival rides and games. The Chamber of Commerce puts on this event every year. This is will be the new CEO, Chris' first year, and I told him I'd offer my support.

As I walk down the long row of vendors, I mentally take inventory of who is fully set up and who still needs assistance.

"Beth, let me help you with that," I say, coming up behind the older woman, bringing one of the signs to place outside her tent.

"Oh, Jasper, you're the best," she says, letting go so I can bear the weight. "Thank you."

"No worries." I nod in her direction.

"Which one do you think will be the favorite this year?" I dive the metal spokes on the bottom of the sign into the ground. All her flavors of jam are in our local cafés and restaurants.

"Although peach is a community favorite, I think this year blackberry is going to be the big winner." Her eyes sparkle, looking toward me from a hunched-over position.

"Blackberry has always been my favorite."

"I know," she says. "I'll make sure to save you a jar."

I finish adjusting the two signs, then turn to Beth. "Can I help you with anything else?"

"No, I'm good. Thank you."

"Of course," I say, sliding down my sunglasses, expecting the sun to blaze into us now that it's late afternoon.

The vendor rows are filling up fast. I wave at each owner as I pass. Then I spot Easton's booth toward the end of the row.

I head right for my friend. "Hey, man."

"What's up?" he greets me as I approach.

"Just making my rounds. How's set up?" I ask.

He's standing behind the table with two other employees, unpacking paper coffee cups. "We open soon. Shouldn't you change into something more *mayor-ly.*"

I glance down at my board shorts and flip-flops. "Nah."

He laughs. "So, do you think Arizona will show up?"

"Maybe." I shrug, trying not to show how much I want her to. "I invited her."

Suddenly, I get a pat on the shoulder from behind. "Wassup, guys," Bodhi hoots. "I heard your long-lost love is back in town."

I cock a brow at him.

"We need to give Jasper some sympathy. It's been a hard few days for him," Easton spits at my expense, then places a finger in the air. "And she's engaged to someone else."

"You're an asshole," I say, jerking his hand off my shoulder.

Bodhi laughs. "I want to say hi to her. Where's she staying?"

"At the Hannah beach house."

"Damn, that's like two houses down from yours." Bodhi's eyes widen. "Has it been tempting not to sneak over there?"

Annoyed with my friends, I roll my eyes. "No. It's fine. Many years have passed. It's all good."

Bodhi asks the barista standing next to Easton for a latte, then turns back to me. "So, what's she here for?"

Easton and I glance at each other. He smirks and then turns away, implying that I need to tell Bodhi why Avery was suddenly back in town. "She's come back to ask for a divorce."

Bodhi's mouth drops. Speechless, he scratches his chin, like he realized that jokes aside, this was something very real and very legal. "Oh fuck."

Rubbing my lips together, I nod in the shared gravity of the situation. "Yeah."

"I thought you took care of that years ago?" he asks.

"He didn't." Easton tosses over her shoulder.

"Well, no shit ..." Bodhi pauses mid-sentence, his focus captured by something in the distance. "Speak of the devil."

My head whips around to see Avery walking up the narrow sidewalk next to City Hall—the same place we were married eight years ago this summer. *Fuck me.* Her brown hair is loose, and she's wearing a tight black summer dress that makes my dick jump.

"There she is," I mumble to myself.

"Are you going to stand here or say hi to her?" Easton pokes with amusement at my expense.

But I ignore him, keeping my eyes trained on her. "I'll be right back."

"I want to say hi, bring her to us!" Bodhi calls out.

I jog across a small patch of grass near the center of the town square, quickly eating the distance between us. "Hi."

"Hi, Jasper." She smiles, leaving about ten feet between us.

I bite back a grin. "You came."

"I did."

Then, as if fate was reminding me of what reality is for us, my eyes darted down to the massive diamond on her finger. *She put it back on.* Avery catches me staring and swings her arms around back, clasping them together.

I blink a few times before rising to meet hers. "I'm glad. You'll have fun."

"I'm sure." She blushes. Falling into step with me, we walk toward the booths.

"Do you want anything to eat or drink?" I ask, shoving my hands in my front pockets. "We have just about anything you could want here tonight."

"Yeah, I'd love to try it all." Her energy is lighter today.

"I was just about to check on the beer garden. Do you want to come?"

She smiles. "Yeah, but I don't want to take you away from your mayor duties."

"The Chamber pretty much runs this whole thing. I'm here to greet people, mingle, and then make a quick speech later."

"Sounds like a pretty relaxed night for you," she says. "Do you still have a booth here for your dad's shop?"

I warm at her memory of it.

"We don't. My dad stopped a few years after you left. He really didn't need to do it anymore. Instead, he gave the employees the night off to enjoy the event with their families," I tell her.

Avery's lips twist and her eyes lower pensively. "Your dad was a good guy."

I sigh. "He was."

There's a brief silence between us before we approach Easton's booth.

"Arizona!" Bodhi yells, then grabs her by the waist and swings her around.

"A little overkill, don't you think?" I quip. Hearing her laugh around my friends is surreal—like no time has passed. *What a mind fuck this is.*

"I hear Jasper won't give you a divorce?" Bodhi blurts out, lacking the filter he should have been born with.

Avery straightens her dress when she's set back on the grass. "He won't."

"We'll talk to him," Easton adds. "Nice seeing you again."

She leans over the table and wraps one arm around him for a half hug. "Breakfast was so good. I had no idea you could cook like that."

"I can't take all the credit," he plays. "We do have a phenomenal chef."

A light wind wears through her hair, and the scent of her coconut shampoo hits my nostrils—*what I would give to bury my face in it.*

"I need to check on Lyle and Janet at the beer garden. Avery and I are going to head over there," I say, resting a hand on her lower back out of habit, but then immediately jerk it away.

"Cool. See you in a bit," Easton says, while Bodhi waves with a mouth full of a strawberry scone from Easton's café.

Avery and I walk side by side through the grass. "Still drink old-fashioneds?"

"I do." She bites her lips, dipping her head down bashfully. "I shouldn't have been drinking them back then, you know?"

Rubbing my chin, I fondly remember the first time Avery had an old-fashioned. She didn't drink wine coolers or fruity drinks with the other girls. She also refused to drink beer like the guys. "None of us should have, but we did."

She laughs. It's still the best sound, and the moment those sweet giggles hit the air, my brain is already figuring out how I could do it again.

"Mayor Collins," Lyle greets me as Avery and I enter the small space sectioned off by artificial bushes.

"Lyle, you can call me Jasper," I correct, shaking his hand.

"I know, I know. But we're new here, and Janet and I want to make a good impression," he politely explains.

"I understand." I turn to the beautiful brunette at my side. "This is my friend, Avery. She's visiting from Arizona."

Lyle's wife, Janet, pops up from one of the tree stump stools and rushes over. "You're beautiful, honey. It's so nice to meet you."

"Great to meet you both." Avery smiles warmly.

"So, you're *friends* with our beloved young mayor?" Her voice is a tad higher this time.

Avery chews on the corner of her cheek. "I am."

Sensing the uncomfortable tension between the four of us, more specifically between my long-lost wife, I say the first thing that comes to mind. "Anyone want a drink?"

Lyle's hand comes out in front of us. "Let me get it. Avery, what can I grab for you?"

"It's a beer garden, but Tommy is back in the bar, and he can make you anything you want." Janet blows a corkscrew piece of hair away from her face before twisting it behind her.

Avery's nose scrunches. "Can he make an old-fashioned?"

Lyle's pupils dilate. "Yes, ma'am. I love a good whiskey drinker."

Janet turns to me. "Anything for you?"

I shake my head. "No, thank you. Maybe later."

"No old-fashioned?"

My hand finds her lower back once again, but this time, I don't pull it away. "I'm not comfortable drinking at events I'm supposed to be representing the town. I may have a glass of wine or two at some, but I typically try to refrain from it."

"I respect that."

A minute later, Lyle returns with Avery's old-fashioned. We say a quick goodbye, then head over to check out the stage again before the event officially starts.

She holds the cup to her lips and takes a drink. "Feels so good."

"What does?"

"The warmth, sliding down the back of my throat." She closes her eyes, savoring the taste. *Fuck. I'm a dirty bastard.* I'd like to believe I have control over where my mind goes next, but I don't.

"I have something warm and smooth for your throat," I say. I know Avery, and even years later, I'm sure it will make her blush.

"Oh my god, Jasper!" she bellows, playfully hitting my shoulder. I laugh but make a mental note of how red her cheeks turned.

"You opened yourself up for that one," I retort.

"I guess I did."

Avery joins me as I check in with the remaining portions of the event. I spend the next hour leading her through every vendor to try the foods and beverages. She insisted on sampling everything. The little giggles she lets out when she tries something she likes and the adorable wrinkle of her nose, squeezes my chest. Avery is still my same girl in so many ways, but also very different. All the qualities about her that I loved so much became brighter. Watching her move, I'm completely captivated.

About ten minutes before opening, I drop her off at Easton's booth and then make my way over to the entrance, where the Chamber of Commerce board members gather to greet people as they arrive. I hang around for a short time before I get anxious to see Avery again. But she's not going anywhere, especially because I left her with Easton and he's probably talking her ear off.

"Hi, Jasper."

I'm saying hello to one of the staff members' sons when I'm startled to hear Melanie's voice. Before standing, I crane my neck behind me to see her standing there. I've been so caught up in Avery the last couple of days, I forgot that Melanie would be here tonight. She and I are just a casual thing, I'm sure it won't be awkward. *Why would it?* Avery is engaged, although she has yet to tell me formally.

I extend my arm for a friendly side hug. "Hi, Melanie. How are you?"

A puzzled look on her face tells me she can pick up that I'm more withdrawn than usual. She told me once she thought I'd be like my dad, growing old alone and never settling down with a woman. The truth is, there was ever only one I wanted to be with, but at the time, she wasn't in my life anymore.

But Avery is here now.

"I'm good." She searches my eyes. "Will I see you tonight?"

Nervously, I lick my bottom lip, then scan the people around us, thinking about how to answer her question. "I don't think tonight."

She shrugs it off, acting unbothered. "It's cool. See you around."

I spend an unclear amount of time mingling with families, members of the town, and tourists before I finally get back to Avery.

"Long time no see, Mayor Collins." She hiccups.

"How many of those have you had?" I playfully gesture toward her empty cup.

Easton laughs.

Her eyebrows snap together, bringing a finger up to her chin. "Um, I think two."

"How about two and a half," Easton corrects.

I smile, leaning in close to her. "Still a lightweight, I see."

Her eyes are glazed over, but she's not drunk—maybe slightly buzzed.

Bodhi appears by our side. "So, Jasper, are you going to give

Arizona a divorce or what?"

Avery looks over at me, running her tongue along her teeth. She's searching for a smart-ass comment but struggles to think of one.

"Maybe," I say, grabbing Bodhi's beer and taking a swig while keeping my eyes locked on my wife.

Avery's light pink lips purse together in a pout, and all I can think of is shoving my dick between them.

Chapter Twenty-Two

Now

Avery

Lights and sounds from the event are now behind us. Although I'm barely tipsy, Jasper insists on driving me home. I might have had more than I thought because I agree. We are silent on the car ride back to my rented beach house.

"Did you have fun tonight?" he asks, opening the passenger door.

Sliding out, I smile at him. "I did."

He gives me a quick, satisfied nod and then closes the door. The air is thick with uncomfortable tension as we ascend the steps to the back door. This goodbye feels an awful lot like a date. I have no idea how to act, and from his constant fidgeting, neither does he.

"I'm glad you came," he says. "It was nice having you there."

His words cause my chest to tighten. "I forgot how much I missed it here."

"I bet. How long are you in town for?" he asks, clearly forgetting that I'm here to get a divorce from him. But I have nothing left to fight with him about. I'm trying to change my approach. The thing is, it's been easier than I anticipated it would be. I want to be kind to him. I want to talk to him—*I want to touch him.*

My eyes flutter at the thought. "As long as I need to be."

"Work won't miss you?" He plays, stepping closer.

"I took leave," I whisper as my breathing picks up.

Jasper's eyes blaze into mine. Every memory, every emotion comes flooding back with a force I can barely control. His comfort makes everything natural, as if no time had passed.

"I guess you're in no rush to get your divorce then." His warm breath floats across my lips. I am startled by a sharp buzz from my phone. It breaks our moment. Jasper pulls back just as I dip my head to slide my phone from the pocket of my dress. *It's Dave.* I need to answer his call, but I want to be reminded of what Jasper's lips feel like on mine. "I'll let you get that."

Turning back to Jasper, I shut my eyes and answer the phone.

"Hey." Dave's voice on the other end is cheery.

"Hi, I'm just getting home. Can I call you in a bit?"

"Sure, of course. I didn't hear from you this morning. I wanted to check in." There's now a slight annoyance in his voice. *We just talked about him giving me some space to handle this yesterday.*

"I know, sorry. I've been trying to take things out here as quickly as possible like I told you I would," I whisper, stepping off to the side. From the corner of my eye, I see Jasper rub the back of his neck and stare at the clear night sky. This entire interaction shouldn't be awkward, but it is.

"I didn't know that meant you couldn't check in with your

fiancé," he snaps.

My eyes lock on Jasper's back as he slowly walks away. Panicking, I rush Dave off the phone. "Yeah, I'll call you tomorrow."

"Jasper!" I yell. He doesn't turn around or respond to me even though he's only a few yards away. Moving into a jog, I quickly catch up and place my hand on his shoulder. "Hey, sorry about that."

He whips his body around to face me fully, with frustration growing by the second. "Sorry for what? That you had to answer a call from your fiancé?"

I run a hand through my hair, speechless. "I guess."

His hands come out in front of us. "No need to be."

"Thank you for driving me home." I'm unsure of what to say. He's unsettled, and so am I.

Jasper flashes me a weak smile, then places his hand on my lower back, ushering me toward the steps to the back door. Anxious, I take them two at a time with him close on my heels.

"Safely at your door," he states, leaning in to press a gentle kiss on my forehead. On instinct, I lift my head, angling my lips toward his. My eyes fall closed, waiting for the kiss I desperately crave.

His jaw tenses. "Good night, Avery."

I can't let this go. My emotions are raging, and my thoughts are a mess. Heat builds in my core. Instinctively, I move my face toward his, letting my lips float past his.

Jasper pinches my cheeks. I watch his eyes darken. Then his mouth crashes into mine. My knees buckle, almost leveling me with the ground.

I black out. His lips move with mine. Losing my balance, I fall forward, only for my body to come into contact with his hard chest. My lips start to tingle, and my world spins, then abruptly, it stops.

Jasper pulls back. His features are firm and ice-cold. "Good night, Avery," he says, giving me his back as he walks back to his car.

I feel it crawl up my throat—*word vomit*. I'm unsure if it's the liquor fueling my bravery or just plain desperation, but the following words come out without hesitation.

"Why did you let me go?" I burst out louder than necessary.

Jasper squares his shoulders, pauses, and then slowly turns to face me. More than a few feet in front of me and underneath the dim porch light, I can still make out the sharpness of his features. "What?"

I swallow a cotton ball lodged in my throat while my hands shake, but I'm determined to find answers. I came all the way here for them and intend to do whatever I can to see closure. "Why did you let me go?"

He scoffs and starts walking back toward the front door. "Why did *I* let you go?" he repeats my words condescendingly.

I firmly place my hands on my hips, trying to show conviction in my question, but my insides are raw from the hurt I've endured. "Yes."

"Why did *you* leave?" he counters.

"You know why I left."

"Do I?"

Tears prick the back of my eyes—a sting of regret for opening this box. "Answer the question."

"You answer it, Arizona," he challenges, stepping onto the first stair. I haven't been called that name in years. It rips through me like a knife.

"I couldn't find you," I shout, a tear rolling down my cheek. "I didn't know what to do."

"And you think I did?" He takes another step.

There are two more stairs until his body is flush with mine on the tiny square porch. "I don't know."

Jasper's nostrils flare. "I didn't either. I was just a kid."

"So was I!" I yell, pointing at my chest. "Why did you let me go, Jasper? Answer the fucking question!"

His expression surprisingly softens. "I knew you wanted more."

Gutted once again, I let the tears overflow and slide down my cheeks. "I wanted *you*."

"I wanted you too," he replies, climbing the remaining steps. "You were my everything."

My stomach spasms as I try to catch my breath. His words unearth years of heartache and regret. "It ripped me apart," I admit.

Jasper's hand reaches the side of my face. "Do you think it was easy for me? It fucking killed me when you left."

The warmth of his skin on mine makes my eyelids fall closed. "But you let me go."

He lowers himself, and suddenly, I feel his nose nuzzling mine. My eyes remain shut.

"I've waited eight years for you to come back to me. No one has even come close to you. You know how hard that was?" His breath dances across my lips. I fight my urge not to dip my head and kiss him.

"How hard it was for you? I haven't been able to love anyone else like I've loved you. You stole my fucking heart, stomped on it, and refused to give it back."

Jasper's lips gently caress mine. Without applying pressure for a kiss, he just lets them glide across the seam. "And I'm not going to."

My fingers hook into the front pocket of his shorts. "You have to. I'm marrying someone else."

"Not yet." The ignition in his voice jerks me back to reality.

My eyes bounce between his briefly before Jasper's mouth crashes into mine. His kiss is powerful. Years of pent-up frustration and hurt all manifested into the behavior we're both experiencing now.

Pushed up against the side of the house, I submit to him like I've always done. Jasper's hand feverishly slides along the outside of my leg and underneath my dress.

"Oh god," I groan, savoring every second of his hands on me.

Desperately trying to get inside of me, Jasper's tongue darts in and out of my mouth, going deeper each time. His palm cups my ass, gripping it tightly and urging me against him.

His hard length prods at my core, and another short groan escapes.

"You like that, don't you, Arizona?" he growls. "You fucking missed me."

I hook my arms around his neck to brace myself from weak knees. "Take me inside."

"You got it," he replies with a hurried response.

Suddenly, the hard surface behind me is gone, and I'm

pushed through the door.

In one swift move, I'm hoisted up as Jasper grips my ass. My legs wrap around his waist.

"Where's the bedroom?" he whispers into my lips without breaking contact.

My fingers comb through his longer on top, dark hair. It's exactly how I remember it. "Down the hall. The first door on the left."

When we get to my bedroom, he slows and lowers me onto the thick comforter. Crawling over me, he follows the movements of my body as I hurry to the top of the bed. My heart is racing. My mind is blank. I can't think outside of this moment.

Jasper traces a line of wet kisses along my jaw. "You smell exactly how I remember."

"You do too," I purr, closing my eyes.

His lips continue down my neck before stopping at my collarbone, letting his tongue linger over the flicker of my pulse. He uses a cooked finger to hook underneath the strap of my dress and gently inches it down my shoulder. My insides vibrate, craving to have him again. It's been almost eight years since we've been together, but I still remember how he touched my body. No one has ever been able to touch me like that since.

One of his legs slides under my knee, spreading my legs further. I repeat the motion with the opposite side. Jasper's hand glides up the outside of my leg, causing my skin to break out in goose bumps. I reach down between us and pull up my dress. His eyes flash to mine while a subtle smirk forms.

With the slight quirk of his upper lip, my panties are soaked. My pussy is throbbing, and my eyes are starting to glaze over. He lifts off of me, but only for a second, to unzip his shorts. I catch sight of his red pulsating cock spring out of his pants, and now I'm fucking feral.

"I need you," I beg and paw at his pants in a desperate attempt to move quicker than we already are.

"Always so needy," he growls. With one fluid motion, he pushes my panties aside, then grips himself and thrusts inside.

"Oh god," I grit out instantly, filled by him—my eyes leak.

Jasper tucks his head into the crook of my neck, burying his nose in my hair. I feel him suck in before slipping into a smooth rhythm with rolling his hips.

Heaving and immobile, my limbs are locked in place. The intensity rumbles through my body. Jasper links an arm under a knee, pushing my leg into my chest to get a deeper angle.

"Fuck, you feel so good," he groans into the sensitive skin on my shoulder.

Jasper continues to thrust a few more times before I feel his orgasm start to build. His body begins to stiffen while his movements become more erratic.

"I'm almost there," I barely squeak out.

"Oh fuck," he grunts.

More powerful than the thousands before it, I release. My climax courses through my veins like a familiar drug. That old comforting sting of when it hits you and your back to achieving the air you continue to crave—a full gulp of oxygen. The shot of utter euphoria makes me black out, only to flutter my eyes to see black spots covering the room.

Panting, Jasper lifts off of me. He flips onto his back, then turns toward me with bloodshot eyes and a damp forehead. I'm jumpy and energized. Not knowing how to wrangle the different sensations, I burst into an uncontrollable giggle.

"Let's do it again," I say, meeting his flaring eyes.

"I need a little more time." Jasper lets out a full belly laugh. "How about some food?"

"I'd love some food." I beam with excitement.

"Wonderful." Jasper pops up. Standing next to the bed, he tucks himself back inside his pants, and all I can think of is that I need it more. "Do you have food here?"

Shimmying my dress down, I shake my head.

"Of course you don't," he playfully quips.

I lower my eyes. "That's not funny."

Laughing, he leans over the bed, resting his palm on the mattress. "I'll make you something."

Since when does Jasper cook? This is nice. I bat my eyelashes at him. "Breakfast."

He twirls a loose hair in his finger, then tucks it behind my ear. "Eleven at night, seems like a logical thing to eat."

Grinning through a blush, I can't hide, even in the dimly lit room. "And a fruit bowl with pineapple."

"You go it." His eyes fall to my lips.

I rise to kiss him with a soft, lingering kiss. I breathe him in before he pulls back. "I'll be back in less than ten minutes."

"Where are you going?"

He pauses at the door. "My house. I have a fully stocked kitchen."

I would love to see Jasper's house. To be in his space, smell, and be engulfed by him sounds like heaven. "Can I go with you?"

Chapter Twenty-Three

Now

Avery

I jump off the bed and slide on my sandals, then grab the only light jacket that I brought with me. He follows close behind me as we head down the hallway. Taking an unexpected right, he quickly locks my front door from the inside.

With my hand on the knob of the back door, I give him a quick side-eye, wondering why he needed to make sure it was locked.

"You can never be too careful," he says with a grin.

"Is your town not safe, Mr. Mayor?" I play.

"Maybe I want to make sure you never leave again."

I roll my eyes with exaggeration. Jasper is close behind when I walk out the door onto the sand. The cool night breeze whips past me, carrying a potent feeling of nostalgia.

"Cold?" he asks, wrapping an arm around me before I can respond.

I tuck my head into his chest, smiling to myself. Fuck, it feels good to be in his arms. *Mentally, I never left.*

We walk along the beach past only two homes before we arrive at his. Following Jasper up the steps of the patio and through double blue doors, I glance over my shoulder at the reflection of the total white moon over the black ocean water.

Endless. *Infinity.*

"Come on in." He smiles, stepping aside to let me enter.

At first, the house looked similar in layout to most of the beach houses along this side of the shore, but then I caught sight of an industrial-style spiral staircase in the corner by the front door. While Jasper walks around, turning on a few lights, I take in his home. He has dark furniture, a little nicer than what you'd usually see this close to the water. It looks like him.

"Three stories?" I ask, pointing at the stairs.

He nods, removing two pots from underneath the counter. "The living space is on the first floor, the bedrooms and bathrooms are on the second, and then the third floor is an open loft."

"All that space for just you?" I say, walking over to the countertop bar.

He arches a brow in my direction. "With all that money your parents left you, I'd bet you have a large penthouse in the city."

Embarrassed by being called out, my cheeks burn. "Yeah. I do."

"I knew it." He continues grabbing ingredients from the fridge and pantry. "And you're probably working and barely spending any of it, right?"

Bashfully, I rub my lips together, fighting a smile. "You don't know me."

"I think I do." He flirts, making my stomach flutter.

Jasper and I spend the next hour cooking and talking. A delicate dance of avoiding bringing up any topic that might kick up our past, we both seem to settle in living in a dreamland.

It's nearly midnight, and now I'm sitting across the table from Jasper, eating pancakes and scrambled eggs. Twelve hours ago, I could have never predicted we'd end up here. We've exchanged multiple gazes that carry more weight than just *thanks for breakfast.* The temptation to have him one more time has exponentially grown.

I rise from the table, feeling overheated. "Do you want me to take that into the kitchen?"

"Thanks," he says, handing me his plate.

I take it from him and make a beeline for the other room. *I need to get out of here.* Being in his house clouds my mind. I set both plates into the sink, then turn on the water. I let it run briefly, planning to grab the rest of the dishes from the counter, but I feel the warmth of Jasper's hands clutching my waist. His front is flush with my back.

God, he feels good.

I let my head fall back, resting it on his shoulder. Within no time, his soft lips find my neck. It's game over for me when he makes contact with my skin. I twist to face him, gripping the counter's edge behind me. Jasper's deep brown eyes blaze with heat. His hands thread through my hair, making my scalp tingle. My eyes close, enjoying the feel of him crowding my space.

Jasper lowers his head, bringing his mouth within an inch of mine. "Thanks for having breakfast with me," he mutters. "And for what we did before breakfast."

My body melts under his touch. "Of course."

"But, Arizona?" he says, gliding his tongue along my bottom lip. Unconsciously, mine darts out and licks the flat part of his. A groan rumbles in the back of his throat. "But I'm not done."

My stomach drops. "You're not?"

"Turn around."

I nip at his lip. "What, no sweet, gentle sex?"

"I'm not a kid anymore, and neither are you. So, bend. The. Fuck. Over," he demands, pausing between each word.

I gasp, and my panties almost drop themselves. Fuck. *How could he have gotten sexier with age?* Before I realize what's happening, Jasper is flipping me around. The cold granite meets my bare skin with a vengeance. I hear him lower to his knees behind me.

Jasper's hands slide up my legs and under my dress. His fingers hook my panties and yank them down while I shimmy my hips until they pile at our feet. The sound of him unlatching his belt buckle ricochets off the vaulted ceilings, but I'm still unprepared for the sheer force of him railing into me.

"Fuck, Jasper." I lunge forward with my palms slapping the counter as I brace myself.

Craning my head up and back, I capture Jasper's mouth. His kiss is hungry and desperate and raw. Our tongues tangle in the agony of making up for lost time. He claws at my hips, moving them back and forth while my insides clench around him. Reaching up behind his head, I pull him deeper. Panting, his quick, short breaths fill my throat. I breathe him in, feral enough to crawl inside him forever, but allowing him to be inside me instead. Slapping flesh fills the room and does nothing more but enhance my need.

Suddenly, Jasper reaches down to massage the bundle of nerves between my legs. The shock on my sensitive area causes my head to drop, but he catches it with his other hand, forcing me to remain connected to his lips. Sharing the same breath, we move together, his touch so similar to before, but with a new commanding way to it.

"God, I missed your touch," I moan.

Panting, he continues to thrust in and out of me a few more times. The sound of pleasure continues to fill this sleepy beach house. *Nothing else matters. Nothing else exists.*

Without warning, Jasper's body stiffens behind me. His movements become frantic. Scared that my pleasure will end with him pulling out, a cloud of lust masks my judgment. I arch my back, forcing him to stay.

A deep, heavy groan thunders through his chest and mine. Tingles weave through my body from the top of my head to the bottom of my feet. I buck into him harder as he spills everything into me. *Fuck.*

"Nothing will ever compare to this." His voice is husky and still laced with need. "I missed you so much."

I lift myself off of him and turn around. "Upstairs?"

His pupils dilate as a sly smile transforms his face. "Fuck, yes."

Who needs sleep anyway?

Chapter Twenty-Four

THEN

Avery

Helen and I spent the entire morning in the city buying furniture and accessories for my dorm room. The day I'd been looking forward to for years was overshadowed by the heavy emotions of knowing in just a few weeks, I'd no longer see Jasper every day.

We haven't spoken about how we will move forward or if we'll continue seeing each other. I can't imagine we wouldn't be, but every time I bring it up, he pushes it aside and says, *we'll figure it out.*

"I'm so excited for you." Helen beams, taking the last few bags of new bedsheets and towels into the house. "Your dorm room is going to be so cute."

I smile. Helen and I have become close this summer. She's like a mom and big sister wrapped into one. "Thank you for coming with me."

Out of breath, she sets the rest of my stuff on the bed in the guest bedroom. "Oh, honey, of course. I love it."

"You don't mind keeping all this furniture and things in here until I move?" I glance around the once-clean space, now littered with household items, boxes, and storage containers.

"Don't be silly." She rubs my arm comfortingly. "I'm so grateful I get to be here with you. It brings me so much joy."

We share a sweet moment in silence before she seemingly wipes a tear that I was unaware had fallen.

"You have been such a gift to me," I tell her, wrapping an arm around her shoulders.

"Oh, Avery." She sniffs. "It's you who's brought light into my life."

I smile with a heart full of love for her.

She wipes her nose again, then palms down on her yellow sundress, flattening the fabric. "What do you want to do for dinner?"

Being consumed by another human can be draining. I haven't seen Jasper all day, and my heart aches to be with him.

I should spend the evening with Helen. I've appreciated everything she's done for me and what she continues to do for me. *Maybe Jasper can come over after dinner?*

"Whatever you want. How about takeout?" I suggest heading across the hall into the bathroom.

"Fabulous." Her voice is distant as she passes my bedroom door toward the kitchen. "And then we can see if there's a fun rom-com to stream."

"That sounds great," I reply, but my thoughts halt. A basket of yellow tampons underneath my bathroom cupboard catches my eye. *Shouldn't my period have been here by now?*

I grab my phone and swipe up to the calendar. Counting back

to the first day of my last period, I go back five and a half weeks. That means I'm almost two weeks late. My period is always on time because I'm on the birth control pill.

Wait. My heart skips a beat, forcing a breath.

I never refilled my prescription!

Oh my god. Oh my god! It's fine. My body is probably off its normal cycle because I'm not on the pill. *Everything is fine.* It will come. *But what if it doesn't?* Jasper and I have had a lot of sex.

Gripping the edge of the counter with clammy palms, my mind races.

"Should I pick up Joe's?" Helen's voice startles me from the other room.

I push off the countertop, pace a few times, and then rest my back against the cold bathroom wall. I squeeze my eyes shut. "That sounds great!"

"Okay, be right back!" she shouts. The sound of clinking keys tells me a moment alone is close. "The usual?"

"Yeah, two chicken tacos and a salad," I rush out. My lungs gulp in deep breaths.

"You got it," she says.

A simple latch of the door is all I need to release. My knees go weak, and I sink to the floor. *This can't be happening.* Burying my face in my hands, I take a few heavy breaths to calm down. *It doesn't help.* I rise to my feet, turn on the sink, and splash cold water on my face. My head hangs low while I attempt to rein in my spiraling anxiety. *This happens to girls all the time. Periods fluctuate. It will be here, it's just a little late.*

If that were true, why do I not feel like it is? My boobs aren't sore, and I don't have those annoying dull cramps I get a few days before.

Fuck. I need a pregnancy test. *Maybe Helen has one?* She and Duke always sleep together, and she's not nearly old enough for menopause.

I yank open the bathroom door and hurry down the hallway to her bedroom. With my lungs constricted, I head for her bathroom and straight to the cabinet under the sink. It makes sense why it would be here. I have to push through containers of cotton balls and Q-tips before I find a pink and white box toward the back.

Blowing a sigh of relief, I snatch the box and leave the room. When I return to my bathroom, I notice a text from Jasper. I set the box down and swipe my phone off the counter.

Jasper: Hey, Arizona. I missed you today. What are you up to?

Well, Jasper, I'm taking a pregnancy test.

Me: Missed you too. I'm waiting for Helen to bring back tacos for dinner.

Jasper: How was your day?

It was good until about ten minutes ago.

Me: It was good. We picked up a lot of things for my dorm while we were in the city.

Jasper: That's great.

Me: How was yours?

Jasper: Busy. We have to do inventory at the shop. Do you mind if I still come to see you even if it's late?

My stomach flutters as I tap out a response.

Me: Of course. I can't wait to see you!

Then I toss my phone through the bathroom door. It lands on my bed. I need to take this test before Helen gets home.

With shaky hands, I quickly skim the directions. *It seems straightforward.* I rip open the rapper, pinch the handle with two fingers, and lift my dress with the other. Placing it between my legs, I let a steady stream flow on the testing strip. I take care to leave the strip in place until I empty my entire bladder. *I'd rather be sure.*

When I'm done, I put the cap back on and set the test on a piece of toilet paper on the counter.

Okay, ten minutes. No worries.

I fix my dress and pace my room for what seems like a lifetime. I forgot to set the timer, but I'll know soon.

Finally, after the longest ten minutes of my life, I walk back into the bathroom, holding what's left of my breath, and glance down at the test.

Pregnant.

Oh my fucking god.

There's no way.

It's got to be a false positive.

Panic whips at my back, causing a rush of lightheadedness. *This can't be real!*

Just then, I hear the front door open and close. Helen is back, and suddenly, I'm comforted by her presence. I swing open the door to the bathroom, tears rolling down my face. I have to tell her.

Helen handled the news better than I thought she would. Through tears and minor hysterics, she made me realize this doesn't have to stop my life and that she'd be here with me every step of the way. She also reminded me that I have options. It was a brief conversation, but not something I'd like to consider.

Now I lie in bed, a million thoughts bouncing around my head while even more emotions wreck me. Jasper texted me about half an hour ago, telling me they'd just finished. I'm expecting him to arrive at any moment.

Helen said I should tell him before she said anything to Duke and suggested that the four of us sit down together tomorrow and discuss what Jasper and I plan to do and how they can help us.

A bang at my window gives me a quick scare. I sit straight up to see Jasper hopping down to the floor.

"You know we have a door?" I say. His hair is windblown, and he has shorts and a T-shirt on. Only Jasper can make dressing like a beach bum sexy. *Maybe it's not such a surprise he got me pregnant.* I shake my head, pushing away the thought of doing the same thing that got us in this predicament in the first place.

"I know." He glides his hands along my hips. "But crawling through your window is more fun."

I bring both arms around the back of his neck and lock eyes with his. "I need to talk to you."

He frowns. "About what?"

I lightly kiss his lips, then pull away and gesture toward my bed. "Can you sit down?"

"Okay," he says with a drawl, worried about what I will say.

I sit next to him, shoving my hands between my legs. "Um." I pause, sucking in a weighted breath.

"What's wrong?" He extends an arm behind me and leans in close.

I refocus my eyes away from his, capturing the small pineapple lamp on the dresser. "I don't know how to tell you this," I begin. *Silence.* "Jasper ..."

"You're scaring the shit out of me." He tries to force eye contact, but I keep looking away. "What's wrong, Avery?"

"I'm pregnant," I blurt out, throwing my hands over my face. *Fuck, that was hard to say.*

Jasper removes his arm from behind me and sits up straighter.

Unsure of what to say, I remain quiet, letting him recover from the bomb I dropped.

Without a word, he bends forward, resting his chin in his hands. "How do you know?"

"I took a test," I whisper.

He nervously runs his fingers through his tossed hair. "When?"

"A few hours ago."

"Only one?"

I shake my head. "Helen had me take three altogether."

Jasper audibly sighs and falls onto his back on my bed. "How far along do you think you are?"

Still fearful of a change in his reaction, my limbs remain locked. "I'm not sure, but I think only five and a half weeks."

"Oh fuck," he grunts.

The panic I hear in his voice causes my eyes to fill. "I'm so sorry."

He abruptly sits up. Before I realize it, he wrapped his arms around me.. "Why are you sorry?"

"Because I told you I was on the pill." I sniff, feeling the weight of my lapse in judgment.

"Look at me," he gently demands, cupping my face. My teary eyes find his. "I love you, Avery. *We* made this choice, and now it's a choice we have to live with."

"I forgot that I hadn't refilled my prescription. I'd never had to worry about getting pregnant before, so it wasn't something I thought about all the time."

"I know—" he begins, but I interject.

"We have options—" Jasper vehemently shakes his head, interrupting me.

"No. I would never want you to do that."

A surprising sense of relief washes over me. *Do I want this baby? But how can we care for a baby together if I'm in Arizona? How am I going to go to college?*

Tears leak from my eyes. "How are we going to do this? We're so young."

Jasper presses a sweet kiss on my forehead and then on my lips. "My life is here in Coconut Grove. I just bought a house. I'm running a very successful business with my dad," he explains, tipping his head up to meet my eyes. Boring into them, I feel his love and security. "You have a substantial inheritance from your parents, and we have my dad and your aunt Helen," he continues. "It's going to be alright."

I hear his words, but my thoughts keep circling back to independence and going to college. It's important to me to go to school and make something of myself outside what my parents have done. I'm not sure if it was being raised all alone that has made me the way I am or the fact that they've always made me feel like a burden. I never want to feel like that again if it takes me the rest of my life to prove I'm enough.

"But what about college?" My voice comes out weak and unrecognizable to my own ears.

Jasper smiles, brushing away the sticky hair from my face. He's beaming with palpable love. "You can go whenever you want. We have great schools here."

Rubbing my tear-soaked lips together, I imagine a future with Jasper and a baby. I love him deeply. I could give my baby a chance at a life with loving parents—one I never had. "Okay."

"Come here," he commands, nudging me down beside him. I rest my face on his chest. His heartbeat echoes in my ears—a sound I can't imagine living without. "We're going to do this together."

"I'm so scared," I mumble.

"I am too," he says. "This is definitely not what I ever thought would happen to me."

"Me either." I rub my nose into the fabric of his shirt. *He smells like home.*

Jasper lifts his other arm and massages his temple. "Fuck."

"I'm so sorry," I mutter with guilt. I can't shake the feeling like this is my fault.

"Avery, this is not your fault," he says firmly. "We both had choices and played our part in this." He sighs once again. "I love you so much."

"I love you too."

Since I was a little girl, I believed I'd forever be alone. I'd accepted that and grew to trust and embrace it fully. But could a life with two others be that bad? *Could I even do it? I'm not sure I have it in me.*

Chapter Twenty-Five

THEN

Jasper

My dad turns off the highway onto a dirt road. I instantly recognize it but ask him anyway. "Where are we going?"

When Avery and I woke up this morning, my dad and Helen had breakfast already on the table. The four of us spoke about our plans now that Avery is pregnant. This is not something my dad wished for me at only nineteen years old, but he was extremely supportive. He and Helen offered us whatever we needed, as I assumed they would.

My dad shifts in his seat, switching hands on the steering wheel. "I figured we could go to the beach house."

They both recognized that Avery and I aren't the typical young couple who accidentally fell pregnant. We're in love. We both have stable futures, and just like I reassured Avery last night, we won't struggle the same way other people might.

"My beach house?"

"Yeah." He nods.

"Awesome." I smile, peering out the window toward the

coast. “I have so many renovation ideas I’d love to talk to you about,” I rush out, excited about the possibility of Avery living here with me. “I haven’t mentioned any of them to Avery yet. I probably should get her approval first.”

The car slows to a stop in front of the weathered beach house. Anyone else might see a pile of wood, worn down from the years of abuse from the wind and salt, but I see so much potential. I see memories to be made and my future.

My dad turns to me. The wrinkles around his eyes look more pronounced this morning. “Let’s go in.”

“Okay.” I follow him around to the driver’s side.

We both ascend the few steps onto the rotted wood porch. He opens the door to the empty living space. My camping equipment, blankets, and bed have been folded in the corner of the room since I stayed here.

“I love this place,” he murmurs as we walk in.

“I know, me too,” I agree, closing the door behind us. “I’m so excited to get started.”

He walks around, looking at the old house. “Flooring is still in great condition.”

I nod. “Yeah. The electrical system is still in good condition as well. Plumbing came up in the inspection, so I know that will be something we’ll have to look into.”

“Oh yeah, I remember seeing that on the inspection report,” he says. His answer is dismissive, as if his thoughts are elsewhere.

I circle the room with my hands in my pockets, still unsure why my dad wanted to bring me out here this morning. “Are you alright?”

“Of course.” He runs his fingertips along the dusty counter.

"You're acting a little strange," I say. "Is it everything going on with Avery?"

"Well, yes and no." He sighs. "How are *you* feeling?"

I shrug my shoulders. "I'm nervous and a little scared, obviously, but like I said at breakfast and I can do this."

"Okay, I guess I just wanted to speak with you away from Helen and Avery because I'm worried you really don't understand the gravity of what's about to happen."

I rub the back of my neck, slightly annoyed but also with a level of understanding for where my dad is coming from. "I get it, Dad, trust me."

"Sit down." He gestures to the old wicker chairs by the wall.

I blow out an audible breath, not purposely trying to have him hear me but also not caring if he does. "Sure."

He follows me over, taking the chair to my side. "When your mother and I had you, we were already married, had been together for years, and were much older."

"I understand that," I say. "It's not like we planned this."

My dad shakes his head. "You didn't, which makes this situation trickier," he says. "Being a father is one thing, but being a partner is very different. Avery will need you more than you realize for the next eight months." He pauses. "Let alone for the next eighteen years."

His words carry weight, and even though I feel the impact of how my life will change, I don't fully understand to what extent.

My dad takes my silence as the okay to continue. "She's lost both of her parents. You, me, and Helen." His voice is empathetic, a tone I don't hear often from him. "We're all she's got."

I lean against the back of the chair, wiping my hands up and down my pants. "I know." Taking a more serious approach this time, I nod in agreement. "I love her, and I will do anything I can for her."

My dad pats my knee. "I know you will, Jasper. And I know how much you love her. I've never seen you like this with any girl." He smiles. "I knew she was special right from the start."

But then his expression suddenly hardens. "For the sake of Avery and the new baby, please continue to monitor your mental health."

I clear my throat, not expecting our joyous moment to take a turn. "Look, I got it. I'm doing fine."

"You won't be living with me, and this will be something you'll have to manage on your own, including the baby," he points out. "She needs to be assured that you won't leave her to handle things by herself."

I stand. "That won't happen. She means too much to me."

My dad rests his chin in the palm of his hand. His eyes glossed over and focused on the ground, looking deep in thought. *Did he hear me?*

"Dad?"

A subtle pull at the corner of his mouth. "I remember when me and your mom found out we were having you." The quirk turns into a full smile. "I was scared out of my damn mind." He chuckles. "Your mom wasn't, though. She was calm and reminded me that it would all be okay—we'd figure it out."

He doesn't tell stories of my mother often, but when he does, I feel much closer to her. "I wish I'd have known her better."

"You were so young when she died," he adds.

I bend, returning to the chair next to his. I take his hand in mind. "I promise I will do whatever I can to support Avery and be the best dad I can be for this baby."

He smiles. "I know you will."

"How could I not when I had an incredible dad like you?"

He scoffs at my compliment. "Now you're just trying to flatter me."

I laugh, but I sense there's still more he wants to talk about.

"You know I'm not good at these types of things." He rubs his chin.

"At communicating?" I sneer.

He chuckles. "Yeah. So, I guess I'm also trying to say that you need to commit to her."

"What do you mean?" I ask, puzzled. We got matching tattoos. That's a pretty big commitment.

His eyes dart around the room quickly, then meet mine. "She needs to know she'll be taken care of."

"Dad, she has an insane amount of money with her inheritance."

He shakes his head. "I don't mean money." Leaning forward, he meets me in the eye. "I mean from you."

Suddenly, it hits me. I know what my dad is implying. "Like getting married?"

"Yes."

I arch a brow, more than a little shocked, as he's suggesting this. "Really? From the man who won't marry the woman he's sleeping with," I quip.

"Fair enough. But Helen and I aren't having a baby together," he counters.

Honestly, I haven't even thought about getting married. But sure, I'd marry Avery. *Why not?* It's not like it's going to change anything.

"It's not the nineteen fifties anymore, but if you think I should, I will."

My dad's palms meet the air between us. "Only if you want to. I'm not trying to pressure you. I just want to have a real discussion with you about everything."

I shrug my shoulders. "I will be with her forever, so why not get married."

"Alight." He smiles with pride. "I'm proud of you, Son."

I smile back. Warmth fills my heart, but it's now joined by a new emotion—*protectiveness. She'll never be alone again.*

Chapter Twenty-Six

Now

Avery

The warm sunlight peeks through the translucent white curtains, pulling me out of a deep sleep. Peeling my eyelids open one at a time, I quickly note where I am—*Jasper's bedroom.*

Smiling, I roll over, hoping to see him sleeping beside me. Instead of Jasper, I find space. *This cannot be a dream.* But then, I catch sight of a piece of paper with a handwritten note.

Went on a jog down the beach.
I'll be back with coffee and food.
J

Of course, he'd leave a note instead of sending a simple text. Flipping onto my back, I stretch my arms out above my head. I suck in a deep breath through my nose, then exhale in relaxation. I need to check in with the girls.

I sift through the clothes piled on the wooden floor and under the bed until I find my phone. Using the white sheet to cover my bare breasts, I adjust myself, looking as natural as I can. I swipe up our group chat. When the camera flashes on the video,

I notice the redness all over my chest and a few scattered bite marks. *Oh my god, Jasper!* Flustered, my back falls against the headboard, partly covered by a shadow. There's no way they're not going to notice. I prepare myself for interrogation.

Bailey answers first. "Hey!"

"Hello, my loves." Piper's glowing face shows up on my screen.

Lina quickly follows. "Why are you naked, Avery?"

"What, no formal greeting, Lina Bina?" I tease.

Bailey's eyes grow wide. "You *are* naked."

"This is going to be good. I need to step out," Piper tells someone off-camera. Then I hear her husband Jack's voice in the background, "Tell them I said hello."

"Are the rest of you alone?" I ask cautiously.

Bailey's standing in the kitchen cutting an apple. "I am. Mason and Luca are at soccer practice."

"Carter is flying," Lina chimes in, falling into an oversized white couch. "Spill it. Why are your boobs hanging out?"

Laughing, I blush. "I tried to cover them."

Piper waves her hands in front of the camera. "You have this energy to you too."

"I know that look! You got laid!" Lina shouts, proud of herself for figuring it out.

I rub my lips together bashfully. "Um, well. Jasper and I—"

Lina clicks her tongue. "Stop it."

"You were supposed to divorce him, not fuck him," Bailey affectionately quips.

Piper's grin is the size of the entire state. "The body wants what it wants, doesn't it?"

"I knew you two weren't done," Bailey comments, shaking her head.

"So, what happened?" Lina anxiously asks.

I sit straighter, pulling my knees into my chest. "I don't know. It was all such a blur, to be honest."

"A sex, lust-filled blur," Piper jokes.

Bailey nervously picks up her hair, gathers it, and then drops it again. "What did he say about the divorce?"

Biting my lip, I attempt to formulate a response. The truth is, I don't know why Jasper is refusing to divorce me. The only rational explanation I can come up with is that even though there is still flaming chemistry between us, he's trying to get me back for leaving him all those years ago.

"I honestly don't know," I admit.

They're silent for a beat before Lina speaks. "Maybe he's not over you."

Bailey and Piper both have the same expressions of agreement on their faces.

"Or maybe he's still upset that I left him all those years ago, that he's getting back at me," I counter.

"But there's enough between you two that you hooked up less than two days after seeing each other again," Piper points out softly.

"That is fast, by my standards," Lina jokes, holding up a finger. "Also, you don't have to like someone to have sex with them."

We all laugh.

"Okay, very funny," Bailey dismisses. "Lina does make a point, though."

With a prideful expression, Lina continues, "We all know you still have major feelings for him."

"I know. They're confusing. In so many ways, I'm still angry with him for leaving me alone. Something he said he'd never do."

Bailey frowns. "We get it."

"Look, people make mistakes. We were so young that I feel guilty for being upset after all these years, but I can't help how it made me feel," I explain.

Lina's face twists with sorrow and empathy. "Now, what happens?"

I shrug. "I have no idea. There's so much baggage between us. All the horrible memories I never worked through."

Piper threads a hand through her tousled red hair. "I know. I'm sorry."

I startle at the sound of the door opening downstairs.

"He's back. I have to go," I whisper.

"Okay, love you," Bailey replies.

Lina and Piper blow me a kiss before I end the call and toss my phone on top of my pile of clothes. I hear Jasper's footfalls as he ascends the stairs to the second story. My stomach flutters with anticipation of seeing him. Maybe I should have used this time to freshen up instead of calling the girls. *Whatever.* Jasper has seen me live without makeup and a bikini. I doubt he'll care.

"Hey, you're up." He walks in shirtless, with only board shorts on, holding two cups of coffee. *Fuck, he looks good—better than I remember.*

I pick my jaw off the floor and take one of the cups from his hand. "I am."

He sits on the side of the bed. "How did you sleep?"

Peace washes over me. "Amazing."

"Good." He smiles.

"Thanks for the coffee," I say, taking a sip.

An awkward silence passes between us.

Jasper cocks his head to the side with his eyebrow furrowed like he wants to say something. "So ..." He pauses. "Do you want to go surfing with me?"

My gut reaction is to jump with excitement like a lovestruck teenager, but my mind quickly kills it. "I don't know."

"Come on, Arizona," he gently coerces me.

Picking at the cardboard sleeve, I avoid eye contact. "I should head back."

Jasper raises a hand and pinches my chin between his thumb and index finger. "Just for a little while. For old times' sake."

My eyes can't help but find his lips. Giving into my natural urge, I lean in and kiss him. A light kiss, but enough to savor him and this moment. "Alright."

"I knew you couldn't turn it down." He runs his tongue along his bottom lip. "Can't wait to see your skills after all these years."

I lower my eyes, giving him a lopsided grin. "I've been in the desert this whole time. Do you think I was able to surf out there?"

"You're saying you forgot everything I taught you?"

"I'm saying I might need a refresher."

"Lucky for you, I have time this morning," he states.

My cheeks burn. "Lucky for me."

My legs and stomach muscles are sore as I follow Jasper to the shore. With the surfboard tucked under my arm, my body pulses with a different type of electricity. Jasper and I were out on the water for hours. We didn't speak much, but we also didn't need to. He was in his element, and so was I.

"I'm surprised by how it all came back to you," he says, laying his board on the sand. His hair is wet and messy. He looks the same as he always has in so many ways, but with slight differences that have come with age. His shoulders are broader, and his chin is more chiseled than before.

"Me too," I reply, pulling down the sleeves of my rash guard.

"I'm also surprised you brought your gear."

I laugh. "Me too. I didn't think I'd use it, but felt I should pack it, knowing I was traveling out here."

Jasper sits in the warm sand, facing the water. I rest my board next to his and take the space next to him.

"Was Helen happy to see you?" He squints from the bright sun, then digs into his bag to grab a pair of sunglasses.

"She was." I pull my legs up to my chest. "I didn't realize how much I missed her until I saw her again."

"I'm sure," he replies, glancing at me and then turning away. "It's been hard on her since my dad died."

My head falls, and guilt bowls over me. I should have been there for her more.

Jasper senses my regret and hooks an arm around my shoulder, nudging me into him. "She has a large group of friends out here and a lot of support."

A tear rolls down my cheek and onto his bare, tanned skin. "I know. But it doesn't make the guilt any less."

"But you're here now," he adds, insinuating I should make time for her while in town. He's right.

"I know," I admit, swiping a few more tears from my sticky cheek. "We chatted outside on her patio the other night. It was nice."

"I'm sure it meant a lot to her."

"I think it did," I tell him. "She was sad when I left." Jasper tightens his hold around me. "I should see what she's doing this evening. Maybe we could have dinner together."

Jasper tips his head toward my forehead and then whispers, "That's a good idea, Avery. I'm sure she'd clear her schedule for you."

"Helen is a social butterfly, though," I play. I blow out a heavy breath. "You know I'm not good with this stuff."

"At what?"

"Feelings." I blink away. "Connection."

"You mean human emotions?" he quips affectionately.

I lightly slap his chest. "That's not funny. But yes."

"We're all products of our upbringing. It's not your fault." He lovingly reminds me with a cheeky grin. "My dad wasn't either. If that makes you feel better."

Jasper always makes the world seem sensible to me. Losing Duke was hard on Jasper too. He mentioned how he felt when we were at the old beach house, but I knew he was holding back.

"I meant it when I said I'm sorry for not being there for you either," I tell him, resting my palm on his leg. He places his large hand on mine, wrapping his fingers around me. I flip over and intertwine my fingers with his.

"You don't need to apologize. We're only able to do what we're capable of," he insists. *And there it is*—the first time I've heard him put into perspective what he could not do and what ultimately solidified my decision to leave that grim August night. Jasper lacked the ability to support me. It's something he was incapable of doing.

Like any response to trauma, my brain automatically blocks it out, replacing the sad memories with positive ones.

"What are you doing later tonight?" I ask, attempting to change the subject.

He smiles with those straight, white teeth and the same dimple I've had my tongue all over. "Whatever you're doing."

I lightly kiss the corner of his mouth and continue with small kisses along the seam of his lips. His chest rumbles with laughter, and simultaneously, his opposite arm swings around me, pulling me on top of him. We both fall into the sand.

"You did really well today out on the water." His hands run up and down both my legs while they straddle him. "What do you say I give you a little reward?"

I stare down into his eyes and watch them darken. I can tell what he has in mind. It isn't just a prize for me. "Absolutely."

Behind Jasper's broad smile are all the dirty things he wants to do to me. And behind mine is that same euphoric lust that overcame me all those years ago.

I jump off him, sprinting through the sand and toward his

house. He's hot on my heels, trudging through the sand behind me.

The pure nostalgia of us together, combined with the sound of the waves in the background and the salty breeze whipping through my hair, is utterly dynamic. I am transported back to simpler times when the only things we worried about were ourselves.

Chapter Twenty-Seven

THEN

Jasper

"Still can't believe you got her pregnant," Bodhi comments, slapping the blanket and laying it flat on the sand. "Have I not taught you anything?"

I roll my eyes, tossing the rest of the pillows under the umbrella. "I love her, Bodhi. I know you don't know what that's like, but when you love someone, you don't worry about things like that," I say, then suddenly I turn to see Easton, Riley, and Bodhi with smirks on their faces. They don't believe a word I'm saying. "Fuck off, guys. I do love Avery."

Easton sets one of the tall lanterns on the side of the blanket. "Oh, we know you definitely love her—" he begins, but then I abruptly cut him off. My friend knows me better than this. They're trying to get me to admit that I fucked up—which I did, but I don't want to think of it that way.

"Fine, it was an accident," I snap. "Happy?"

Riley rests a hand on my shoulder. "Again, did Bodhi not teach you anything?"

"I guess not." I roll my shoulders, pushing it off. "Besides, I'd rather refer to the baby as an unexpected surprise."

"Whatever you want to call it," Bodhi busts once again. "I must say, at least it's Arizona and not some tourist."

"Or worse, a girl from Coconut Grove," Riley chimes in.

I chuckle, fist-bumping both of them. "That's true."

Easton lightly scatters red rose petals on top of the blanket. "How'd Duke take it when you told him?"

When Avery and I spoke with Helen and my dad, he was surprisingly calm. Helen was, too, but she was more concerned with how Avery felt about it. Understandably, her whole life is about to change. During the conversation, I kept reminding her this wasn't something she would do alone. There's an entire network of people out here to support us.

"He and Helen both handled it well," I say. "Later that day, my dad and I took a drive over to the beach house and gave me a heart-to-heart."

"Good ol' Duke," Bodhi muses. "That man is a legend."

Easton tosses the last handful of petals into the air. "So, your dad waited until you two were alone to tell you how he really felt, huh?"

I shake my finger in the air. "You'd think that, right? But our talk was mostly about me and how I need to step up for Arizona. He's very supportive of her."

"Huh, imagine that," Riley mumbles more to himself than to us.

"Out of the four of us, we knew you'd get married and have kids first," Bodhi comments.

Riley grimaces. "I actually thought it would be Bodhi who'd

knock up a girl first."

I huff in frustration. "I didn't just *knock her up*. It's deeper than that."

Riley throws a handful of rose petals into my face. "Aww," he pokes fun.

"Fuck off," I spit, sweeping the petals back onto the blanket with my hand. "A baby just adds another layer to our relationship."

"God, you're making me sick." Bodhi gags with exaggeration.

"I don't know why I asked you guys to help me," I snap.

Riley hooks an arm around me. "Because we're your brothers and love that we're now getting a sister."

We all share a laugh.

As dusk hits, the four of us step back to look at the setup. Rose petals cover the ground of the small area, and an umbrella rests in the middle with two small, dim lanterns on either side.

"Are you sure you want to do this?" Easton presses, his eyes trained on the romantic spot my friends helped me create.

"Absolutely," I state, without a doubt in my mind. I don't see any negatives about this whole situation. I live in the town I love, have a network of supportive people, and I'm taking over a family business I love. My life is set. Avery and the baby were the missing pieces. "Is your brother waiting for us at the courthouse?"

"He is," Riley says. "If she says yes, he's waiting on standby."

I run a hand through my hair. "I'm so fucking excited."

"What a hell of a summer this is for you, Jasper." Easton takes his turn at wrapping a friendly arm around me.

"A life-changing summer," I mutter. Just then, my phone

vibrates at my side. I slid it out to see that it's a text from Avery.

Arizona: I'm here. Where do you want me to meet you?

Me: Just stay in your car. I'll come and get you.

I tap out the quick response, then put my phone away.

A few minutes later, I'm walking with Avery down to the shore.

"You're not going to throw me into the ocean, are you?" Avery asks, a thick blindfold tightly around her eyes.

My hands are on her shoulders while I lead her through the sand. "I would never."

"Yes, you would." She giggles sweetly.

"That's true, I probably would." I laugh. "But then I'd come in after you."

"You've been blindfolding me a lot lately." Her voice is airy and light.

"I have, haven't I?" I flirt. Glancing over at my three friends, each one with shit-eating grins on their faces. They're continuing to make me regret including them.

As we approach the blanket covered in rose petals, my heart pounds against the back of my ribcage. I am ready to marry Avery. I love her. "Okay, Arizona."

Her fingers come over mine, and we both pull the blindfold off her head. She gasps. "Jasper."

"Avery."

She looks stunned and confused when she turns toward me

with her palms covering her mouth. "What is all this?"

A calmness cloaks me—one I've never known except from the sea. I smile and bring my hands to her cheeks. "Avery Thomas," I begin. She sucks in a sharp breath. "My dad met my mother when he was fourteen years old. He knew he would marry her from the moment he saw her." Avery's almond-shaped green eyes bore into mine. "I might not be fourteen, but I *am* nineteen. And I knew from the moment I hit you with that volleyball you were like no other girl I've ever met."

"When you hit me with the volleyball you knew?" she whispers, slight humor in her voice.

I chuckle. "Yes."

She smiles, letting me continue.

"Others like to say that people our age don't know what love is or is about, but I *do* know. It's how my body feels when I'm connected to you. It's how I can see into your thoughts and how we can simply lay in silence for hours without feeling the need to fill it with empty words."

"Love can be quiet," she whispers. A single tear escapes from under her eyelid and rolls down her face.

"Yes." As my body warms, I lean into her, bringing my forehead to hers. "Now, I'm going to ask you something, and I want you to know I'm more than sure I want to do this." Then I pull away, lowering to one knee in front of her.

"Fuck yeah, dude!" Bodhi calls out from a few yards away. I crack a smile, pushing his wails away. And when Avery does the same thing, I am even more sure of my decision.

"Avery." I swallow hard, barely able to catch my breath, as the nerves finally hit me. "Will you marry me?"

Everything around us blurs. I stare at her from the position at my knee and watch in slow motion as a quick rise in her chest results in what I can only describe as a low-pitched shriek. "Oh my god."

"I love you, Avery Thomas."

She sucks in a breath. "I don't want you to think, just because we're having—"

My index finger reaches her lips, hushing her words. "Stop. That's not why I want to marry you. It might be happening sooner than I thought." I chuckle. "But I knew I always would."

"Oh, Jasper. Yes! Of course, I will marry you," she shouts in a high-pitched tone.

I anticipated this answer, but hearing it with my ears is an entirely different emotion. "Yeah?"

"Yes." She bends, bringing her lips to mine. "I love you so much!"

Overcome by pure euphoria, I quickly rise, gripping her by the hips and lifting her into the air.

"The ring!" Easton yelled in a reminder of a crucial piece I had forgotten.

"Oh yes!" I laugh, lowering Avery into the sand. I shove my hand into the front pocket of my shorts and remove a small black velvet box. Silence surrounds us, the moment drowning out the wave rolling through the shore. Avery and I lock our gaze onto the box as the lid pops open. I've seen this ring many times, but now I see it through a new lens. "It was my mother's."

Avery's hands fly to her chest, clutching tightly. "Oh wow."

I take the two-carat oval-cut diamond ring from the box and reach for Avery's shaky hand. "It's yours now."

Raising her hand to get a closer look, she gazes in amazement. "I can't believe how beautiful it is."

"Can we come over now?" Bodhi bellows with annoyance.

"My brother is waiting!" Riley adds. Instead, the three don't wait for a response and jog directly over to us.

I ignore the guys, turning back to my fiancé. "I want to be with you every single step of the way. I want you to experience nothing with this pregnancy without me."

"I'm so glad we're doing this together," she answers distantly, still staring at the diamond on her finger.

Taking two fingers, I pinch her chin, forcing eye contact. "Riley's brother is at the courthouse waiting for us."

Her eyes grow wide. "Wait. Now?"

I nod. "Yes."

"Um. Wow. Okay. What about Helen and your dad?" she asks, biting her bottom lip—valid questions, but I don't want them trying to talk us out of it. Even though my dad insinuated this, it might make him rethink his stance if he finds out I'm actually going through with it.

"You're my family now." I bring my palm to her belly. "This baby. Us."

Avery nervously pulls her bottom lip between her teeth while her eyes bounce between mine. She cycles through all the reasons why we should wait or whether we should do this. "I love you so much, Jasper. I didn't grow up knowing what love looked or felt like. But you've shown me what it's about." She pauses, gazing upward, filling her lungs with salty sea air. "Let's get married."

"Fuck yes!" Easton chuckles, pulling Avery into a hug.

"We're all coming," Bodhi states, his arms folded at his chest.I slap his friendly shoulder. "I knew you would."

"Is that why you wanted me to wear one of my black sundresses?" she asks, blowing a few strands of hair away from her face.

"Yes. I knew you'd want to get married in black," I reply, pulling her back from Easton. She tucks into my arm.

Avery pinches her eyebrows together wearily, looking at me playfully. "Wearing a black wedding dress isn't bad luck, is it?"

"I guess we'll find out," Bodhi quips, shrugging his shoulders.

I laugh. "I doubt it."

"Texting my brother." Riley holds his phone in front of him. "I'll tell him we're on our way."

"Is the courthouse even open right now?" Avery looks puzzled.

Easton cocks his head to the side. "Look, Arizona, when you've lived in a small town your whole life, you gain connections at all levels."

She cocks a hip in his direction. "I should have learned that by now."

"Easton is very proud of his small-town upbringing," I retort at my friend's expense.

Bodhi flashes her a toothy smile. "You'll have plenty of time to learn because now you'll be here forever."

I glance in Avery's direction, and I can't miss the brief change in her expression. *Is it one of panic or contentment?* Her eyes flicker to mine, catching me staring, but she lovingly smiles as if I didn't see her subtle apprehension. I try to brush it off, chalking it up to my nerves.

"I guess so," Avery says.

"What are we waiting for?" Riley barks at the group. "Let's go get you two married."

My eyes fly back to Avery's one more time to make sure she wants to do this. I'd be heartbroken if she changed her mind, but I'd respect it. "Are you sure?"

She presses her lips together, forming a tight smile. Her cheeks redden before she replies. "Yes. Let's do this."

"Fuck yeah!" I say, planting a rough kiss on her head.

Avery and I follow the guys out to the parking lot.

"My car is here, but I want to ride with you." She frowns.

Scratching my nose, I regret not thinking this all the way through. Of course, she and I should ride together. "I guess I didn't think that far ahead."

"I rode with Riley, so I'll take your car back to Helen's, Arizona," Bodhi offers, extending his arms and cupping his hands for Avery's keys.

She glances at me with an unsure look. "I'd be nervous to give Bodhi my keys as well," I say, shooting Bodhi a side-eye. "But he'll take care of it, I promise."

"Fuck you." Bodhi punches me in my side. "I'll take it to the courthouse, and then Riley and I will drop it off."

Avery pauses with apprehension before tossing Bodhi her keys. The five of us pile into our cars and make a beeline for the courthouse.

I'm getting fucking married tonight.

Chapter Twenty-Eight

THEN

Avery

"I can't believe we just did that!" An excitement-filled scream bubbles from my throat.

Jasper hooks an arm around me, yanking my body into his. "I've never felt so good."

"We're going to be a family, Jasper." I lovingly look up and smile.

This is my chance to create the family I never had. The dark hallways and empty rooms will not be something I will experience again. Holidays will no longer be a source of utter loneliness. I won't have to watch other families make memories and establish traditions together. I will get to experience it myself.

Apprehension still knocks on the back of my skull, but this is the best decision. The fear of history repeating itself, leaving me once again in a puddle of sorrow and despair. *When does life ever go as planned anyway?*

"We are." Jasper's fingers weave through my windblown hair,

pushing it away from my face. "Even though the guys couldn't stop cracking jokes the entire time, I'm glad they were there."

I nod. "They're like your brothers. Of course, they should've been there for this moment."

Just then, I hear rapid footfalls behind me as the three guys come barreling out of the courthouse.

"When are you going to tell Duke and Helen?" Riley pants as soon as he reaches us. His eyes bounced between Jasper and me, directing the question at us both.

Jasper turns to look at me before answering. "Now?"

My heart rate quickly escalates. Helen is not like either of my parents, and I am eighteen now, which makes me an adult. I can make my own decisions. *But why is my initial reaction fear and judgment when it should be the comfort of knowing Helen is not like my parents?* She's kind and understanding and wants to support me. *Old habits die hard, I guess?*

I smile at my *now*-husband with confidence. "I think it can wait until morning. I'd like to spend the night with my husband."

Jasper's face brightens even more than it already is. "*Your husband*," he repeats my words. "I like hearing that."

My stomach flutters. "I like saying it."

"So, where are you guys going tonight?" Easton suddenly comes to our side, bringing up an obvious question.

Seems like Jasper and the guys had everything planned, from the proposal on the beach to Riley's brother at the courthouse, but they completely forgot about the *actual* wedding night.

"Okay, enough." Bodhi sneers. "You two will have all night to bang."

"Not if they don't have anywhere to stay," Easton quips.

"I thought you had everything planned, Jasper?" Bodhi bites, cocking his head to the side.

Jasper shoots him a few daggers. "I just got married. Can't you lay off me for one night?"

He pauses and gazes, angled upward like he's considering Jasper's question. "Nope."

I chuckle, enjoying the banter between them. The friends and family I'm only now experiencing. I get to share them with Jasper and I couldn't be happier.

A beat passes before Jasper turns his attention back to me. "How about the beach house?"

"The beach house?" I ask, knowing there's not a single piece of furniture in that place."Yeah." Jasper smiles, his gaze falling to my lips and returning to meet my eyes. "I still have the floor bed and blankets from when we were there for your birthday."

I grin. "Sounds like a plan."

"That's great. Now we have you two figured out, can we talk about food? I'm fucking starving," Bodhi complains, crumpling his shirt, showing off his toned stomach. "I need some grub soon."

Listening to Bodhi mention food causes my stomach to growl. "I could go for something to eat too."

Easton raises his eyebrows. "Wedding night dinner at the burger shack?"

"Yes, Jasper, let's get some big-ass greasy burgers," Riley yells, slapping Jasper's shoulders.

Jasper turns to me with his top lip quirked up. "You want a burger to eat on our wedding night?"

I shrug my shoulders, smiling. "Honestly, double decker sounds good right now."

Jasper's eyes widen. "This is why I married you."

"Because I'm cool."

"Ehh." Jasper's eyes lower. "A little bit."

I scrunch my nose. "I am."

"That's a stretch, Arizona," Riley adds playfully.

Easton shoves me. "Nah, you're cool."

"Tolerable at best," Bodhi comments with a smirk.

"Fuck you guys." I laugh. "I'm the bride. Find me a burger."

"I'm nervous about Bodhi with my car," I admit. Jasper is a couple of steps behind me as we approach the wooden beach house door.

With a couple water bottles and a bag of snacks clutched in his hands, he shrugs. "It'll be fine." Then he unlocks the door with his free hand. "He likes to fuck around, but he's trustworthy."

"I know." I sigh, breathing in the musty, humid air. I can't explain why the unpleasant scent of sea air breaking down old wood bathes me in comfort, but it does. I watch Jasper use his cell phone as a flashlight in this dark, abandoned house on the surf's edge. I've only been here twice, and both times now have been an adventure.

"And you can just buy a new one anyway, can't you?" He

flashes me a quick smirk over his shoulder, followed by a cheeky wink.

I roll my eyes while kicking off my sandals. "That's not the point. I like that car.""I get it. I've had my truck since I was sixteen." Jasper unwraps the floor bed and lays it flat in the middle of the living room—the same spot where I gave him my virginity, only a couple weeks prior.

"It's the first thing I've bought myself," I tell him.

Jasper's eyebrows furrow, and his face softens. "Really?"

I nod.

"Well, it won't be the last." He smiles.

A quick vision of our future together dances across my mind, and an unintentional smile breaks. Jasper catches it and slowly walks over to me. His palms cup my elbows while he brings me close to him. A whiff of sunblock and a hint of cologne hit my nostrils when my face meets his chest.

"We have our entire lives for you to do whatever you want with your money, future, and time. I'm happy with what I'm doing and where I'm at," he says, sliding his hands over to my abdomen. "Your job is to focus on your happiness and our baby's."

"Thank you, husband." I tilt my head, my eyes meeting his.

Jasper smiles. "My wife."

We stand silently together for a few emotional moments, listening to the faint sound of waves outside.

I'm the first to speak when a question lingers in my thoughts. One that I answered the morning we told Helen and Duke I was pregnant, but now, with us suddenly getting married, it makes more sense to rethink our living arrangements.

"So …" I begin, unsure how to invite myself to live with him or if he even wants to take that step yet. "Will we live here together?"

Jasper's two fingers lift my bashful expression. "I would love that."

My heart flutters. "Really?"

"We're married, Arizona." He smiles. "We chose each other. Why wouldn't we live here as a family?"

Swallowing hard, I try to rid my throat of the dryness that's cloaked it. "Yes, I guess—"

"You'll have to stay with Helen until I can make this house livable," he jokes, glancing around the run-down space. "It'll be easier for your pregnancy as well. Then, when it's time for the baby to come, the place will be done and ready to bring him or *her* home."

My mind races with all that's happened in the last few months—well, the week. Jet propulsion at full speed, I thrust into a brand-new existence, leaning into an entirely different life.

"That sounds perfect," I whisper, staring deeply into his eyes.

"Good."

Another beat passes with the distant sound of the surf. "Can I have input on the designs?"

"Of course," he says, slipping behind me. Jasper wraps his arm around me and stacks them on my chest. With his chin resting on my shoulder, he gently rotates me to face the living room and kitchen. "What are my wife's thoughts on our new home?"

A giggle bubbles beneath my lungs, and a quick zip of excitement shoots up my back. "Well, I do love pineapples," I begin.

"Ah, yes. Pineapples."

"I'm not suggesting we make the entire place pineapples themed—"

"That's good because I might have to push back on that," he quips.

"But they're my favorite fruit."

Jasper runs his nose across my cheek. "Okay, fine, a pineapple house it is."

I laugh. "I'm kidding."

"Really? Because it was starting to grow on me."

"Maybe the bathroom?"

"That can be done," he says, releasing me slowly. Jasper walks over to the kitchen.

I take a few quiet steps toward him. "I do want the house to reflect the freshness of the beach. Island-themed with an organic touch. Elements like driftwood and greenery," I continue as he circles the eat-in kitchen.

"I love it." Jasper opens one of the broken, white cabinets. It falls off the loose hinge and clashes with the floor. "Shit."

Startled, I jump back, but with a brief glance between us, we both start laughing.

"It might take longer than expected." He chuckles.

I approach the peeling wallpaper to my side. "And a lot more than a simple coat of paint."

"Yes." He laughs. "I was thinking about painting the outside of the house blue and white."

I shut my eyes, imagining what it would look like with those colors. A picture of Jasper and me with a baby in my arms, standing at the door, flashes behind the darkness of my eyelids. I barely recognize myself in this vision. *It feels right, but why is it so hard to imagine it could happen to me?*

I open my eyes to Jasper standing before me with his eyes on fire.

"Sounds perfect," I squeak, recognizing his flame.

"Now, what do you say we get started on more important things," he says, slipping his hands around my waist. The warmth from his touch causes an outbreak of goose bumps to span my body.

"I think that's a great idea." I pull my bottom lip between my teeth and wrap my arms around the back of his neck.

"I can't believe we got married tonight," he says in a husked voice, pressing a gentle kiss on my forehead.

My eyes fall closed, savoring his touch. "I know. I can't believe you got me to do that."

"You weren't that difficult to convince."

"That's true." I giggle. "You're a hard guy to say no to."

"Arizona?" His voice is a little sharper than before.

I tuck my face into the sweet-smelling cotton of his shirt. "Yeah?"

"Take off your black wedding dress."

Chapter Twenty-Nine

Now

Jasper

I pace back and forth, wearing down the same spot on my hardwood floors. I wonder if Avery will want to see me again after her dinner with Helen. She has come barging back into my life, and the sheer terror I feel about losing her once again manifests into a light hum of panic.

My phone chimes on the kitchen counter. I practically jumped over the back of my couch to grab it, hoping it was her.

Easton: Avery is having dinner next door with Helen.

As if best friend telepathy, he knew I'd be wondering where she was at.

Me: At Marv's?

Easton: Yeah. Shouldn't she still be holed up with you instead of eating pasta?

I roll my eyes.

Me: She hasn't seen Helen in years. They're just catching dinner together.

Easton: You two are done with your little weekend trip down memory lane?

Me: First of all, the weekend isn't over, my friend. Second of all, I'm headed to meet them now.

A lie. But his words get to me. This weekend can't end yet. I need more time with her. I don't know if that makes a difference, but right now, I'm obsessed with soaking up as much time with her as possible. Once she gets hit with a reminder of reality, my fantasy is over. She'll still be in need of a divorce and back to another man. Fuck, that makes me ill.

Easton: Okay. If you say so. Don't forget, we're meeting Bodhi and Riley for a beer later.

Me: I forgot that rich fucker is back in town.

Easton: YEP. See you later.

I slip my phone back into my pocket, swipe my keys off the counter, and head out the door. My stomach is in knots the entire ride over to the restaurant. Not because I'm showing up but because I fear my time with her is running out.

I pull into the back parking lot at Marv's Italian restaurant a short time later.

"Hey, Jasper." One of the cooks greets me with a cigarette dangling off his bottom lip.

"What's up, man?" I return, extending an arm to open the black wrought-iron door into the kitchen.

"Do you want me to have them pack up your usual to-go order?" he asks.

"That'd be great. Thanks," I toss over my shoulder as the heavy metal slams behind me.

The kitchen is busy with people in black-and-white uniforms scurrying around. Classic rock plays in the background, lightly overshadowed by the line cooks calling out orders. As I walk toward the front of the restaurant, I get a few hellos from the staff.

"Jasper!" Standing at least a foot shorter than me, Marv comes barreling out of the office. "I didn't know you were coming! Did you already call in your order? I didn't see it yet. Annette!"

"No, I didn't call in an order," I interrupt his frantic spiral. "No one forgot anything, don't worry."

Marv nods his head vigorously. "Okay, okay. That's good."

"Busy tonight?" I comment, scanning the room for Avery and Helen.

"Yes." He smiles, calmer now. "Can I get you anything?"

"No, I'm good, Marv." I pat his shoulder. "I'm here looking for a few friends."

"Lady friends?" His mouth curls into a high smile.

"Sort of." I laugh, glancing behind me to sweep the dining room again. "It's Helen and her niece Avery."

"Oh yes. They have the table in the corner." He points to the opposite end of the restaurant. "I'll take you over."

"No, I don't want to interrupt them. I just wanted to see if they were here," I tell him.

Hearing those words reminds me I had no plan for after I got here. *What was I going to say once I saw them?* I would never want to intrude on Avery's dinner with her aunt—they haven't seen each other in years.

I stand here confused but not willing to leave yet. *Am I worried losing sight of Avery could cause me to lose her entirely again? Am I chasing her or our past?*

Maybe both.

Marv shrugs his shoulders. "Okay. Well, since you're here. Can I get you a glass of wine?"

I'll wait until they finish, then follow Avery to her car. *That's not weird at all.* I repeated this to myself a few times before responding to Marv. "Sure. I'll just hang out here at the bar."

"Wonderful. I'll grab you something from my reserve." His voice is spritely.

I climb onto the bar stool, keeping Avery and Helen in my peripheral. "Sounds good."

The door to the back flings open and then shuts as Marv pushes himself through.

"Mayor Collins." The tall, blonde bartender says my name smoothly. "What can I get for you?"

"I'm good. Marv is grabbing me something from his personal stash," I say.

"Of course he is." Her eyes drop to my lips and then back up. "Can I get you anything while you wait?"

I shake my head, seemingly declining more than just a drink offer.

"Suit yourself." She rolls a shoulder, turning in the opposite direction.

"Jasper?" A feminine voice from behind me. It's not the one I'd prefer, but it's familiar.

I whip my head around, coming face-to-face with Melanie. I knew it was a bad idea to date a local. "Oh, hi, Melanie."

"Haven't heard from you in a while," she states, clutching her purse.

I knew I wouldn't be able to avoid her for much longer. Coconut Grove is a small town, and I am the mayor, for fuck's sake. Melanie and I were just a casual thing, but the moment I saw Avery walk into my office that day, a switch flipped.

"I meant to call you, but I've been busy." I give her a canned, empty response. It's a dick move. My mind can only focus on the tattooed brunette from my past.

"Of course," Melanie dismisses my reply, knowing as well as I do it's a bullshit excuse. She opens her red lips to continue, but Marv is suddenly at her side.

"Jasper! Here is my favorite red," he begins as if not realizing he's walked into our conversation. Grateful for his electric personality, I sigh a breath of relief. "Iris and I use it as a table red whenever we have people over. Yes, it's a simple blend, but just perfectly spiced." he slips around the back of the bar and pulls two wine glasses off the hanger. "Well, here, you just have to try it," he continues. "Oh, you have company!" he says, reaching for a third glass.

"She's not staying," I blurt, extending my arm in front of us.

Marv pauses, his hand suspended in the air. His eyes dart over to Melanie, and they exchange uncomfortable looks. I get the urge to explain or apologize—*or something*.

Heat burns the tips of my ears. "I meant that I'm meeting someone soon."

"Stalking me, Mr. Collins?" The last voice I ever want to hear is suddenly behind me. I slowly craned my neck, knowing Avery had joined our uncomfortable group. My situation got a hell of a lot stranger. I can't tell them all a different story, and now the restaurant owner—one of my constituents, my ex-fling, and the love of my life—are all staring at me, waiting for me to answer their simple questions.

"Avery, hi," I say causally.

"What are you doing here?" Her hand rests on the back of my high-back bar stool.

"Okay, four glasses of my favorite red are coming up!" Marv's excited voice and clanking glasses provide a brief reprieve.

"Hi, I'm Melanie." Melanie shoots her arm out with a smug look, swiping me across the face.

"I'm Avery." I catch the subtle furrow of Avery's brow as she returns the gesture.

I open my mouth to speak, but the way Melanie's eyes bore into Avery's, it won't matter what I say. So, instead, I sit and sweat.

Melanie clicks her tongue. "And how do you know Jasper?"

Avery's lip quirks up with a devious smile. "Oh, we used to fuck."

Damn.

Melanie's face reddens, and then she takes a hard swallow and replies, "So did we."

This isn't going well, but what should I expect?

"Look—" I begin, but I'm quickly dismissed.

"But not anymore," Avery replies with a condescending tone.

I should be nervous by this exchange, but every single nerve in my body lights up with each of Avery's comebacks. *Fuck. I missed her.* She's tame, but there's an intoxicating little spark and confidence in her now.

"Listen, I don't know who you are—" Melanie snaps.

I jump off my seat, positioning myself between them. "Okay, okay—"

"Wine for everyone!" Marv rushes over, carrying four glasses on a black tray.

I turn to him. "One moment, my friend." Then I shift to Melanie. "It was great running into you, Melanie. I'll see you around sometime."

Her hand flies to her hip. "That's how this is going to be?"

"Melanie," I say, lowering my voice. "We've discussed this."

From the corner of my eye, a subtle smirk on Avery's face tells me everything I need to know about where we stand.

Melanie snatches one of Marv's glasses of red wine, takes a hefty swig, and then flashes me a glare before stomping out of the restaurant.

"Please come back for our buy one get one pasta deal next time!" Marv smiles wide. "More for us."

"Thank you, but the lady and I need a few moments alone," I tell him, removing two glasses and handing one to Avery.

"Of course," he says. "Your takeout will be ready soon. And please, everything is on the house."

"You're the best, man."

Lowering her eyes, Avery stiffly climbs into the chair next to me. "Again, stalking me, Mr. Collins?"

I smile. "Sorry about the Melanie situation."

Her eyes fall to the glass in front of her. "No need to explain."

Leaning in, I take two fingers and gently pinch her chin. Tilting her head until we make eye contact, my expression slowly changes. "Melanie and I are not currently sleeping together."

Avery jerks her head away, scoffing it off. "You don't need to explain, Jasper."

"But I do. I want you to know," I say. "We went out a few times, but it was casual."

"How long?"

"It's been a few months," I admit.

She lets out an audible sigh, pausing for a moment before speaking. "Okay."

Her response catches me off guard. I don't know how I wanted her to react, but I'd assumed I'd at least be able to get a read on it. "Okay? That's it?"

"That's it." Avery's lips purse together as she swigs the cabernet. "So, what are you doing here?"

I look away, hiding the grin on my face. "I came for you."

"You did?"

"Yes," I say.

"Want to go back to my place?" I ask, not entirely convinced she'd come.

Avery downs the glass of wine. "Let's go."

Excitement courses through my veins. We're not done yet. I get more time with her, and I can't be more relieved about it.

Chapter Thirty

THEN

Avery

"So, she was just *fine* with it?" Cassie asks with disbelief.

I pull out the rest of the racerback mix-and-match tops from one of the freight boxes. "She seemed to be."

"That's interesting." Her comment is disconnected, as if she didn't intend for it to be heard.

"What do you mean?"

Cassie's hand flies up to her hip while she cocks a brow skyward. "Hear me out."

Unsure where this is going, I agree now and am curious about what small-town two cents she offers me.

"Okay ..." My voice drawls.

"Well, you just came to live with her, and within a few months, you get pregnant and married to a guy you barely know."

Cassie is the closest thing I have to a friend in this town—besides the guys, so I try to rein in my immediate defensiveness. "I know Jasper very well. And just because things like this happen, doesn't mean it's anyone's fault—especially

Helen's."

"I get it. I'm just saying that she must feel a little sad about it."

Heat pricks the tips of my ears. *Who is she to pass judgment on me?* Or have an opinion about my life, for that matter?

"Why would it make her sad? What about being in love would be sad?" I challenge with a clipped tone.

Cassie turns back to the plastic hangers, continuing to clip each string of the bikini top in place. "Look, I'm not trying to offend you. I'm just stating the obvious."

"And that is?"

"Come on, Avery, I haven't known you that long, but what I have known about you is that you are intelligent, independent, and have dreams of your own. That must be hard for your aunt to see your future disappear." Her words slice through me even though her tone is soft.

She is right. I know it, and I feel it. Sure, this isn't the life I envisioned, and it's true. I constantly worry about getting caught up in a fantasy that isn't reality. But my half-friendly coworker is not someone I can open up to about my anxiety and fears of the unknown. Jasper loves me. I can feel it. I need to trust it.

I toss the ball of empty bags into the trash. "My future isn't disappearing. It's just changed a little."

"I get it. You're young and in love, but does anyone find their soulmate at eighteen anyway?" she asks more like an assumption than an honest question.

I haven't dated a whole lot. None of the guys I knew in high school ever interested me—or me in them. Most thought I was the reclusive rich girl who wore too much black and wasn't allowed to leave the compound that I called home.

After my parents died, their attorney asked me what I wanted to do with the house. Only two words came to mind. *Sell it.* I was ready to say goodbye to the lonely prison I called home for most of my life.

"With all due respect, Cassie, it's none of your business," I reply over my shoulder as I leave the backroom.

I get back onto the floor and catch sight of the time—close to four pm.

"Avery?" Cassie's timid voice is behind me.

I whip my head around to see her standing only a few feet away. "Yes?"

"I'm sorry." She sighs. "It is none of my business, and I shouldn't have inserted myself in it." She tucks a corkscrew curl behind her ear. "I'm sure this is hard for you. I shouldn't be making it worse."

Cassie is apologizing, but I still feel there's a backhanded comment threaded in her words. *Why does she think it's hard for me?* I love Jasper. My pregnancy was a surprise, but I chose to marry him.

"I appreciate the sentiments, I do, but I love Jasper, and I refuse to believe that we're not meant to be together. The most significant sign of that is this pregnancy." I defend myself.

"We're the same age, and I know I'd feel worried if I were in your position, even if I was in love with the guy." I open my mouth to speak, but she interjects. "And it doesn't take love to make a baby," Cassie adds with a friendly wink.

Her intentions are in the right place, but I'm frustrated with the tone of this conversation. I blow out a heavy breath of air. "I know you mean well, but butt out, okay?" I snap, then turn on my heels. I gather my things, clock out, and head to my car.

As soon as I open the door to Helen's, the sweet scent of pineapple chicken hits my nose. My stomach rumbles.

"Hi, Helen. I'm home," I say, dropping my purse on the table by the front door.

"In the kitchen," she calls out.

When I get to the kitchen, she's standing over the stove, stirring a large wok filled with chunks of chicken, pineapples, and spices. "I made your favorite pineapple chicken."

"It smells amazing in here." I smile and climb onto the bar stool at the island. "You didn't have to do all this. We could have just ordered takeout."

She flips a dish towel over her shoulder. "When you said you'd be here tonight and not with Jasper, I got excited to spend dinner just the two of us."

"That's sweet. Thank you."

"Where is he tonight?"

"He had to work late at Duke's. They're preparing for that artist to come in," I tell her.

Helen places a bowl of chopped fruit on the counter in front of me. "Oh yeah. He's the one who's going to design a bunch of custom boards for them, right?"

"Yeah. I know Jasper is excited about it. He believes it will be another way to bring in tourists," I say, popping a slice of mango into my mouth.

"Same with Duke," she replies with a smile.

While my aunt cooks, I replay my conversation with Cassie at work. I shouldn't let her get to me, but she is. Helen has been more than supportive and understanding about the pregnancy and that Jasper and I eloped. If she and Duke have any reservations, they're hiding them from us—well, at least me.

"Aunt Helen?"

"Yeah?" she replies, pouring dry rice in a pot.

"Can I ask you something?"

"Of course," she says, pausing her movements to give her full attention.

Nervously, I bite the inside of my bottom lip. "How do you honestly feel about everything going on with Jasper and me?"

She glances around the room for a second before circling back. "What do you mean?"

"Are you disappointed about me getting pregnant?" I begin. "And then about him and I running off to get married?"

She sighs. "That's a tough question."

"You haven't really expressed any real feelings about it."

Walking over to the island, I see her throat bob with a hard swallow. "I just want you to be happy. That's all. And if this is what is going to make you happy, then I'm supportive."

"Yeah," I say, unsatisfied with her answer. *Am I looking for something more? Validation? Or for her to say I'm too young for any of this?*

She leans over the counter and cups her hands over mine. "I know what you want me to say. The pregnancy *and* you eloping with Jasper is bittersweet. On one hand, I get you here all the time now, and I've never really had family around." The corners of her eyes wrinkle with a soft smile.

"It's a whole new exciting world I'm looking forward to." She pauses, thinking through her next thought. "But I also know how bad you wanted to get back to Arizona for college, and this isn't the life you saw for yourself. So yes, it is a mixed bag of emotions for me."

A weight lifts off my chest, hearing her true thoughts. I appreciate them more than she knows. "I have those same feelings. It's more of the unknown I'm unsure about."

Helen lifts a hand, placing her palm on my cheek. "Sometimes not having everything figured out can be a wonderful blessing."

My aunt's words fall heavy on my heart. "I understand that, and I do love Coconut Grove."

"And you're in love with a very special surfer out here too," she says, lovingly pushing my hair to the side.

"So are you," I quip with a cheeky smile.

"Yes. But Duke and I are a lot more complicated than you and Jasper." I hear a subtle sniff as she walks back to the stove to check on the rice.

After dinner, Helen and I are sitting on the back patio, listening to the waves roll in. "I can't believe I'm going to call this place my permanent home now."

"It's absolute heaven here. A little slice of paradise," she adds, keeping her focus trained toward the midnight waters. "I can't imagine living anywhere else."

"What brought you here?" I ask, vaguely remembering that she ended up here by accident.

She lowers an eye in my direction with a smirk. "A boy."

My brows raise with surprise. "A boy?"

"Yes." She sips from a glass of red wine. "A surfer boy."

My head falls back in disbelief. Laughing, I turn in my chair to face her fully. "Well, isn't that interesting?"

Helen folds her arms at her chest and leans in. "We were married for a few years when I was young. We came to Coconut Grove for a training camp he was attending. I was supposed to stay only eight weeks, but when it was time to leave, I couldn't. He left without me, and we managed a long-distance relationship for a number of years before things just fizzled out."

"I'm sorry. That must have been so hard for you."

Her lips pursed together. "It should have been, but it wasn't. I made friends here, I loved my independence, and I unintentionally created a life for myself. We were also very young."

The word *young* rings in my ears like a church bell. *Will Jasper and I have that same fate?* If I want to go to college after the baby is born, will we drift apart? *Will I resent him later for having to give up my life?* I love Jasper with a force, and it guts me even to imagine losing what we have.

"And how did the whole Duke thing happen?" I ask, craving to know more about this woman who I've come to admire deeply. I never realized how strong and self-aware my aunt was.

Helen laughs before answering. "Duke was more complicated."

"Tell me," I press, tucking my knees under myself on the patio chair.

Her cheeks redden. "It had been a number of years since Jasper's mom had died, but he hadn't moved on yet. I ended up taking surf lessons from him. Jasper was his priority, and I respected that. We grew to enjoy each other's company over time and became partners of sorts."

"The dynamics of your relationship are unconventional," I

comment with astonishment.

"Yes, but it works so well for us. As I mentioned before, when you first moved in, we meet each other's needs, and I couldn't be happier about how things are."

I smile warmly. "I love that."

"Me too."

Helen and I sit in comfortable silence for a few minutes before I start to get tired. I'm sure Jasper will be calling to check in soon.

I rise from my chair to head to my bedroom when I get hit with a sharp pain in my lower abdomen. It's unlike anything I've ever felt, but I know it's a cramp-like sensation.

"Ow," I grit out, slightly bent over.

Helen jumps to her feet, rushing over to me. "Are you alright?"

"Yes—ahh." It hits me again. Similar to a period cramp, but much worse. The deep pain sends a wave of nausea through me.

She's hunched over, meeting me at my level. "Avery, are you okay?"

"I think so. I don't know what's wrong," I manage to say before falling back into my chair. Suddenly, I feel a wetness in my panties. *My period? It can't be.* I took four tests three weeks ago.

"Avery, honey, you're bleeding!" Helen's frantic voice causes my head to spin. I barely see her bend down and wipe the blood off the inside of my leg with a napkin.

"The pain is getting worse." My breath is labored. I lay over the chair's armrest, unsure how I will get up.

"We need to get you to the doctor right now," she tells me.

"Stay right here. I will get you a pad and shorts." The cramps are increasingly getting worse while panic zips up my spine.

"The doctor?" I ask, worried. "Everything is okay, right?"

Her expression hides more emotion. "Just stay right here."

She's back quickly and slides both items on under my dress.

"Thank you," I whisper. "What's going on?"

"I don't know." Helen slides her arm underneath mine, lifting me from the chair. "It's a short walk to the car, honey, so don't worry. Just stay focused on getting there."

In a daze, with my vision blurry, I barely remember making it to the car—or throwing up in there on the way to the emergency room.

A quick flash of two nurses sprinting around the check-in desk to capture me as soon as my legs weaken is the last thing I see before I make contact with the cold, tiled floor.

Then everything went black.

Chapter Thirty-One

THEN

Jasper

The pounding of my heart pulses inside my ears. It blocks out everything else as I sprint down the stale, empty corridor of the hospital. Helen called me less than fifteen minutes ago. The second I heard her say the words *Avery* and *emergency room,* I ran out of the surf shop. My mind was spinning the entire way here. In my state of panic, I barely made out when she tried to explain that Avery was bleeding and they needed to find out why.

"Excuse me, sir." The attendant at the desk stops me. "Can I help you?"

Out of breath, I say, "I'm here to see Avery Thomas."

"Are you a family member?" she inquires, prepared not to let me behind those double doors.

"No—" But then it dawned on me. *We're married.* Smiling with pride and relief, I answered confidently, "Yes, I'm her husband."

"And your name is?"

"Jasper Collins."

Just then, Helen emerges from behind the automatic doors. "Jasper, honey. I'm so glad you're here."

I give her a quick hug. "Is she okay?"

The puffiness around Helen's eyes tells me this is something serious. "A little shaken up, but the worst is over."

She leads me into a long, sterile hallway. "What happened?"

"I think it's better if you speak with Avery." She frowns.

Now I'm really concerned. What could have happened where Helen can't even explain it to me?

"Okay." I swallow hard, forcing a breath through the nerves constricting my throat.

We pass only a few rooms before we get to Avery's. Helen and I round the corner to see her lying in the bed beneath mounds of white sheets and thin blankets. Her head is turned to the side, facing the night through an open window. She looks so vulnerable. It scares me.

"Avery?" I whisper her name. Her beautiful eyes slowly drag across the room until they land on me. They're laced with panic. Sadness covers her usually bright face. "Are you okay?"

"Oh, Jasper." Her body shakes, wracked by sobs. "I'm so sorry."

"I'll give you two a minute." Helen pats me on the shoulder before exiting the small room.

Taking each step in stride, I carefully walk over to my wife. I lean over the railing and press a kiss on her forehead. "What happened?"

"I lost the baby." Her voice cracks. Tears roll down her swollen cheeks.

What? My eyes rapidly blink, and my brain can't process what she's just said. "Wait. What?"

Her hand slips into mine. "I lost the baby."

"What do you mean?" I ask, confused by her wording and what this means.

"I had a miscarriage," she tells me, wincing like the words alone cause her immense pain.

How could that have happened? Avery is young and healthy. I'd only heard of these things happening to older women—and I've never known anyone in person who has experienced this. My only knowledge of when women lose a baby comes from what I've seen in TV shows and movies.

"Oh my god." My head falls into my hand. "Fuck." *My mind is spinning, trying to make sense of this. What happened? What caused it? Was it something I did wrong?* "So, the baby is gone?" I ask, fearful of her confirmation.

She nods, tears down her cheeks.

Pinching the bridge of my nose, I gather my thoughts. "How do you know? Did something cause it?"

"The doctors don't know why. They just said sometimes these things happen in the early stages of pregnancy."

I blow out a heavy breath. "When did this happen?"

Avery slips her hand into mine. "I was sitting on the back patio with Helen after dinner, and suddenly, I started getting painful cramps. And not soon after, I started bleeding." She brings our clasped hands to her chest. "Helen rushed me here."

"Oh my god." I can barely form words. My heart shatters. *How can this be? We were just planning our life together as a family.*

"I'm so sorry, Jasper," she cries.

I shake my head vigorously. "This is not your fault."

I don't know much about miscarriages or the medical side of things, but I do know this wasn't something she did. "It's going to be okay. We'll get through this." My words contradict the hurt I feel.

"Are you still on your medication?" she asks cautiously, breaking the dense silence in the room.

I whip my head around. "What?"

"You heard me," she states, but her voice is unsure. "I'm worried about you and this news."

Frustration and hurt and anger crawl up my back. *She's the one who just experienced losing a baby, but is she worried about me?* I'm her boyfriend—*husband.* It's my job to take away her pain. I'm her protector.

"I'm fine," I snap, but the walls slowly close around me.

"I'm sorry." A few more tears fall.

I immediately regret my tone. *I'm such an asshole.* I can't believe I'm getting defensive. She's been through so much. The last thing she needs to worry about is me and my unstable emotions.

Leaning in, I thread my fingers through her hair and bring my forehead to hers. "No, I'm sorry. This is a lot for me too."

Avery wraps her arms around my back, pulling me down onto her. "This is awful. I can't believe it's happening to me." She pauses. "To us."

I feel my breath become labored. *I need to get out of here.* "What can I do for you? Can I get you anything?"

"I'd love something sweet." She gives me a weak smile.

"You got it." I kiss her lightly on the lips. On contact, she begins to sob. I squeeze my eyes shut, unsure how to help her.

"When you leave, can you send Helen back in? I don't want to be alone."

"Of course," I say, grabbing the door handle. But before I twist the knob, I turn back to my new wife. "I love you."

She smiles, but the hurt is still there. "I love you, too, Jasper."

I left the hospital room with every intention of returning. But after speaking with Helen, I ended up back in the parking garage instead of the cafeteria in search of Avery's sweets. When I reach my truck, I'm in a daze. I stop right before the driver's side door.

"What the fuck!" I scream into the dark, empty garage. Bending down with my hands planted on bent knees, I inhale a heavy breath. *Fuck.* My chest tightens. *No baby? No family?*

Suddenly, my phone rings. I quickly wipe the tears from my sore cheeks.

It's my dad.

"Jasper? Are you alright?" His voice booms through the phone before I can say hello.

"Oh god, Dad. I don't know," I admit.

"I just got off the phone with Helen." He sighs. "I'm so sorry."

I wipe a hand down my face. "I'm still trying to get my head to process it."

"I'm sure. This is a tough thing." He clears his throat. "Are you at the hospital with Avery?"

"I am. Well, I was." I rub my eyes, tears fall. "I guess I still am. I'm in the parking lot."

"Are you still taking your meds?" he asks timidly.

I push off the side of the truck. "Why does everyone keep asking me that? I'm fine."

"Jasper, this is a traumatic event. I only want to make sure you're in the right state of mind to support yourself and Avery."

"I realize that, Dad," I spit. I'm frustrated by the people around me thinking I'm not strong enough to support myself—and Avery during this time.

"I know you don't like to talk about it, but both of you are going to need each other right now." I hear keys wrestling in the background. "And, of course, Helen and I will be here for whatever you two need."

"I get it," I say, climbing into the truck. "I need to clear my head."

I should go back in, but Avery has Helen, and at this point, I need to save myself from falling down an endless black hole.

"Okay."

"Are you heading over here?" I ask him.

"I'm going to meet them back over at Helen's. She wants some support in all this as well," he says.

"I'm sure. I'm going to take a drive along the coast to clear my head." I start the vehicle without a clear direction on where I'm going. "Then I'll head over there."

"Sounds good, Son. Call me if you need anything," he says before we end the call.

I toss the phone onto the passenger seat. The silence is deafening. Sadness and regret and anger bubble over. I loosen my grip on the steering wheel, swing my arm back, and punch the center console. It takes a few more good swings before I feel any relief.

Pulling out of the hospital parking garage, I'm a mess with emotions. A few more tears fall before I reach the highway. Lynyrd Skynyrd's "Freebird" comes on the radio as I plow down the dark road. In less than three months, my life has been turned upside down in the best way, and now, to have a portion of it taken away is unfathomable.

I drive for an unclear amount of time before I realize I'm at the beach house.

Pulling into the vegetation-covered driveway, I park my truck and head inside. Everything is precisely how Avery and I left it after we'd gotten married. This place doesn't even feel like mine anymore. It's a ghost of what once could have been. My family. My life. *Will Avery want to stay married now? Will we have no reason to stay together? Will this mean she'll now move to Arizona for college? I'll be losing my baby, my wife, and my future with them both.*

> Dad: Just checking on you. We're back at Helen's. Avery is asleep.

I start to tap out a quick response, but the heaviness in my chest combined with the lack of interest in communicating with another human is enough to slide my phone back into the pocket of my shorts, ignoring my dad and the rest of the world.

Chapter Thirty-Two

THEN

Jasper

Each episode, unlike the one before, I'm sent into a tailspin the last couple of days. This one came on faster than they typically do. When I arrived at the beach house two nights ago, I was going to stay for a few hours to clear my head, mourn, and then head back to Helen's to be with Avery. But I didn't. I was gutted and in disbelief, but then slowly the emotions melted away. They transformed into a painful weight pressed on my every limb, but in a way, I couldn't feel anymore.

I roll over to the side of the bed and snatch my phone from the wooden floor. I've kept it off since I got here, only checking it twice. Pressing the small button on top, I watch as my phone turns on—and with it, a slew of concerned text messages.

Dad: Where are you?

Arizona: Just got home. Your dad said you'd be here soon.

Arizona: Where are you?

Arizona: Is everything okay?

Arizona: I'm getting worried. Where are you?

Arizona: Text me back. I need you.

Dad: Got worried. Drove up to the beach house.

Dad: I see your truck here. I'll give you space. Please let me know if you need anything.

At least my dad knows now.

Arizona: Jasper? Please answer my calls or text back.

I should be bothered by her pleading, but I can't get there.

Arizona: I'm sad. I miss you.

Her words mean nothing in this moment, and I hate myself for it.

Arizona: I can't stop crying, please come cuddle me.

Dad: Avery is worried. I won't tell her where you are, because you seem to need space, but I'm only giving you another day and then we're coming to get you.

Arizona: Spoke with your dad. He reassured me everything is alright. He doesn't seem worried.

Arizona: Does he know where you are?

Arizona: Jasper, I need you. Please.

This isn't always how things go, but the more I thought about Avery leaving, the more I fell deeper into myself. When I knew she was going to move back to Arizona, my mind had already accepted it. I began looking for ways for us to still be together. Because I knew we would. But then after finding out she was pregnant and believing she wouldn't actually be going away just to face the possibly that I was going to lose something I hadn't yet been able to experience was like being submerged underwater with no way to find the surface.

Arizona: I can't sleep. I miss you.

Arizona: I feel so alone.

Dad: Twelve more hours.

He's counting down until he breaks into my house, I know it. I glance at the time and date. I haven't even been gone for forty-eight hours, yet.

I need to respond to them, but there's not enough motivation in me to do it. I drop my phone back onto the floor, then roll back on my side and yank the blanket over my head, falling back asleep.

A pounding on the door wakes me from the darkness. Unsure if it's a dream, I close my eyes again. The rapping at the door grows harder and quicker. *Maybe it's not a dream?* Is it my dad? I consider not answering it and burying my face into the thick comforter of the floor bed.

"Jasper!" I hear her yell my name through the wood, followed by another impatient rhythm.

Avery. *Avery!*

I should want to see her. I love her, but when I'm in this state, everything outside of lying in bed is nearly unbearable. I doze off for an unclear amount of time. But then, there's a banging on the glass door to the back patio.

Sucking in a deep breath, I peel myself off the floor and drag my feet over to the back door.

"What the fuck, Jasper!?" Avery storms inside the beach house. "Is this where you've been the last forty-eight hours?"

I can tell she's upset, but the fog in my brain prevents me from empathizing. It angers me to my core.

"Yes," I say, gripping the handle on the door.

"Your dad told me you were here." Avery's hair is thrown into a bun, and her eyes have dark circles underneath them.

"I figured he would," I say in an even voice.

"I shouldn't have had to hear it from him!" she snaps. "I should have known. You're my husband!

"I'm sorry," is all I can offer.

Her shaky arms fold across her chest. "How could you just leave me like that?"

My head falls as I squeeze my eyelids shut. "I'm sorry, Avery."

"You said this was something I wouldn't have to do alone." Her voice cracks with desperation. "I trusted you!"

"I know." Closing the door, I walk right past her and back to the bed. She needs comfort and wants to be held tight, but I can't find the urge to do it.

"You promised, Jasper." Tears fall from her eyes.

I drop to the floor, almost missing the side of the low bed. "I know that too."

"That's all you have to say?" she presses, losing her patience.

I want more than anything to give her what she wants. I also want to explain when these episodes take control, I feel powerless to stop them. Like those intrusive thoughts say, *what would happen if you swerved to the left ever so slightly into oncoming traffic?* But then, the rational voice always overpowers, preventing you from following through. How can I explain to her, at this emotional time, that the sensible voice inside my head is nowhere to be found?

"I'm doing the best I can." I run a tired hand through my dirty hair. "This is hard for me too."

"But if we can't lean on each other during hard times like this, how will a marriage ever work?" she counters.

My brain sends panic signals pulsing through my veins, but it simply feels like a dull buzz easily shaken off. *Fuck, I want to feel. I can't even remember what it was like to feel.*

"Everything will be fine—"

"Will it?" She paces back and forth in front of me. "Because I'm starting to think it might not be."

"It will."

"Have you been taking your meds?"

I want to tell her so badly, but the truth is—I haven't. I've been so happy that I thought I was better with everything between us. I thought I could handle it. And now that I'm thinking about it, no wonder why I'm crashing so hard right now. It's been a little over a week since my last pill, and usually, by now, I start to feel all the physical and mental symptoms much more heightened.

"I've got it handled, okay?" I snap.

"You don't." She lowers to the bed, taking the space next to me but maintaining at least a foot between us. "You're struggling."

"I told you, it will pass. It always does."

Her hands swipe the wetness under her eyes. "If we want to build a life together, I need to be able to trust you."

"You can."

"I can't."

I exhale a heavy sigh in frustration. I hate that we're going through this. I hate that I have this darkness I can't control.

"I'm sorry. I can't control it," I plead.

"Yes, you can," she spits. "You can take the medication your body desperately needs."

"It's not that simple," I mumble, resting my head in my hands.

"What do you think would happen to someone with epilepsy who stopped taking their medications?"

"It's not the—"

"They'd start having seizures again." She steps forward, then drops to her knees in front of me. "You have an illness. Treat it like one."

My head aches. "Fine, Avery."

"I needed you." Her shoulders bounce as the sobs come once again. "And you weren't there."

I wrap an arm around her shoulders, pulling her into me. She continues to cry into my chest.

Fuck.

"I lost our baby." She heaves, falling into my lap. Her face was buried in her hands. "I didn't grow up with loving parents. This was my one chance to create the family I never had, and I ruined it."

"This is not your fault."

"I never should have believed I could have a life like that," she says. "I went against my better judgment and got swept away in love and the dream that now seems impossible."

Frustration crawls up my spine. The heat is unbearable as I muster everything to fight for her. "We do love each other, and you do deserve a life that you want."

"I don't want to be alone anymore."

"You're not going to be. I'm here."

"But you're not," she mutters.

"I'm sorry." Depression or not, Avery has to choose me. Yes, I come with the constant fear of a black cloud lurking for a storm to brew. I don't know what it's like for her to be experiencing this loss, but what I do know is that I have to handle it myself as well. And right now, I have no fucking idea what to do. Defeated,

I offer her the only real thing that pumps through my veins. "I love you with all that I have."

Her neck jerks away, allowing me to catch a glimpse of her side profile. Her cheeks are shiny with moisture, and pain overcomes her usual bright hazel-green eyes. "I love you, too, but I also love me."

Fuck.

In a blur, she rises from my lap and gives me her back.

The echo of a slamming door is the last sound I hear before I drift into oblivion.

Chapter Thirty-Three

THEN

Avery

It's been a week since I found Jasper at the beach house. I haven't heard from him either. It's better this way. My heart is broken, and I can't wait to leave this town. The summer whirlwind I've experienced is enough to send any healthy person into a spiral of sadness.

"How are you feeling?" Helen asks, standing at my door.

Pulling my lips to the side, I fight against the quivering of my chin. I've cried for seven days straight. I let myself mourn. It's time to take my control back.

"As to be expected, you know?" I say, sitting on the edge of my bed.

Helen shuffles over, moving a stack of clean clothes, ready to be packed, to the opposite side of the bed. "I am just so sorry you're going through this."

She has been more of a mom to me the last couple of months than my birth mother was during my childhood.

I lean into her just as she wraps both arms around me in a

sweet embrace. “Me too.”

She sniffs a few times. “I’m definitely going to miss you.”

“I’m going to miss you too,” I say, hugging her side.

We hold each other for a silent beat before she slowly pulls away. Clutching both of my shoulders at a distance, she smiles through the sadness. “I know it will be difficult, but it is the right choice for you. It’s what you’ve wanted.”

“I’m a mixed bag of emotions,” I admit. “But yes, it’s what I need to do.”

“And to think, we almost withdrew you from the college last week,” she comments with relief.

“Yeah.” My heart clenches as I try to push off regret and the images of what might have been. “I guess I need to trust the timing of my life.”

“Everything happens for a reason, Avery, even if it causes heartache,” she adds.

I stand, then walk around to the other side of the bed to continue packing the last few things. “Seems like it.”

“Have you spoken to Jasper?” she asks timidly.

I shake my head and swipe a tear from my cheekbone. “Not since I found him at the beach house last week.”

“He knows we’re flying out tomorrow morning?” she confirms.

I asked Helen not to interfere with what was going on between Jasper and me—a hard thing to ask of her based on the relationship she has with Duke, but a necessary one for my mental health. I need a clean break. It might not be the choice someone else would make, but it’s the one I have to.

Rubbing my lips together, I imagine the calendar on the wall in his bedroom with today circled in red marker. *He knows.*

"He does."

A sigh slips through her tight lips. "Once we arrive in Phoenix, we'll pick up your car from the shipping location, then head up north, right?" she asks, clearly wanting to change the subject. I appreciate it.

"Yeah, I got the confirmation from the moving company that all my stuff was officially delivered to the storage unit on campus." I swipe up on my phone, confirming the information.

"These were not this convenient when I went to college." She chuckles. "You have been able to ship your furniture and car out there seamlessly. It's amazing."

"Beats us having to rent a moving truck and drive all the way to Arizona. Besides, I didn't want to put the miles on my new car anyway," I say.

She slaps her legs, then rises to her feet. "I'm going to let you finish packing the rest of your things. What do you want for dinner?"

I filter through all the wonderful food I've had here, living by the coast, but only one dish comes to mind that I'd like to have on my last night. "Pineapple chicken?"

Helen's smile is wide. "I would love to make that for you tonight."

My heart warms. I'm going to miss her so much. I will miss everything about this town, but I won't miss the pain that also comes with it. "Thank you."

Helen turns on her heels and walks toward the door but stops short of the hallway. She slowly faces me. "I know you've thought about this. You're such a smart woman, honey, but what are you going to do about your marriage to Jasper?"

I want to tell her nothing. I want to tell her this was all a dream and none of what happened this summer actually occurred, but it would be a lie.

The pit in my stomach grows. "Bill, our family lawyer, who has helped with my parents' trust and my inheritance payments," I tell her. My words come out like poison. "I'm sure he can get it taken care of."

A weak smile appears on my aunt's face. "That's good to know. And please let me know if you need anything through that process. I'm here to help you."

I nod. "I know. I appreciate it."

Helen has known Jasper for years. She loves and cares about him and Duke. I can't imagine how hard this is for her as well. This fantasy we were all living in completely blew up in our faces. I never expected to fall for her partner's son, but it happened. And now I have the emotional scars to prove it.

Jasper made me believe my life could be different. I could have a life of security—one where I wouldn't have to be lonely anymore. But it was all smoke and mirrors. That life does not exist for Avery Thomas. I have to accept it.

I fold a few more articles of clothing into my suitcase when I hear a rapping sound outside of the window.

Jasper? Oh fuck. I can't see him. I can't talk to him. My hands start to sweat with nerves as I walk over to the cracked slats in the window.

"Arizona?" A male's voice I recognize, but don't place right away.

"Yes?" I say, unable to see into the dark night.

"It's Easton. Can I talk to you?" he says.

Oh, Easton. Emotionally drained and barely able to keep myself from crying, I fear talking to Jasper's best friend won't help the situation. But Easton is my favorite one of the guys—he's the most caring.

Against my better judgment, I agree. "Sure. I'll be right out."

"Come around the back," he tells me.

I slip on my shoes, then walk past Helen in the kitchen. "Just stepping outside for a bit. Be right back," I say, opening the back door.

"Okay," she calls out.

As soon as my feet hit the sand, I see Easton's dark figure only a few feet away.

"Hi, Easton." My voice comes out weathered.

"Hey," he greets me as I approach him. "Sit with me?" He gestures next to him while he lowers into the sand.

I follow his lead. It feels nice seeing him again. Somehow, sitting beside Easton makes me feel closer to Jasper.

He brushes two rogue hairs away from his eyes. "How are you holding up?"

"I'm alright," I say. "It fucking sucks. This whole thing, you know?"

Easton rests his arms on bent knees. "I can only imagine."

I can't explain what comes over me, but a wave of emotions roll over me. "I love him," I say, through a spontaneous outbreak of tears. "Easton, I love Jasper so much."

His face softens. He lays a friendly hand on my shoulder. "I know. He loves you too."

"How could he just leave me like that?" I beg, craving to have answers when there aren't any I'd understand.

"I'm so sorry," Easton says. "Jasper has suffered with depression for as long as I've known him," he explains. "When we were in middle school, he'd retreat into himself for no clear reason. He'd lock himself in his bedroom and sleep for days."

I sniff. "That must have been difficult for him to understand, being so young."

"Oh yeah. Especially for Duke. He didn't know how to help him," he says, glancing over at the dark, endless ocean. "At first, he thought it was because they lost his mom, but by the time we got to high school, Duke had more information."

My heart aches for Jasper but also for myself. "I'm sorry he has had to deal with this, but what I went through—" I pause to wipe my leaky nose. "It was hard for me too."

"And I understand that," he reassures me. "Look, I'm not here to try to make you feel bad or justify Jasper's actions in any way, but he is like a brother to me, and I know how much you mean to him."

I squeeze my eyes shut, sucking in a desperate breath. "I don't know how to be there for him. It was simple when I didn't need anything in return, but I did."

"I know," he whispers.

"Does he know you're here?" I ask.

"No."

"Do you know where he is?"

"Yes."

I shove my face into my hands. "I'm only eighteen. I shouldn't have to deal with this," I complain, unable to control my emotions.

"You've been through a lot too." He empathizes in a small voice. "I get it."

With my heart pounding on the back of my chest and panic coursing through my veins, I do the only thing I know how to do—protect myself. I love Jasper, but I'm also a realist.

I straighten my posture and sniff one more time to pull myself together. "I appreciate you coming by, Easton. Jasper is lucky to have you," I say, then with bile creeping up my throat, I slide Jasper's mom's ring off my finger. "I want you to give this back to him."

Easton's eyes are as large as saucers. "Avery—"

I shake my head. "No, he deserves to have it back."

His eyebrows snap together. "I can't give this back to him. He'll be crushed."

I lick my lips, then rub them together. "I know. But I'm leaving for college—"

"And the summer is over," he finishes my thought as he knew where I was going.

I hold out the ring with a shaky hand. Easton gently takes it from me with an understanding, yet solemn expression. "Time for you to move on?"

"Yes," I admit with a heavy heart.

Easton and I share a quick, heartfelt goodbye. I hug him with everything I've got. Our embrace encompasses emotions of my farewell to Coconut Grove, this summer, and more importantly, Jasper.

"Goodbye, Arizona," Easton says, his eyes swelling.

I squeeze him one more time, fighting the tears threatening to fall. I use him to release so many things. The emotions of what

I've gone through in such a short amount of time combined with the emotions of saying goodbye to a life I would have had.

It's all too much.

Chapter Thirty-Four

THEN

Jasper

It's been almost a week since I've been back on my medication. The clouds haven't entirely lifted, but the first few hours after my first dose of the day, I get a little burst of energy—a transient effect that will level out over time, like it has many times before.

I overheard my dad on the phone with Helen, discussing Avery's decision to return to Arizona for school. That conversation ripped me open and sent me to sleep for about two days afterward.

"Jasper?" My dad knocks softly on my bedroom door. "Can I come in?"

I peel my face from the sticky cotton pillowcase. "Yes." I'm relieved when I answer that it doesn't physically hurt. *The medication is working. This episode is passing.*

My dad opens the door but doesn't walk in. I see his shadow only as he stands in the doorframe. I know it's daylight outside based on the sun shining through the slits in the shutters on each window.

"Easton is here," he tells me. "Would you like to see him?"

I roll onto my back, another activity that doesn't come with pain. *Thank god.* The fog that's clouded my thoughts is also dissipating. "Sure."

My dad nods, then walks away. He's heartbroken by the events of the last almost two weeks. What Avery and I have been going through has unintentionally strained my dad and Helen's relationship. Helen wants to support Avery, and my dad intends to help me. And as I've overheard a few of their conversations, those two things don't always align.

I pull myself up to lean against the headboard of my bed. Blinking a few times, the furniture in my bedroom looks crisper than in some time. I can make out the sharp lines and the textures of each item. Another sign is that things are passing.

"Hey," Easton greets me as he walks through my door.

I reach my arm out to shake his hand. "Hey, man."

A somber expression has taken over my best friend's face. Normally happy and going with the flow, his demeanor is unsettling.

He sits at my desk on the opposite side of the room. "How are you feeling?"

I shake my head with relief. "I'm feeling better. Thank god."

"That's good," he says, avoiding eye contact. *What's going on?*

"What's up, dude?" I bluntly ask, knowing there's something on his mind.

He leans back and rubs his palms across the top of his legs. "Have you spoken to your dad about Avery?"

My heart aches. "I did, briefly. He mentioned she decided to go back to Arizona. I'm going to try to go back there tonight. I remember she was supposed to leave in the next few weeks."

Easton's eyes dart over to the calendar on my wall, then back to the floor. "I saw her last night."

My ears perk up. "You did?"

"Yeah," he says, nervously picking at a loose piece of denim on the seam of his jeans.

A heat pulses through my veins. "And?"

"She wanted me to give you this," Easton says, reaching into his front pocket. He pulls something out. With his palm face up, my eyes land on a yellow-gold diamond ring: *my mother's—the one I gave to Avery.*

My breath hitches, and my heart shatters. "Fuck," I let out, and my head drops into my hands.

"I'm so sorry, Jasper," he mumbles. Easton steps up and puts the ring safely on my nightstand.

"What am I going to do?" I ask painfully.

With his forehead puckered with empathy, Easton rests his hand on my shoulder. "I don't know."

"You saw her last night?" I ask.

He nods. "I went to her house. We talked outside for a bit. She's broken, Jasper."

"Fuck!" I squeeze my eyes shut. "Why am I like this?"

"The whole thing sucks," he says.

"I need to talk to her." I rise to a stand on wobbly legs from spending days in bed.

Easton's hands come up to stop me. "That's the other thing—"

"What?"

"She and Helen left this morning for school." He grimaces, the words like poison to him.

"Shut the fuck up," I warn, my limbs locked in place.

"I'm serious," he tells me. "She told me last night they were catching a flight out this morning."

"What the hell? Why the fuck didn't my dad tell me?" I yell, panic whipping my back.

Easton's forehead mists. "Avery asked Helen not to tell your dad."

This cannot be happening. Heat pricks to the tips of my earlobes. This is just a fight we're having. Everything is going to be alright. Avery can't leave yet. She's not supposed to go for another couple of weeks. We have to work it out. Avery and I are meant to be together.

She's my fucking wife.

The room spins as I rush toward the door. "Dad!"

Easton is hot on my heels. I quickly turn to face him. "You knew last night? Why didn't you tell me then?"

"I tried to call you like a thousand times," he defends himself. "I know how you get during these episodes, and honestly, I thought it was just a threat. But then, when I went by her house this morning, and they were gone, I knew she was serious," he rushes out. "And then I came directly here."

Blood boiling, my heart pounding on my ribcage, I gather my thoughts. "Dad!"

I sprint toward the back door, but my dad grabs my shoulders.

"I just got a text from Helen," he says, my back to him. "I

came straight home from the shop to speak with you."

Adrenaline coursing through my veins, I shove my dad aside. "Get the fuck away from me."

I open the sliding glass door, jump down the steps, and onto the sand. Making a beeline for Helen's house, I run full speed down the beach. The hot sand burns the bottoms of my feet, forcing me to pick up my pace even more. My heart lodges in my throat until I reach the cottage's back door. Taking the stairs two at a time onto the patio, I fight to catch my breath.

"Jasper!" I hear Easton shout from the beach. He followed me.

I bang on the door. "Avery!"

My knuckles slamming into the wood.

Easton is suddenly at my side. "They left."

I bang on the door until my skin cracks. The rapping vibrates through my chest. Blood drops onto the painted white wood at my feet, but I don't care.

"Avery!" I scream, my voice more desperate this time.

"She's gone, Jasper." My dad's steady voice is now behind me as well.

Avery left me. Did everything that happened between us mean nothing to her?

She fucking left.

Tears spring from my eyes as my legs give out underneath me. I pull out my phone and tap her name. It goes straight to voicemail. I call her ten more times before I feel my dad's hand on my shoulder.

"Maybe try to call her in a couple of days," he says.

I let my head hang between bent legs and drop my phone.

"She left me."

Easton sits at my side, with his back against the house. "I'm sorry, man."

Soon, my dad takes the spot on the other side.

"What do I do? I love her," I plead to my best friend and dad for answers—ones they can't give me.

"I don't know." My dad's kind voice does nothing to comfort me. "You need to take care of yourself right now."

"I love her," I mutter. With my heart shattered and my mind facing a whirlwind of emotions, I try to think about my future, but there isn't one without Avery in it. How can I convince her to be with me? How can I ask her to choose a life with a broken person like me? I couldn't even support her during one of the most traumatic events of her life. What type of *man—husband—father* would I be if I'm incapable of putting the people I love first?

"Do you want to go after her?" Easton asks more like a suggestion under his breath.

Go after her?

But Avery chose. She wants more. *She deserves more.* She never was supposed to be a young wife and mom. Avery wants other things. She wants independence and solitude. It was selfish to ask her to marry me, and I could have done more to prevent the pregnancy. But I didn't. I was caught up in being in love. I know she is the one for me, but what if she isn't sure I'm the one for her?

I shake my head, swiping a tear from my cheek. "I can't go after her."

"Why?" Easton challenges. "Get her back. Tell her you're

sorry."

Swallow hard. "I can't."

I hear an audible sigh from my dad. "Just give her some space. You need to get your depression under control before you think about anything else."

"I thought I had it taken care of," I say.

"I know, Jasper. I did, too, but it's alright. It's going to take some time," he replies.

"I get it." Easton runs a hand through his hair. "It's just that you're my best friend, and I've never seen you that happy." He fights on my behalf. "There's more to her than just summer love."

I smile and hook an arm around my friend. "You're a good guy, Easton. Thanks for being my friend. But right now, I need to accept her leaving, which I have no idea how to do."

How do I move on? Will I ever?

Chapter Thirty-Five

Now

Avery

"Breakfast?" I ask, running my hand through Jasper's hair.

He flips the cotton bedsheet from over his head. "I think I've just had my breakfast." He emerges from between my legs and crawls over my torso. "But." He pauses, his lips are now on my collarbone. "I'm still hungry."

"I need real food." I giggle, grabbing his bare ass. "And I'm sure you'll need some energy if we ever want to leave this bedroom."

Jasper raises his head, arching a brow. "I have no plans on leaving this bed, let alone the room."

My belly rumbles with a laugh. I would love to stay in bed all day, our limbs intertwined with one another, but I am extremely hungry. "That sounds like the best idea, but I'm starving."

He lifts above me, looking down with a smile. "I forgot how much you eat, Arizona."

Every time he calls me *Arizona*, it hits me with a cyclone of emotions. "I can eat a lot. And with how much late-night cardio we've been engaging in this weekend, I will need it even more."

"You got it." He lowers to kiss the tip of my nose before pushing off the bed. "I'll order us breakfast and then pick it up after I catch a few waves."

"That sounds perfect," I say, sitting up. I pull my legs close to my stomach, keeping the sheet around my breasts.

"Don't hide those," he playfully warns, grabbing at the edge of the sheet.

Laughing, I fall backward, holding the cotton in place. Jasper crashes down on top of me, capturing my face between his two hands. "I don't want to leave."

"I'll be right here when you get back." I lift my head and kiss his inviting lips.

"Promise?"

"Of course."

He rolls off me, grabs his pants from the floor, and slides them on. "Be back in a few."

"I'll be waiting," I answer in a high tone, flipping onto my back.

Jasper takes off down the stairs, but not before turning to flash me a knee-buckling wink.

Once I hear the front door shut, I pop out of bed and head for his closet. I'm craving everything about him. My body yearns to be bathed in his scent like it used to be. I finger through his collared shirts, board shorts, and sweaters before I find a simple white button-up. Gently, I pull it off the hanger, then slip my arms through. Bringing both sides of the shirt up to my nostrils, I inhale deeply. Every ounce of my being electrifies under the heavenly nostalgia.

Wearing nothing but his shirt, I make my way around his room. I scan every area of the place he's been for so many years. The endless nights I stayed up wondering how he was. I thought about his life and whether he'd gotten married or had kids.

I jump at the loud ringing of my phone on the floor to the side of his bed. Scurrying over, I don't think twice about who it could be and instead bring it to my ear.

"Hello," I answer.

"What the hell, Avery?" Booms the masculine voice on the other end.

Dave.

I cautiously sit on the side of the bed and cross my pantiless legs as if he can see me. "Oh, hi. Dave."

"That's it? Just a *hi*?" he growls. "I didn't hear from you again! I almost called one of your friends."

My eyes drift out the open window, falling onto the steady ocean waves. *Stability.*

"I'm sorry," I say. "It's been harder being back than I expected."

"What the hell does that mean?" he snaps. The anger in his voice is unmistakable.

I sigh, then pause for a moment to gather my thoughts—and words. "There are a lot of memories here—"

"Oh my fucking god," he interrupts me. "There's another guy, isn't there?"

I swallow. "Look, Dave—"

"Don't, Avery. I know where this is going."

Panic shoots up my spine. I care for Dave. He's stable, and I can count on him. There's an unspoken agreement between us. We're transactional and that works for me.

"There's no one else. Everything is fine." I sigh, rubbing my eyes. "It's just been an emotional weekend. Well, week."

"What does that even mean?"

I lift off the bed, still in Jasper's shirt, and walk back to the open window. Closing my eyes, I let the salty mist pepper my face. It feels good, but it also feels like heartache. "This town holds a lot of memories. That's what I meant when I told you I have unfinished business out here."

"I'm trying to be understanding."

"I know. I appreciate it."

"As long as there's no other guy getting time with *my* fiancé, especially when she should be here supporting me, I can give you the space."

"It's not that I need space from *you,*" I begin. But then I quickly realize it doesn't matter how I explain things to him. He won't fully understand. No one can. I need to get this wrapped up with Jasper to leave this place and return to my secure, controlled life. "Thank you, Dave. I'm sorry I've been distant. I'll try to catch a flight out tomorrow."

"I don't want you to leave sooner than you need to. Besides, tomorrow isn't even our day together anyway. I'd like you to finish whatever you need to do, so it doesn't come into our marriage."

His comment makes my skin crawl, but I shake it off. "That's fine."

"Good, I'm glad we're both back in agreement." His voice is stern. It catches me off guard, but I get it. I'd be annoyed if I were him.

"We are."

Dave and I say a quick goodbye, and then I toss my phone onto the bed. A quick glance at the ocean behind me, I reassure myself this is for the best. I must close this chapter for good. My little escape from reality is over.

I stand in the window, enjoying the sea breeze for some time before I hear Jasper's footsteps on the wood staircase. My stomach twists with what I must talk to him about—*playtime is over.*

I need my fucking divorce.

"Look at you," he says, holding a take-out bag. "Found my closet?"

I fight back a blush. "Can we talk?"

"It might be difficult while you're wearing that." He smirks.

My eyes flick down at my bare legs. "I'll change and then meet you downstairs?"

Jasper's expression changes slightly, sensing my distance. "Sure."

As soon as he's downstairs, I grab my clothes and dress as fast as possible. An urgency takes over my nerves. If I don't get a hold of my fantasies now, I'll be free-falling down the same bottomless hole that got me eight years ago.

I take the steps two at a time and round the corner into Jasper's kitchen to find him standing behind the island, where our breakfast takeout awaits.

"Check out this spread." He extends his arms like he's presenting a meal he cooked himself. *It's fucking adorable.*

Keeping my head down, I approach one of the high-top

chairs. I grip the leather's back to release some tension but fail miserably. I suck in a breath and blurt out the next four words, "I need a divorce."

Jasper's head drops. He leans over the side of the counter without responding. A beat passes, causing bile to creep up my throat. *Don't throw up. I need to let him speak first. He deserves to respond.*

"You still want a divorce?" he asks, but it comes out as an accusation.

I squeeze my eyes shut. "Yes, that's why I came back to Coconut Grove."

Suddenly, Jasper slams his hand into the granite countertop. "Did this weekend not mean anything to you?!"

"Of course it did." I pinch the bridge of my nose, holding back tears. "But it was also irresponsible."

"Irresponsible?" he repeats. "What the fuck do you mean?"

"I'm engaged, Jasper."

"No shit, *Avery*." He pushes off the counter. "I'm reminded of it every time I see that god-awful ring on your finger." He sneers. "Which is not even your taste."

I hate that he's right. "I'm sorry." I hear the sadness in my voice as it cracks under the dense pressure of my emotions.

"Why can't it be us?" he begs, pain woven into his words.

I pause, mustering up the courage to spill everything I've felt for years—the reasons why it couldn't be all those years ago, the reasons why it can't be now. "Please, just sign the papers so we both can officially move on with our lives."

"No." Jasper quickly rounds the corner of the island, stopping only a few feet away from me. "My life has been on hold since I showed up at Helen's house that morning looking for you, only to discover you were *really* gone."

"Like you were surprised!" My patience is growing thin.

We're back there now.

We're back to that day all those years ago, finally addressing what we never did.

Maybe this is the closure we both need.

"Yes! I was gutted. I lost my baby, my wife, and my entire future in a couple of days." His hands clasped behind his head. "You threw me aside like one of your expensive shoes."

"How can you say that? I was willing to give up my entire life to be with you at only eighteen years old!"

"So was I!" he shouts. "I thought we had something special. But I was wrong. Who finds their soulmate as a teenager anyway?" he bites angrily.

"I did love you! I lost all of that too!" I scream in return. "*I'm* the one who lost our baby." I point a finger at my chest, then turn it toward him. "Not you. I have had to live with that guilt for eight years, all alone."

"That was your choice. You didn't have to do it alone." Jasper's Adam's apple bobs. "I was there! And I am here. I always have been."

"You left me in that hospital room to cry and mourn by myself," I squeak, tears spilling from my eyes. "I was fucking alone! Do you know what that feels like?"

Jasper runs his hand down his face, and his eyes swell. "I grieved alone too."

"It's not the same," I whisper. "It was my body. *My job*. And I failed."

"You didn't fail. There was nothing you did wrong. Sometimes, bad shit just happens," he argues with a softer tone.

I hear his words, but they don't scratch the surface of the trauma I've carried with me. "It changed my whole world."

Jasper's eyes lower. "I've never been the same either."

"I need a divorce." My stomach clenches. "I need to move on. From you, our baby ..." I sniff. "Coconut Grove."

"Don't do this. Please." His eyes are begging, pleading. *It fucking kills.*

"You're putting this on me like I'm the one who made this decision."

Jasper rubs the back of his neck, pacing between the counter and the dining table. "You're the one who left me."

"I had no choice. Your depression was difficult for me to understand back then. I was young." Another desperate tear rolls down my face. "But you never came after me."

Jasper's jaw twitches. "I know it was a lot. I was still trying to understand it myself. And maybe a part of me felt guilty about forcing you to carry that darkness too." He pauses, his eyes darting out the window. His struggle is written all over his sharp features. "I wanted you to choose me for all I was. Just like I chose you."

I'm barely processing our conversation. It's emotionally charged and painful. "You know where I've been since I left. And chose to stay here and move on." I suck in a desperate breath. "But I haven't. I never did."

"*I* never moved on." He takes a couple of cautious steps toward me. "My love for you has been like a ghost. It has never died." The wind is knocked out of me. My heart plummets from my chest. "And you're the one who's engaged!" Jasper's words hold disgust. I know I shouldn't be ashamed, but I am.

I purse my lips together, swallowing the hurt and guilt and fighting to protect my heart forever. "I am."

Jasper's expression darkens, hardening under the midmorning sunlight. He abruptly turns and pulls out a drawer behind him. A yellow manila envelope emerges, clutched in his hands. I stand frozen, immediately recognizing what the document is.

The divorce papers.

He rips it open, flips to the last page in the back, and removes a pen from the same drawer without making eye contact with me.

My breath halts. A dense ringing in my ears drowns out every single background noise. In what feels like slow motion, I watch as he signs his name next to one of the sticky pink arrows.

"Now leave me the fuck alone," he warns, shoving the stack of papers across the island. Then he leaves, slamming the front door and leaving me alone in his house.

I gasp, forcing a breath. Keeping myself together, I snatch the documents with shaking hands.

I take one more painful look around his house before leaving.

Chapter Thirty-Six

Now

Avery

I slam my back into the door, mirroring my confusion over a week ago when I accepted Dave's proposal. I never thought I'd be coming back from Coconut Grove feeling more unsure than I was when I left. I went to move on from Jasper, and I stupidly let him get into my head. *He got into my soul.*

My eyes scan the entirety of my dark penthouse. It looks like no one lives here. Everything is clean. The place lacks color, personality. There are no earthy tones like the crystal blue water of the ocean or the buttermilk sand dotted with small green plants and seaweed.

This is the life I've created. This life fits me more than one with him.

I shake it off, swipe a tear from my cheek, and peel myself off the wood.

"Finally, you're home. We were getting worried." I hear a recognizable woman's voice in the background. Startled, I jump back, tripping on my suitcase.

"Relax, babe, it's just me," Lina says, emerging from my guest bedroom.

"You scared the shit out of me." Clutching my pounding heart, I'm relieved it's just my best friend. "What are you doing here?"

She shuffles down the stairs in an oversized T-shirt and pin-striped shorts. "Didn't you get the building notification on your phone?"

I shake my head. "No."

Lina walks past me and into my kitchen. She removes a handle of bourbon and two glasses from the cupboard. "Or on your door cam?"

"No."

She cocks a brow and pours a shot of whiskey in each glass. "Didn't your security system alert you that your alarm was turned off?"

I roll my eyes, sighing. "Maybe. I haven't been in a good mental space since I left Coconut Grove this afternoon."

"I figured," she quips, handing me a drink. "That's why I'm here."

I stare at the amber liquid, knowing I'm about to feel much better temporarily. "Cheers to my fucked-up life."

Lina purses her lips together, humoring me. "Life is what you make it. This is your story."

We both take small sips, then walk to my couch. "Jasper signed the papers."

Her eyes widen. "He did?"

"Yeah." I nod, my chest tightening.

"The girls and I tried to give you space, but it was almost

impossible," she complains.

I chuckle. "I bet it was, but I appreciated it."

"So, spill. What happened? How are you feeling now?"

I pause, unable to answer. "I don't know. It all happened so fast."

"How did you feel being back there again?" she asks.

I sigh. "A million emotions. It's strange how it was just a small sliver of time in the grand scheme of my entire life, but it had a bigger impact than any other time before and after."

"I understand." She smiles weakly. "So, was the sex not enough to make you question everything, though?" she asks, grabbing the glass with her whole hand, like a warm coffee mug. "It literally took you two less than forty-eight hours to jump back in bed together."

"The sex was ..." My eyes find the window and the scattered city lights below. "Indescribable."

Lina rapidly blinks and throws her hand into the air. "What?"

I look away.

"How is *that* not enough to show you you're with the wrong guy?"

"It's complicated." I wave her off.

She huffs, tucking her legs underneath her. "I get it. You know how stubborn I can be."

"Yeah, let's not talk about how much you fought back against your sick love for your dad's best friend," I retort, rubbing the condensation from the side of the glass.

"We can call him Carter, now." She winks.

"Oh, is that his name?"

"Ha. Ha," she mocks playfully.

A beat passes between us as we look down at the busy city streets below.

"I have to marry Dave," I whisper.

She shrugs. "Well, you have some time."

I click my tongue. "What's that supposed to mean?"

"Look, you don't have to decide now."

"I have decided."

Lina's hand goes up. "Okay."

"You don't believe me?" I snap, straightening my back. "He's going to offer me security. And since he doesn't have my heart, he'll never be able to break it."

"I believe you, but I also know you," she counters, glancing at the tattoo on my wrist.

I feel her eyes bore into my skin. Self-consciously, I flip my wrist over and tuck it under my thigh. "Whatever. Why did you come over again?"

"To be with you." She smiles, wriggling into the cushions on my couch.

My high heels click on the tile floor as I slip through the crowded restaurant. I'm meeting everyone at *The Poppy* tonight for dinner. Piper and Jack are in town from California, Lina is bringing Carter, and I'm sure Bailey's boyfriend Mason will be there since he owns the place. A little more than a year ago, it was just the four of us girls. Now, my friends have all coupled up. I would bring Dave, but I rarely bring him to casual things like this. He's never shown much interest in getting to know my friends—and sadly, I prefer it that way.

"Avery!" Bailey's brother Harry waves at me from behind the bar.

"Hey!" I wave back, plastering a smile on my face to hide the turmoil boiling inside me.

"Everyone's outside!" he shouts, pointing to the patio, reminding me that the group is at the table he and Mason typically reserve for us.

It's been over a week since I returned home from Coconut Grove. During that time, I've worked constantly and stayed as active as possible. This is the first day I haven't traveled since the night I returned. Oddly, Dave contacted me every day when I was in Coconut Grove, but I've barely spoken to him since I returned. Even while traveling for work, he'd been distant.

I step onto the patio, crane my neck to the left, and spot my friends. Bailey sees me approach the table first. She smiles and gives me a quick hug.

"I'm so happy to see your face," she says, squishing her cheek against mine.

"Scoot over." Piper's pregnant belly pokes me from behind. "Let me into this."

I swing my arm around to hug her from the back.

"Now I'm jealous." Lina sets down her martini, gets up from her chair, and wraps her arms around us from the side.

"Okay, you four," Mason says, bringing over a plate of appetizers. "You act like you never see each other."

We all laugh at his comment, then release. While we all take our seats, I quickly greet Jack, Piper's husband, Carter, Lina's boyfriend, and Mason, standing next to the table with his arm around Bailey's shoulders.

"So, where's the dentist?" Mason asks, gazing at the eighth chair, which is next to me and empty. I'm engaged to him. He should be here with me. Suddenly, emotion from the last couple of weeks weighs heavy on my chest. *How do I tell them I don't mind? How do I tell myself that if it were Jasper, we'd never want to spend that much time apart?* I don't.

I rub my lips together, my heart still clenched inside my chest. "It's not our night tonight."

A blanket of awkward silence covers the table. The girls know about Dave and me having nights off from each other, but I don't think the guys are aware.

"What does that mean?" Jack asks, softly picking up on its sensitivity.

A server places an old-fashioned on the table in front of me. I glance at Mason, knowing I haven't ordered yet. He shoots me a friendly wink.

I smile appreciatively before taking a sip—the chilled drink leaving a warm trail down my throat. "We have an understanding that certain nights of the week, we don't see each other." The guys give puzzled looks while empathetic expressions are on the girls' faces.

"But what if the only time you're home from flying is on one of those nights?" Carter asks, his voice low. "Do you still not see each other?"

I shake my head. "No."

"And you don't mind?" Jack seeks clarification.

"No."

Everyone is silent for a beat, processing what I said and probably being grateful they aren't in a relationship like that.

Lina slips her hand over my knee, giving it a soothing squeeze. "So, Piper Moon, how are you feeling?" she asks, changing the subject.

Piper beams. "I feel really good."

"Avery, how was Coconut Grove?" Mason asks. *Can these guys not take a hint?*

I sigh, giving in to my friends. It's hard enough for me to open up to the girls, let alone their significant others. But Mason, Carter, and Jack are part of our circle now.

I rest my hand on top of Lina's, which is still comfortably placed on top of my knee. Glancing over at the empty chair to my other side, I find myself wishing Jasper was here with us.

"It was fine," I say, frustrated with myself for not being good at stuff like this. I should open up to them. Each one of my friends has been in vulnerable positions like this, and each time, the rest of us rally around to show support. *Is this what they're doing for me? Do I not need to carry everything by myself anymore?*

"Just fine?" Mason asks sympathetically.

Carter's forehead furrows. "I'm sure it was hard for you." *These girls gave them all the details. I know it.*

I straighten my posture and clear my throat. "Well, it sucked. I got married when I was eighteen, had my heart broken into a thousand pieces, and never got a divorce." I take in a breath. "I went out there to ask for the divorce, but when I got there, all the feelings came back, and my estranged and I ended up in bed together less than forty-eight hours after I arrived. He finally gave me one, but now I feel shittier and more confused than I did before I went."

Bailey lovingly looks over in my direction. "I'm proud of you, babe. It's a lot to deal with."

I clamp my eyes shut, being put on the spot, but not in the way one might think. I feel comforted by them, and in this moment, although brief, I don't feel alone.

"That's a lot," Jack comments. "Give yourself some time. I'm sure you'll figure it out."

Carter leans forward, looking past Lina to give me a soft smile. "Thank you for sharing that with us."

I breathe a sigh of relief. "Can we order food now?"

The table erupts in a rumble of laughter.

"Yes!" Mason exclaims.

As we all order our food, I spend the night conversing with my friends, who have now become my family. I feel complete, but a piece of me is still missing. Trying not to get bothered by the annoyingly cute banter between Bailey and Mason, or how it's impossible for Lina and Carter to keep their hands off each other, or how my Piper Moon and Jack seem to exist in a world of their own.

I will never have this with Dave. But I also will never be hurt again like I was. Sometimes, to keep out the bad, you must keep out the good too. A painful sacrifice I'm willing to make.

Chapter Thirty-Seven

Now

Avery

Dave's family will be on vacation in Southern France, so they've requested a short engagement. When everything is said and done, Dave and I will marry in three weeks. They have family friends who own a golf course in Scottsdale and would like to have the wedding there.

I agreed. It took me a while to send the divorce papers to my lawyer. It was a difficult decision, but I forced myself to do it. I know Dave is the safer choice. I'm not a risk taker, and he's not a risk.

Thank goodness my lawyer was on vacation with his family, so he didn't charge me extra time since the documents would have arrived later than we'd agreed on.

I pace outside in front of the bridal studio, waiting for Lina, Bailey, and Piper to arrive. A day that should be filled with excitement and champagne, but instead, there's a dark cloud looming over my every move. An exciting day for any bride, but it lacks the enthusiasm it should.

Bailey's heels click on the ground as she steps onto the curb. "What's with this rain?"

"It's not monsoon season," Piper adds as she quickly approaches us.

"I don't mind the rain," I comment, holding my arms to them. The three of us embrace.

"No hugs without me!" Lina's high-pitched voice is distant until she jogs up the sidewalk.

"Here," I say. Piper and I open our arms to let Lina in.

Lina squeezes us tight. "Okay, Avery. Let's find you the most beautiful wedding dress in the world."

Bailey glances over at me. "One that's fit for a dentist's wife."

"What does that even mean?" Piper laughs.

"I don't know. I couldn't think of anything else to say." Bailey shrugs.

We release.

"How are you feeling today?" Lina turns to me.

I twist my lips. "Good."

Simultaneously, all three of my friends look at me with unsure expressions.

Piper is the first to speak. "We're doing this?"

I never had good friends as a child, but these women are my family, *sisters*. They know me very well, better than I'd like.

"Let's go." I sigh, ignoring Piper's question.

They exchange glances, and then Lina steps forward to open the doors. The three of us enter the upscale bridal studio in downtown. Dave's mom, Christy, is friends with the owner, so she was able to get us in early even though the studio's appointments were booked three months out.

"Hello, ladies, I'm Jan." A petite blonde woman in a dusty pink three-piece pantsuit walks up. "I'll be assisting you today."

We all smile and greet her.

"Hi, Jan. I'm Avery," I say, introducing myself.

Jan flashes me a wide smile with perfectly bleached teeth. "Oh, hello, Avery! You're more beautiful than Christy lead on."

Lina flips her hair back. "Of course, a woman like that wouldn't want to acknowledge that her son is marrying up."

Bailey rubs her lips together.

Piper pats Lina's shoulder. "Okay, how about we look at some wedding dresses?" she suggested, lightening Lina's condescending comment.

"Okay." Jan pauses. "Alright, well, for what it's worth." She lowers her voice and dips her head in my direction. "Your friend is right."

"Thank you."

I take the compliment. I appreciate it. But why does it feel like one more thing the universe is doing to twist the knife about Jasper? *Dave is marrying up,* meaning he typically wouldn't deserve a woman like me.

Jan leads us into a backroom lined with racks. Each one displays beautifully designed wedding dresses.

Lina slumps over onto the white, silk ottoman. "Why is my champagne hand empty, Jan?"

Piper laughs. "Excuse our friend. It's three in the afternoon and apparently time to drink."

"I like that." Jan straightens her skirt. "You ladies are going to be fun, aren't you?"

Bailey brings an arm around me. "Do you have bourbon?"

A puzzled look crosses Jan's face. "Not here, but I can have my assistant go next door and grab some?"

"Perfect." Piper wraps an arm around my other shoulder, pushing my hair to the side. "I'll take a sparkling water."

"I do have that!" Jan exclaims before quickly nodding and scurrying away.

Lina cranes her neck over her shoulder with her palms pressed into the silk. "So, what do you like?"

I shrug. "I have no idea."

"Let's look." Bailey steps away and starts fingering through one of the racks.

"What did you wear to your wedding with Jasper?" Lina asks. Bailey shoots her a warning glance for bringing up Jasper.

Lina looks back at me. "Sorry."

"It's okay." I smile at the warm memory of that night. "I wore a black sundress and sandals."

Piper's face softens. "Oh, Avery. That's so you."

"True," Bailey adds. "What'd Jasper think about it?"

"It was his idea for me to wear black," I say, feeling the heat of Lina's concentrated stare from across the room.

"He knows you," Lina whispers.

My friends mean well. We always do when it comes to one another. But I'm not one to beat around the obvious like they do. I'd instead address the awkward elephant in the room now so we can focus on the day.

I place a hand on my hip. "Alright. I get it. It's clear you guys have never thought Dave was the one for me," I begin. "But you don't know how hard it is to move past something traumatic that's happened to you."

Bailey walks over with a dress draped over her right arm. "What about what happened to Lina in high school?"

Piper nods her head, glancing at Bailey. "And Bailey with her ex, Tyler?"

"And Piper with her upbringing and her mom," Lina comments. "We've all been through shit. Who hasn't?"

"It's not the same," I argue. My voice remains low because they're right. What my friends have gone through—what we've all gone through—changed us. "Trauma rewires your brain."

"Yes." Bailey nods affectionately.

"It makes you believe your only worth is defined by what another person thinks of you or how they treat you," Piper says.

Lina tucks a loose blonde hair behind her ear. "Or a single event."

Without realizing it, a tear rolls down my cheek.

"Oh," Piper whimpers, hooking the dress back on the rack. She walks over to me and pulls me in for a hug.

"Okay, ladies!" Jan bursts into the room. "I have whiskey!"

No words at this moment could make me feel better than those three. "Thank god." I wipe the moisture from my face, then grab one of the glasses from her gaudy decorative tray.

Once all four of us have our drinks, we raise the glasses and Piper with her water for a brief cheers before two of Jan's assistants emerge from behind ornate double doors with various styles of dresses in each hand.

"We brought you sweetheart and halter necklines," the shorter one on the right says.

The other one chimes in, with her arm extended before me. "And form-fitting, cocktail, and ballgown styles."

I take a generous sip of my whiskey, preparing to try on all these bright white dresses. They blind my eyes.

Bailey steps in to answer for me. "Do you have any that aren't white?"

The two assistants exchange confused looks.

"We have cream." Jan's voice, coming from behind us, is unsure.

Lina grimaces, hiding her face behind her cup.

I can't wear a cream dress. That might be worse than the white ones. I honestly don't know what I want. Truthfully, I'm not even sure I want this big wedding anyway. It's more for Dave's family.

"The white is fine," I say. Then I notice Jan and her assistants staring at me, possibly waiting for me to pick a style to start with.

Piper walks over, grabbing a few hangers from their hands. "We've got this. Thank you for your help."

Then Lina raises and grabs the rest of them. "We'll call you if we need you."

"Oh." Jan's surprised look tells me everything I need to know about her clientele. "Let's give these ladies some time." She claps at the two girls. "Call us if you need anything."

"*So* awkward," Piper comments.

"Thank god they're gone." I sigh in relief. "I hate being waited on."

Bailey playfully frowns. "Aww, does it trigger your privileged upbringing?"

"Ha. Ha," I retort, tossing crumpled-up tissue paper at her.

"Well, let's get this party started then!" Piper says.

Suddenly, my phone buzzes inside my purse. I hold one finger out. "Hang on," I tell them, then step to the side to answer it.

"Mrs. Thomas?"

His voice startles me. I wasn't expecting to hear from my lawyer after I mailed the divorce papers to him two weeks ago. "Mr. Fritz."

"I'm just returning from vacation and trying to catch up on everything. My apologies for not calling sooner," he says, sounding slightly out of breath.

I step into one of the small changing rooms, lowering my voice when I speak. "He signed the papers. We're all good."

"You didn't, my dear."

My heart stops. "What?"

"You never signed them."

What the fuck? "So, technically, Jasper and I are still married?" The pounding in my chest speeds up. Sweat mists my hairline.

"Yes. But lucky for you, if I overnight them back, we can have this filed by the end of the week." He plays it off, sounding more upbeat this time.

Confusion, apprehension, and panic bounce around in my mind. "By the end of the week?"

"Yes, so it shouldn't mess up anything with your upcoming nuptials in three weeks."

The walls in the dressing room move in closer, causing my breath to pick up. "I never signed them?"

He pauses. "No."

"What?"

I whip my head around to see Piper, Lina, and Bailey standing in the open door frame.

Lina's eyes are the size of saucers. "You never signed them!"

I never signed the papers.

Jasper and I are still married.

"Oh my god," I gasp, falling onto the silk tufted stool in the dressing room.

"Avery!" Bailey shrieks. "This is a sign."

I can't think straight. My mind is racing, and my heart is thumping against my chest. *How did this happen?* I know I signed them first.

"I'll call you back, Mr. Fritz." I don't wait for a response, quickly ending the call.

"What are you going to do?" Piper asks in a whisper.

"Get the fuck out of the wedding dress shop," I reply, rising to my feet.

Jan appears from her office with a wide grin on her face. "Like any of them so far?"

With the girls hot on my heels, I bolt in the direction of the front door. *I have to get of here.* I subconsciously didn't sign those divorce papers. That has to mean something.

From my periphery, I see Lina's arm dart out, grab one of the drinks, and down it. "You have been most helpful, Jan, but we really can't stay."

"All the dresses are beautiful!" Piper calls out as we're flung onto the sidewalk of the busy downtown street.

The cars pass us with speed, the pressure causing my ear drums to throb."Avery," Bailey pants, out of breath from our unexpected sprint.

I flip my hair to one side like it's going to help me form a cohesive thought. "I know. I know."

"You can't marry the dentist," Piper admits, shaking her head.

My eyes dart over to Lina, whose hands are firmly placed on her hips. "I love you, Avery, but we can't let you do this."

"It was hard enough going along with it before, but now with this?" Bailey chimes in. "It's bigger than us now."

Unable to catch my breath and with adrenaline pumping through my veins, I break down. Tears spill from my eyes. "I don't know what to do."

"Oh, babe." Lina wraps a friendly arm around me. "Yes, you do."

Bailey rests her head on my shoulder just as Piper embraces me from the front, engulfing me with love.

"We're going to miss you," Bailey whispers. "But your home is not here anymore."

"It never really has been," Lina adds quietly. Her voice barely close enough over the busy street.

Burrowing my face in Piper's neck, I take comfort from my best friends.

They're right. I have to follow my heart—even with all the risks.

Chapter Thirty-Eight

Now

Jasper

The last couple weeks have been rough. If this were a couple of years ago, I would have sunk into a deep depressive episode. Now, I've learned ways of managing it.

When I returned to my house, hours after I left Avery with the signed divorce papers she pleaded for, I wasn't surprised she was gone. Of course, I hoped she'd realized how much she loved me and how it would be a mistake for her to marry anyone else.

Avery left me for the second time, and now I'm numb to it—broken down and defeated again. She wonders why I never went after her, because I knew she wanted more. Just like now. She desires something else, and whether it's going to make her happy in the future or not, unfortunately, we're both caught in the crossfire.

I walked right into the house, got one last whiff of her scent before I knew I'd be gone forever, then headed back to the waves. I spent the entire day on the water.

"I can't believe she left again." Easton empathetically hands me a beer.

Neither can I. The past couple of weeks have been hell. I might be stronger than I was when I was nineteen, but it still cuts like a fucking knife—a gut punch that repeatedly hits whenever I'm flooded with an old memory. And now, I have more recent ones to add to the rolodex of pain.

"I know. It fucking sucks," I admit, then take a large gulp of the cool beverage.

Riley sits back in his chair, crossing his arms against his chest. "I know that you two love each other. For something to have lasted as long as it did—"

"Especially with you not seeing each other for that many years," Bodhi interjects.

"Exactly. It surprises me that neither one of you is fighting harder," Riley continues.

I grip the handle on the beer mug, bringing it to my mouth again. *It doesn't even taste good. I hate beer.* "I can't convince my wife to be with me." I wave the server over. "Can I get an old-fashioned?" I ask when she reaches the table.

Bodhi exaggeratedly rolls his eyes. "The fact is that you still refer to her as your wife—"

"She *was* until two weeks ago," I spit.

"Did you honestly think she would just stay married to you forever?" Riley asks condescendingly.

Easton shakes his head in disapproval. "You fucked up, man."

"She left me." I defend myself. I shouldn't need to. My friends were around for the aftermath of her leaving the first time. And now, I'm hanging on by a thread. "Twice."

"I'm not trying to be a broken record, because we all know

you've heard this before, but she needed you back then." Easton brings up a painful truth about our past. "What she went through was scary as hell. And before you get upset at me, yes, I remember what it did to you. I also remember suggesting to you back then you should have gone after her."

For years, I held on to a tremendous amount of regret about what happened. What my friends don't realize is that Avery is going to do what she wants to do. And even if I had tried to go after her, would she have wanted me to? What if she would have come to resent me at some point? I couldn't live with myself. I felt it was better for me to stay here and wait—for her to return or eventually get divorce papers.

"If you're trying to make me feel better, you're failing miserably." I turn to Bodhi. "A little help?"

Bodhi sips his beer, looking in the opposite direction.

I slam my hands on the table. "Fuck you guys."

"You love Arizona," Riley states matter-of-factly. "On your first anniversary, one year after my brother married you guys." He pauses, sipping his light beer. "You said the one regret you had was not fighting harder."

I'm flooded with a brief memory of the day I drove over to Helen's looking for Avery when I found out she was gone. Easton had spoken to her the night before. He thought he was being a good friend by coming to the beach house to tell me she was leaving—and he was. But the moment he handed me my mother's ring back, I knew it was over. Avery had chosen, and there was nothing I could do to change her mind.

"Here's your fucking chance, you chickenshit," Bodhi snaps, waving the server back over to our table. "I'm starving."

"You guys are not making this situation any better," I say, although my friends are right.

We order an unnecessary number of appetizers and take turns talking about our jobs before the conversation comes back to Avery and me.

"I heard about the run-in you had with Melanie and Avery," Easton mentions with a snug look.

Bodhi takes a bite from his poke bowl. "When did this happen?"

"When she was here a couple of weeks ago. We all sort of ran into each other at Marv's," I say.

Easton chuckles. "You mean when you followed her and Helen to dinner?"

Riley clenches his jaw, smirking. "Why am I not surprised?"

"You three are starting to piss me off with all this shit-talking," I threaten, tossing my napkin on the table.

"Good," Bodhi quips. "Get your fucking girl."

"Don't you think I would have done it already if it were that easy?" I retort. "I can't force her to be with me."

"Look, I hear you." Riley's arm extends across the table. "But you've dated off and on for years, and no one has come close to Avery."

"She's the only one we liked too," Eason adds.

Bodhi rubs his jaw, his eyes facing upward. "I liked Melanie."

"No, you didn't," I correct him.

He shrugs his shoulders. "She was hot."

Easton nods his head in agreement. "Yeah, you could be with her. Who knows. She could be the next future Mrs. Collins."

"Mrs. *Mayor Collins*," Riley jokes.

The thought of any other woman having my last name makes me feel sick. It was Avery's first, even though she never formally changed hers.

"Absolutely not," I say, swirling the spherical ice around in my old-fashioned.

"Why not?" Bodhi presses.

Annoyed once again, I huff in frustration. "Because she's not Avery!"

Fuck. They're right. There will be something wrong with every woman I try to be with—none of them will ever be Avery. I will continue to find reasons why they aren't for me, listing all their imperfections.

I was clear with my intentions that day in my kitchen. Was it enough? Does she need me to make up for my absence that day in the hospital? I don't know. But what I've done until this point has not allowed me to move on. And with what happened between us when she was here, is there any indication about where her heart is? That should be my answer.

I swam the last of the whiskey from my glass and slam it onto the table. "I'm going to go to Arizona."

"Are you going *to* Arizona, or are you going to *get* Arizona?"

My eyes narrow. "*Get*. I'm going to get her."

"Finally," Easton comments, wiping a hand down his face.

I give him a quick fist bump and say an even quicker goodbye to Riley and Bodhi. "I'll keep you guys updated."

By the time I exit the restaurant, I'm already on my phone looking up flights to Phoenix.

Chapter Thirty-Nine

Now

Avery

Fuck. Fuck. Fuck. I can't believe what I'm about to do. I thought about it constantly all night. Sleep was not going to happen, so I just gave up, spending the entire night staring at my dark ceiling and listening to the air conditioner hum when it turned on and off.

When I left the girls yesterday at the wedding dress studio, they had more than enough questions to make my head spin. To appease them, I said I needed time and would speak with them in a few days. But knowing my friends, they'll be banging on my front door soon. I can't tell them what I'm about to do. I need to do it fully on my own.

"Hello, my bride." Dave answers on the first ring.

"Hey." I nervously scratch my forehead. "Are you free for dinner?"

"Uh, yeah. It's not our night, though." The running water is in the background, and the distant sound of his voice tells me he's still at work.

A bit of our relationship the girls always give me a hard time about. They've never been comfortable with Dave wanting to be alone twice a week. It never bothered me because I never had that *need* always to want to be with Dave. The more I thought about it, the more I realized it was strange.

"I know, but I need to talk to you about something," I say straight out. It's no use being cryptic.

He sighs, pausing briefly before responding, "What is it now?"

"Can we meet at the pizza parlor down the street from my building?" I ask, understanding his frustration but choosing not to bring attention to it.

"You're not going to tell me?" he presses, his voice clearer this time. Maybe he stepped away from one of the patient rooms and into his office.

"I'd rather just talk about it in person," I say, anxious that he'll continue to push back.

"I can come by your place when I get off work," he offers. I'd rather be in a public place. Not because I'm scared of Dave but because I want to keep things clean cut and to the point.

I think of something on the spot. "It's a new restaurant, and I've been wanting to try it for some time." *Not completely a lie.* "I figured this would be a good opportunity."

"That's fine," he replies with a clipped tone.

I don't blame him for his feelings. I'd feel discontented as well. I've put him through a lot in the last few weeks. Hopefully, getting what I need off my chest will comfort us both. I'm ready to move on from the previous eight years, and my patience is growing thin.

"Thanks, Dave."

"I'm just finishing up with my last patient, and then I'll head over there," he tells me.

"Okay, see you—" Dave instantly cut off my words by hanging up the call. I squeeze my eyes shut and fall back onto my couch, not bothering to call him back.

Over the next hour, I drift in and out of sleep, passing the time before I'm sure Dave has left his clinic. I peel myself off the couch and head directly into the kitchen. Taking a sharp left and turning toward the wet bar, I grab a bottle of bourbon. Forgoing a glass, I take a swig right from the top. The warmth rolls down my throat, eventually coating my stomach.

"That's better," I whisper to myself, smiling down at it as I would an old friend.

With extra courage, I slip on my shoes, swipe my keys off the counter, and head out the door.

As soon as I round the corner in front of the pizza parlor, I see Dave leaning against the hedge next to the entrance. We make eye contact. He nods quickly and pulls me in for a stiff hug. He suspects something is up.

"Thank you for meeting me," I say, brushing off the nervousness whirling in my stomach.

"Yeah, sure," he murmurs, leading me into the restaurant.

The hostess escorts us to a corner table by a window.

Dave and I take the seats on opposite sides.

"Thank you," I say taking the menu from her.

Dave opens it and closes it quickly. "I guess I'll be getting pizza."

I chuckle uncomfortably at his sarcasm. Dave isn't an

informal guy. He would feel more comfortable sitting in a dress-coded, white table linen establishment.

"I think I'll start with the salad and then get a personal cheese pizza," I tell him, making small talk.

He nods silently and doesn't speak until the server comes over to take our order. When Dave and I are alone, he places his elbows on the table and clasps his hands beneath his chin.

"Okay, let's get this over with," he says. "What's going on now?"

I practiced explaining everything to him at least a dozen times in my bathroom mirror, yet in this moment, I find myself at an utter loss for words. Suddenly, I'm second-guessing how to tell him and if I should say anything. *Does it benefit to know more details, or is it better to be straight to the point?*

I suck in a heavy breath. "I want you to know, I think you're a great guy and—"

He jerks his head away, pushing back in his seat. "Oh my god. Where is this going?"

Maybe not the best way to approach this conversation—very cliche, but it's not like I have much experience with this. Speaking from an honest place is all I can do.

I curb my patience, reminding myself he'll need time to process what I'm about to say. "Can I finish?"

"Continue." He waves a hand in my direction.

I take in a breath and start again. "I've been thinking lately that I want to take some time for myself."

"What does that mean?"

He's going to make me say it. "I don't think we should get—"

"Are you actually doing this?" He cuts off my thought.

"Look, Dave—"

His palms fly into the air between us. "Save it, Avery."

"Can you just let me talk?" I snap, sitting straighter.

"I already know what you're going to say."

"Well, if you already do, it shouldn't shock you," I reply.

He crosses his arms at his chest, taking a defensive posture. "Are you just trying to call off the wedding, or are you breaking up with me?"

Rubbing my lips together, I glance around the room. My eyes darted from one couple in love to the other. It looks like they can't get enough of each other, with most sitting close and even cuddling in this romantically lit restaurant.

I've never felt that way with Dave.

"I think both," I grimace.

"Both?" He scoffs, arrogance taking over his expression. "My mother was right about you."

Wait. What?

I can't engage with her unkind comments. We'll lose track of what I'm trying to do. "I'm sorry she was right about me," I offer, trying to keep our conversation civil. "I just—"

"So, what's wrong? What happened?" he asks more like a statement rather than seeking to understand.

Here's my time, to be honest. Tell him everything. *Deep breaths.*

"The thing is, Dave, I've never been able to give my heart to you fully." I pause to gulp a generous sip of my old-fashioned that was just placed on the table. "You did nothing wrong. It's not you."

"Then what is it?" he pressures.

"We both deserve to be able to give our whole heart to someone, ya know?"

"That's what I thought we did." His eyes soften slightly. "I care for you, Avery."

"But are we really in love?" I ask. "Or has it been just something easy?"

"That's what I need," he replies matter-of-factly. "I need a wife who wants her own space and isn't overly emotional about things. You're never bothered when I work late or if I'm grabbing a beer with my friends." He goes on to attempt to list my positive qualities, but they only act as a reminder that I've never been completely invested in this relationship.

"Aren't couples supposed to *want* to spend a lot of time together?" I challenge. A brief silence settles between us as our food arrives. We both take a few bites before I decide to continue. "It's not fair of me to marry you, knowing I don't feel that palpable tension and desperation to be with you. You as well, apparently."

He tosses his napkin into his lap. "People aren't really like that. Marriage is transactional. It's a partnership in life and not about that romantic stuff you see in movies and TV." This is Dave. A perfect summation of his view on life and love. But I know marriage can be so much more.

I ignore his condescending comment. "Dave, I want to be madly in love with the man I'm married to, and I want him to be madly in love with me."

"At some point, maybe we will?"

What? No. That's not how love should be. I'm getting nowhere with these points because none of them would be deal-breakers for him. I need to be more honest than I want to be.

"I can't marry you because my heart already belongs to someone else." Even with the confidence I try to elude, my words still appear insecure and small. Shoving my hands underneath my legs, I wait for his response.

Dave stiffens. His jaw clenches, and he leans forward as if not hearing me clearly the first time. "Fuck, Avery."

The emotional weight of the past eight years crushes my chest, forcing a breath. "I gave my heart away long ago, and he's never given it back."

"Does this have to do with your trip to California?" he accuses, the vein on his left temple being more pronounced than before.

I promised myself I'd tell him the truth. Some details will stay with me, but he deserves to know the rest. *I'd want to.*

"Yes." I nod, swallowing hard. "So, the reason why I had to fly out there was because I'm already married."

The color drains from Dave's face. "What?"

"I got married when I was eighteen. Right after my parents died."

"And you've been married this whole time?"

"Yes," I admit but quickly explain more. "But we haven't been together or even spoken with each other since then."

Dave's head falls back as his hands come up to cover his face. "Don't you think this is something you should have said a year ago when we started dating?"

Valid question. "Yes. But we were just casual most of the time when we were together. It only just recently became serious—"

"After I proposed?"

Nodding, I rub my lips together. “Yeah.”

“I don’t even know what to say right now,” I say, dropping his fork into the salad bowl. “I need to get out of here. I need to process this.”

My chest is tight. Despite my feelings toward Dave, this is a very difficult and emotional situation for both of us. “I’m so sorry.”

“It’s fine,” he rushes out, trying to maintain his composure. “Can I have my ring back?”

“Yes,” I say. A tear of sadness rolls down my cheek. I bring my arm up to the table to remove it, but from the corner of my eye, I catch Dave’s arm extending. He clasps my hand in his. Staring down at the beautiful pear-cut diamond on my finger, a flash of sorrow changes his expression.

“This is a beautiful ring,” he mumbles, slipping it off my finger.

I smile. “It really is.”

A bit of sadness moves through me as Dave takes his ring back. It’s a bittersweet feeling. The possibility of a loveless, secure future is still difficult to pass on. I’m sure for other women, it would be a clear decision, but a broken heart changes the way a person thinks and acts—especially how they view the world.

Society places this invisible barrier on kids in love. We’re taught to believe it can’t be real until you’ve reached some ambiguous number and are deemed ready to be in love.

I know without a doubt that what I experienced with Jasper that summer on the beach was love. We made memories by the shore that changed who I was.

I loved him then as I do now.

Chapter Forty

Now

Jasper

When I signed the papers in front of Avery that morning in my kitchen, I quickly noticed her address on the upper right-hand side of the document. I wasn't sure at the time why I slid one of the extra copies into my drawer, but I'm glad I did because now I have the address for her penthouse.

I caught the first flight out this evening. I've waited eight years. I could have waited until tomorrow, and it would have saved me from having the last seat on the flight, which, of course, was in the middle. I knew I'd get nervous and change my mind if I delayed this any longer.

Now, four hours later, I'm in Phoenix, Arizona, on the way to her place. I'm not sure if she's *actually* home, and my decision to leave abruptly was purely rash, but I had to do it.

"Here, sir?" the driver asks, pulling to the curb outside a tall residential building in a bustling part of downtown Scottsdale.

I'm trying not to think of the outcome and only live in the moment because that's precisely what I did the summer I met Avery. She changed my life.

I did book a hotel room nearby in case she's not home on my first attempt. I plan to come by every day until she is.

"This is it," I say, glancing up at the nine stories before us.

"Love this part of town," he comments as I pay through the app.

I nod, climbing out of his SUV. "Looks nice."

"All the rich finance guys live down here."

That's nice. I purse my lips together in a tight smile. "Okay, well, thanks for that."

I give the driver my back as he peels away, and then I turn my sights on the locked glass doors in front of me. It looks like I will need a key card to get in. But to my luck, I only have to wait a few minutes before a group of people chatting loudly walks up the entrance. I'm able to sneak into the building behind them. The lobby is wide open and looks expensive. A stark contrast from the simple life of Coconut Grove.

I hop into the elevator and stare at the endless buttons. I find a set of six at the top, each with a number and a capital "P" at the top. I know Avery's is Penthouse 3 based on the divorce papers. With confidence, I hit P3 and watch nervously as the doors close.

My breath halts until the chime alerts me that I've reached her floor. The automatic doors open, and I face a short hallway with a large window on the left. I step out and walk toward two black double doors with a small camera on the right side. *She'll know it's me.* Flipping up my hoodie, I attempt to hide my face even though this might appear creepy. I'll give it a shot.

I knock on the door a few times, then ring the bell—*no answer.* I switch between knocking and tapping the bell. Not ready to give up for the day, I continue for an ambiguous amount of time.

After repeatedly knocking and ringing, I decide to give up for the day. *Maybe she's traveling?* Suddenly, the elevator opens behind me. Heart pounding, I whip my head around, half expecting it to be her.

"Whoops," she says. "Wrong floor."

"Actually, I'm headed down," I tell the woman, slipping into the elevator. She's young and looks about our age. *Maybe she'll know Avery?*

"Do you live in this building?" I ask.

She gives me the side-eye. "I'm not going to tell you if I live here. You're a stranger." I sense a playful tone to her voice.

"Sorry, let me introduce myself," I offer, extending my hand. "I'm Jasper. I know the tenant in P3."

Her eyes widen. "Oh, Avery?"

I knew it.

I turn to face her fully with a warm smile. "Yes. We go way back."

"Of course you do." She rolls her eyes. "Avery always gets the good-looking guys."

Shoving my hands in my front pockets, I lean against the railing in the elevator. "She gets a lot of guys?"

The woman puts a hand on her hip. "She did until she started dating the dentist last year." She continues to be forthcoming with information. "But the odd thing is, I don't think she's that into him."

I can't help but feel a flush of satisfaction when I hear that. "Interesting," I breathe out. "I'm trying to surprise her. Do you happen to know where she is?"

"Oh yeah! I just ran into her and her fiancé at the pizza place a block from the apartment."

She's with him. Why did I hope that her weekend with me left her with the relaxation that something was missing? *Did she not tell him she slept with me? Maybe it was a test that I didn't pass.* Avery and I have incredible sex. It wasn't that.

"A block down, you say?" I confirm. A slow pit grows in my stomach.

The doors open.

"Yeah, when you walk out of the lobby, take a right, then it's about two or three restaurants down." She points out of the doors in the direction she wants me to take.

"Thank you," I toss over my shoulder, jogging through the lobby. Not sure why I'm running.

In the distance, I hear her call out, "What was your name again?"

I don't turn around, ignoring her as I enter the warm evening air. With purpose, I dart around the crowds on the sidewalk, passing a Greek restaurant and a small café before I see the pizza parlor's white-and-red-checked tablecloths.

I stop before I reach the small outside patio to collect my thoughts. *I have no plan. What am I going to do? Profess my love for her in front of her fiancé?* Fuck. Maybe I'll just confirm it's her, then come back in the morning now that I know she's in town and not working.

My palms are clammy in this desert heat. I'm not used to it. *How do people live here?* I swipe a few drops from my moist hairline, then creep around a bush and peer into the restaurant through one of the floor-to-ceiling windows. Scanning the place, it only takes me a second to find her.

My heart leaps from my chest. I spot Avery sitting at a small two-seater table in the corner. A guy in a buttoned-up collared shirt and a blindingly expensive watch is positioned across from her, rolling her massive engagement ring between his fingers.

She's laughing.

It's a gut punch. I rip my eyes away, ready to claw them out. *They look happy. She looks happy.* The woman who was my wife first. The woman who chose me to give herself to that night at the beach house. I loved her then. I've loved her since. But I didn't fight for her. I didn't follow her to Arizona. I never got on that plane to chase after her. I was a young kid back then, but what was my excuse in the years that followed?

Fuck.

Crouching behind this bush, I try to hide myself. The visceral feelings of regret hit like they never had before. *Did I think she'd wait for me for this long?*

It's my fault. I wanted her to *want* me as much as I wanted her. I've been blinded by the fear of her one day regretting giving up her life to stay in Coconut Grove, and I lost track of what was important to me.

It's not fair for me to fight now. All I ever wanted was for her to be happy. Now it seems she is.

Chapter Forty-One

Now

Avery

The world is complete with colors of bright blue and deep green. The sun holds many different hues of yellow, and the open and fresh sky welcomes me as I drive down the coast from the airport to the small town that's done nothing but make the biggest impact of my life.

As the sun sets over the horizon, I pull my rental to the side of the street. I hope he's home. I had Lina call the mayor's office this morning using a disguised voice to make sure he didn't have any events this evening. He doesn't. Which means he's probably out on the water behind his house.

With a steady calmness washing over me, I step onto the ground. I close my eyes and let my nostrils absorb the warm, familiar ocean breeze. I'm done fighting against this town.

When I was sent to live with Helen, I was a lonely young girl lacking a sense of belonging and authentic love. It might be difficult for someone who didn't grow up how I did to understand a story like mine or why I decided to marry a guy

I barely knew at only eighteen years old. But I wasn't living for anyone else. I was finally living for myself.

A loud silence fills the narrow streets as I walk up to his doorstep. Knocking on the door a few times, I'm surprised I still haven't been hit with nervous energy. My limbs are all relaxed. They move smoothly.

As most eighteen-year-olds, Jasper and I were impulsive and stupidly in love. The hurt that I experienced that summer was unlike anything I'd ever want someone to feel. Or maybe if they had, they would have made different choices. Maybe someone else would have accepted Jasper for his flaws or knew how to handle them. But I didn't grow up with healthy role models, people who cared or took the time to educate me on the world. I was born into a life where I was at no fault of my own.

I deserve a life of love and trust. I don't know what the future holds, but what I do know is that it has Jasper in it. There is no world without him. I don't exist in any universe without the boy who taught me what unconditional love is, a boy who only wanted the best for me, a boy who stole my heart and refused to give it back. A boy who became a man which I desperately want to call my own forever.

After a few minutes without an answer, I decided to walk around the back. As I walk past the back patio, I glimpse the space next to the back door, where his surfboard is usually propped against the wall. *He is on the water. I know him so well.*

My eyes make a full rotation around and quickly spot Jasper with his surfboard tucked under his arm, walking through the sand toward his house. His wet hair drips in front of his face while his head is angled toward the sand at his feet.

My pulse quickens, causing my heart to skip a beat. It only takes him a few steps until he sees me. I gulp. *Will he be happy to see me or turn me away?*

He approaches with a puzzled yet hardened expression.

"I already signed the papers." He walks past me, avoiding eye contact.

"Jasper?" I say, turning on my heels to face him.

Water drips down Jasper's defined shoulders as he pauses. "There's nothing else left," he mumbles, then takes the steps two at a time on the back patio.

"Jasper." His name rolls off my tongue like I'm begging for a basic need. I follow, right on his heels. "Would you please talk to me?"

He stops, then turns to face me with his jaw clenched, a million emotions painted on his face. *He still loves me.* "I have nothing to say to you. It's over. It's done. I gave you what you wanted. We're all good. You can move on with your fucking life. And your fiancé, which I saw you so happy with yesterday."

He saw me yesterday? How? Suddenly, what I had to say could wait. I need an explanation of what he's referring to.

"What are you talking about?" My eyebrows pinch together with confusion. "What do you mean you *saw me yesterday*?"

Jasper forcefully tilts his board against the wall. "I flew to Phoenix, Avery. I went to your house to say that I'm sorry for never coming after you."

"You came to my house yesterday?" I repeat in disbelief. "I had no idea."

"Yeah, you should probably get your camera fixed if you didn't even know," he snaps.

"When did you see me?"

"I ran into a woman in your building who knew you. She said she saw you and your fiancé at the pizza place down the street," he exclaims in frustration.

"You saw me with Dave?"

His eyes lower. "I don't need to know his name."

"Jasper," I say softly. "It wasn't what it looked like."

"You two looked pretty cozy." His eyes flick to mine before he opens the backdoor. "You shattered my heart once again. I gave you what you wanted. Now leave me alone."

I can't help the smile that pulls at the corner of my lips. "I didn't sign the papers."

Jasper's body stiffens. "What?"

"I didn't sign the divorce papers." I rush up the steps to him.

His face is weary but curious. The dusk glow highlights every curve, including his defined jawline. "What do you mean?"

"I got a call from my lawyer a few days ago. He told me I sent them in without my own signature."

"And?"

"We're still married," I whisper, bringing my fingertips to his bare chest. His skin pebbles under my light touch.

Jasper sucks in a breath. "So, that means you can have one last fuck session with me and don't have to feel guilty about it?"

The steady rise and fall of my chest do nothing to help curb the intoxication I feel from standing this close to him. "It means I don't want to get divorced."

Still putting the pieces together, Jasper is silent for a moment.

"What about your fiancé?" he asks cautiously. The back of his knuckles finds my cheek. He caresses me tenderly.

I lean into his touch, craving it more than water. "When you saw me at the restaurant yesterday, I was breaking up with him."

Relief that's palpable washes over Jasper as he sucks in a heavy breath of air. "You were leaving him?"

I nod, smiling sweetly. "Yes."

"And what does that mean for me?" Jasper's other hand meets my face.

"It means no one else exists," I say.

"No one else has ever existed." He rubs his nose against mine. "You were my first and only love, Arizona. When I met you, I was young and knew nothing about how to be a partner, but what I did know was that I never wanted to live without you. My love for you is both steady and chaotic, just like the Pacific." He slowly glides his fingers into my hair. Threading them through, he fists a handful. With a gentle tug, my head tilts upward. "Say you're mine."

"I'm yours." With my eyelids filling with moisture and my heart in a death grip, I release those two words like I'm taking an oath.

His eyes leave mine for a quick glimpse down to my lips and back up. "That's better."

"You were my first love, Jasper." My voice cracks. "Your touch, your laughter, and your commitment are the only things I know are real in this world. I'm sorry I didn't understand how to support you either, but I plan to spend the rest of my life learning how because I only want to live for us."

Jasper's mouth comes crashing into mine. A kiss more desperate and promising than any other before it. His tongue finds mine, weaving into my mouth and mapping like it's his own. I swing my arm around the back of his head, pulling him deeper into our embrace. I never want to let him go ever again.

"I love you, Avery," he mumbles.

Tears stream down my face, but we stay connected, and somehow, I make out the words, "I love you too."

A small chuckle rumbles through his chest before he releases my hair then slips both palms to my cheeks. Our gazes remain locked.

"This is it," he tells me. "No going back. No running away."

I shake my head through a smile filled with tears. "Never. I'm never leaving you."

His expression showing signs of either shock or disbelief. I haven't figured it out yet. "And you're moving back to Coconut Grove?"

I thought about this constantly the last twenty-four hours. And the real question that I should be asking myself, which should have been addressed many years ago. *Are Jasper and I going to be a moment or a lifetime?*

"Yes," I say with a confidence that bleeds from my soul. "I don't want us to be a small moment in time. I don't want our memories by the shore to be only that—memories." I lick my salty lips. "I want us to be a lifetime."

For only the second time I've seen tears fall from his eyes, Jasper blinks, forcing a single drop to escape from under his eye. "A fucking lifetime."

I fall into him, letting his body engulf mine in an all-encompassing, future-building, panty-dropping kind of way. He holds me tightly.

His lips graze across my collarbone. "Arizona?" he whispers

into my skin.

The light dusting of his breath leaves goose bumps in their path.

"Yes," I breathe out, my knees weaken.

"You need to change your last name," he gently demands, slipping his hand underneath my dress and gliding up my leg.

I giggle. "I know."

"Oh, and Arizona?" he whispers, caressing the thin cotton barrier between us.

I swallow hard, bucking into him. "Yes?"

"Take off your clothes," he growls, diving a crooked finger into the wet heat between my legs.

"It would be my pleasure, Mr. Collins." I smile.

I'll never be alone again.

Epilogue

Six Months Later

Jasper

"Don't tell me how to decorate the tree," Avery plays, adding another ornament too close to a group of others.

Wrapping my arms around her, I reach over and remove the shiny red ball from her hands. "How about you go make us some drinks, and I'll finish the tree."

"Mr. Collins." She clicks her tongue. "I never would have suspected you to be one of *those* people."

I furrow my brow, leaning in to kiss the soft tip of her nose. "Who are *those* people?"

She giggles, tucking herself under the crook of my arm. "People who take tree decorating very seriously. You know, the ones who get bothered if the ornaments are clustered together when other parts of the tree are empty?"

"You mean basic symmetry?"

Avery rolls her eyes, ducking her head underneath my extended arm. "It's supposed to be fun. There shouldn't be order to it."

"You feel very passionately about it, don't you?" I smile.

She shrugs. "Growing up, we always had professionals come in to decorate our Christmas trees. I was never able to do it."

Now I feel shitty. "Well, when you put it that way. Go crazy."

She laughs, spinning on the balls of her feet. "I love telling you stories of my childhood that make you feel guilty."

"You're good at that, aren't you?"

"It was normal life for me," she plays.

Avery slowly starts to accept herself and her childhood for what it was. I love that we can now tease each other about it. It brings light to a situation that wasn't ideal for her. We're now replacing all she was missing. I will continue doing it for the rest of my life.

"Not anymore," I reply.

Avery smiles warmly. "I'll go make us a drink."

"Perfect."

I continue evenly placing the red and white ornaments on the tree that sits in the main living room of my beach house. Now that Avery has officially moved back to Coconut Grove, we're searching for a larger home. Her good friend, Piper, convinced her to keep her high-rise apartment like she did, so we'll have a place when we visit Arizona.

We've been back once a month since she moved here. She can't stay away from those girls.

"Hey, babes!" I hear Avery's excited voice from the kitchen.

They're probably Facetiming again. I'm happy Avery found her circle. I've always had the support of Easton, Bodhi, and Riley—my brothers whom I grew up with. But Avery didn't have that as a child and now, to experience this type of friendship as an adult, it's irreplaceable.

Avery pops back into the room a couple of minutes later with two old-fashioneds in her hands.

"Piper is in labor!" she exclaims.

"That's wonderful," I say. A flash of envy steals my moment of joy.

With her face beaming and watery eyes, she hands me a glass. "I can't believe it. I'm so happy for her. Thank goodness Dupara Wine Country is only a few hours away. We can head over once she and Jack are home from the hospital."

"That sounds great," I say. "Perfect time for Christmas too."

I set my glass on the table, then turn to Avery. Trying to form the right words, to ask her what I've been thinking for some time. She might turn me down, and that's alright, but I'm as sure now as I was back then all those years ago—she is my world. I have wanted to be a father since I found out we were having a baby for the first time.

Taking both hands and grazing the smooth skin on the sides of her face until I can thread them through her hair, I piece together the proper words.

"Avery." I smile, my eyes bounce between her hazel-green sparklers. The beautiful eyes I'm sure our baby would inherit.

She wraps her arms around my waist and gazes up at me. "Yes?"

"I love you more than anything in this entire world," I begin.

"I love you too," she drawls, unsure where I'm going with my words. "Are you alright?"

"I waited for you for eight years," I say softly. "I don't want to wait any longer."

She pulls her mouth to the side. "We're already married, if that's where this is going."

I bite my lower lip, trying to keep a straight face. "You asked me yesterday what I wanted for Christmas."

"I did."

"And I told you, I have everything I could ever want."

Avery slides her hands up the back of my shirt, caressing my skin. "Yeah?"

I cup her cheeks, tilting her head to force eye contact. "I want to try for a baby."

A sharp rise of her chest alerts me she wasn't expecting that. "Oh, Jasper." Avery's eyes dart away. Her fingertips fall from my back. "What if I can't give you one?"

"What do you mean?" I ask, unsure why she'd think she wouldn't be able to have a baby.

Avery backs away and shuffles her feet to the couch. "I've already lost one. I don't know if I could do that again."

There it is. Fuck. How can I convince her to try again if what happened when we were young still haunts her today?

I slowly blink, gathering my thoughts. "I understand." Taking the space next to her, I pull her in and hold her close. "I understand why you'd be scared."

"I want a baby with you so much, and I finally feel like I'm at a time in my life when it would be an amazing adventure," she says, her voice slightly cracking. "But what if I fail? What if I can't?"

We lie back against the couch, her curled into my arms. "Then we'll get through it together. I promise."

"I'm nervous."

"I am, too, but we won't know unless we try."

With a deep sigh and relaxation of her muscles, she turns her head toward me. Avery's eyes flare with fear but a hint of excitement. "Alright."

I can't explain the happiness that takes over me. "Yeah?"

She nods, a tear rolling down her cheek.

Epilogue

Avery

Jasper and I finally finished decorating the tree. A task so simple but meaningful at the same time. We cooked dinner together, which is a nightly thing now. *Who knew living with another person could be this fun?*

When Jasper asked me if we could try for a baby, my first reaction was worry. I wanted to say no purely from fear of possibly experiencing what happened before. But nothing with Jasper has ever been thought out. Every decision I've made with him has been made from raw emotion, and this time is no different. I wholeheartedly agreed.

While Jasper finishes the dishes, I'm heading upstairs to shower. I just arrived back home this morning from a three-day trip, and I am craving my own shower—*well, his.* I love living in his house and his space, and I'd be willing to leave my things in storage forever if he'd let me. I have no attachment to material items except for the piece of precious jewelry comfortably placed back on my finger.

His mother's ring, and I couldn't be more grateful for it.

Slipping off my jeans, I'm interrupted by a buzz from my phone on the dresser.

Helen: Hey, honey, I can't wait to see you and Jasper at the holiday party tomorrow night.

Since moving back, Helen and I have spent a lot of time together. I apologized for being away so long, and in true Helen fashion, she was comforting and reminded me she'll always be here.

Me: Me too. I'm looking forward to wearing the dress we picked out last weekend.

Helen: Your first official function is as a mayor's wife.

I smile, warming at the thought.

Me: I know. I hope I do alright. The guys have been giving me a hard time about it.

Helen: Don't let them get to you. I'll be there to keep them in line.

Me: Thanks, Helen.

Helen: Tell Jasper I said See you tomorrow.

Me: See you tomorrow!

I lay my phone back on the dresser, then finish undressing

and get into the shower.

Letting the warm drops cover my body, I lean my head back and breathe out a heavy sigh. It's been six months since Jasper and I got back together, and there hasn't been one second out of this entire time I have not thought about pinching myself. I'm happy and extremely grateful. I miss the girls, but luckily, I was able to stay with the same airline, so I still see them often. Since Piper and I live out of state, the four of us get together virtually for a weekly happy hour.

Like they did before, Easton, Riley, and Bodhi have accepted me into their group once again.

A light creak of the door tells me Jasper is on his way in. Butterflies flutter in my stomach.

I turn my head around to see him standing on the other side of the glass without any clothes on. "Can I join you?"

"Of course," I say. "I've been waiting for you."

Sliding the door open, he steps in and immediately hoists me up with two hands. A rumble of laughter vibrates both our chests.

"I missed you so fucking much," he growls into the sensitive skin on my neck.

With my legs wrapped tightly around his waist, I wriggle my hips, trying to find his cock. "I missed you."

Jasper's lips crash into mine, his hard length rubbing against my core. Desperate for him to slip inside, my pussy throbs. Water droplets fall onto my face, creating wetness not only from our kiss but from the arousal between my legs.

With one arm bracing my leg, he reaches between us to stroke himself. Clenching my muscles tightly, I keep myself upright as the inside of my thighs grow slick.

"I need to feel you, Jasper," I beg, running my tongue along the seam of his lips.

"So needy, aren't you?" he says right before slamming himself into me.

"Oh." A guttural groan forced from the back of my throat the moment I'm filled by him. His arm returning to my other leg, he clutches my ass and uses my body to get himself off. Back and forth with a force that takes my breath away. Heavy panting fills the air.

"Fuck, Avery," he moans, slipping in and out of me with a wild hunger.

My fingers comb through his wet hair. The heat from the water creates an apron of lust around us. A bubble unable to be penetrated, we cling to each other. Rolling his hips along with the deep arch of my back, we fall into a familiar rhythm.

"I love you," he breathes into my lips.

"Don't pull out," I gently demand.

"I'm not going to." His voice is dark and confident. It sends chills up my spine and directly to the bundle of nerves at my core.

Quickly, his mouth finds one of my breasts. Opening wide, he devours the entire thing, sucking hard while he releases everything into me. My head falls against the tiled wall, my pussy clenching, squeezing, and locking him in place.

"Yes," I purr, euphoria taking over. Jasper's body softens as he stills. His face is now buried between my breasts while his labored breaths fill the room.

"Do you want me to wash your hair?" he asks. And all I can do is smile.

First love always deserves a second chance.

Acknowledgements

First, I want to thank the readers who have taken a chance on this love story and me as a brand-new romance author. The series came to me while on a flight to Las Vegas with my husband. I knew I wanted to write a story about four flight attendants who are close friends and their very unique love stories.

To my husband, thank you for putting up with my endless conversations about plots, character ideas, and scenes that seemed to jump into my head at the most inconvenient times. Thank you for putting up with my inability to stay stationary, as I'm consistently running at full speed through life. I love you and all of the ways you show up for me every day.

To all of my beta readers, Nicki, Melissa, and Morgan, thank you for reading Memories by the Shore and making it the story it is today.

To Melissa, thank you for loving Avery and Jasper just as much as I do and ensuring their deeply personal story is ready for the world.

Thank you to the incredible indie authors who have become a network of resources, knowledge, and support. Lauren, Jay, and Jenna. I'm so grateful to call you my friends.

To all the romance authors who have shared their love and creativity with the world, thank you. Your stories inspire me and provide an escape from the rest of the world. Please don't ever stop writing. We need those happily ever afters.

About the Author

M.J. Huxley is originally from Los Angeles, California, but resides in the Southwest. When she isn't jamming to 80s music, eating tacos, or hanging out with her family, she's writing about the characters she loves.

M.J. Huxley strives to tell authentic stories of imperfect love. She writes emotional romances with banter & spice. M.J.'s books will always have a happily ever after, but that doesn't mean her characters won't have to work hard to get there.

Keep in touch with M.J.

Newsletter: bit.ly/3U6EXxW
Facebook Readers Group:
https://www.facebook.com/share/g/1B9iSqUyNt/
Instagram: https://www.instagram.com/authormjhuxley/
TikTok: https://www.tiktok.com/@authormjhuxley
Goodreads: https://bit.ly/4aouWSG
Pinterest: https://www.pinterest.com/authormjhuxley/
Website: https://www.authormjhuxley.com

MEMORIES BY THE SHORE

Also by M.J. Huxley

Tangerine Sky Series

Light Behind the Lies

Check out Bailey and Mason's steamy brother's best friend, enemies to lovers, and single-parent romance.

Love Beyond the Illusion

Check out Piper and Jack's steamy accidental Vegas marriage, forced proximity, and fake relationship romance.

Beauty Beneath the Sorrow

Check out Lina and Carter's age gap, dad's best friend, and pilot/flight attendant steamy romance.

Get the books here:

https://amzn.to/4jwUC4v

Scan for books here:

www.ingramcontent.com/pod-product-compliance
Lightning Source LLC
Chambersburg PA
CBHW030019060826
49398CB00031B/145